THE MECHANICS' INSTITUTE REVIEW
ISSUE 9 AUTUMN 2012

GW00703414

The first Mechanics' Institute in London was founded in 1823 by George Birkbeck. "Mechanics" then meant skilled artisans, and the purpose of the Institute was to instruct them in the principles behind their craft. The Institute became Birkbeck College, part of London University, in 1920 but still maintains one foot in the academy and one in the outside world.

The Mechanics' Institute Review
Issue 9 Autumn 2012

The Mechanics' Institute Review is published by MA Creative Writing, Department of English and Humanities, School of Arts, Birkbeck, Malet Street, Bloomsbury, London WC1E 7HX

ISBN 978-0-9547933-9-5

Project Director: Julia Bell

Editorial Team: Sue Betney, Dane Buckley, Sarah Cumming, Natalie Fletcher, Marlowe Harris, Zoë Ranson, Antonia Reed

The Editorial Team would like to thank Russell Celyn Jones, Julia Bell, Sue Tyley and Anne-Marie Taylor for making this project possible.

For further copies or information, please contact Anne-Marie Taylor, MA Creative Writing, Department of English and Humanities, School of Arts, Birkbeck, Malet Street, Bloomsbury, London WC1E 7HX. Tel: 0203 073 8372. Email: a.taylor@english.bbk.ac.uk

Website: www.writershub.co.uk/mir.php

Printed and bound by CPI Group (UK) Ltd, Croydon, CR0 4YY

Cover design and typesetting by Raffaele Teo

The Mechanics' Institute Review is typeset in Book Antiqua

Table of Contents

What we call the beginning is often the end
And to make an end is to make a beginning.
The end is where we start from.

T. S. Eliot, *Four Quartets*

The Trojan Horse Mixtape
TERENCE JAMES EELES

*"*The Neil Young *original? Over* the Saint Etienne cover? Are you crazy? No *way,"* Poppy splutters, tucking vinyl-black hair behind an ear while her laughter just slays and buries you somewhere far away in an unmarked grave. "No way *ever,* New Guy . . ."

The mixtape playing isn't yours but you could have made it. These living-room walls aren't home but they somehow feel it – and already, as rain teems down outside, you know Poppy's bed is a good and safe place to be.

"*Only Love Can Break Your Heart*" – she tries swaying your heart with hers, her body bouncing on the broken sofa close enough to smell her hair's flowers and fruits – "it *has* to be Saint Etienne's. End of."

Poppy wears sneakers, not trainers. Her clothes are thrift-store new and her South London flat is high enough above the shop units below to fall and survive with shattered legs. At night passing strangers gawk up at her lit windows, "Glimpsing," she said, "a ceiling fan that doesn't work, cacti I overwater, and the poster for a subtitled film that everybody seems to hate apart from me."

But here you are, and all your fault – your perfect date. Poppy's flatmate is out and the place is yours: mixtapes, cheap red wine, and conversations with an awfully pretty girl.

But sometimes perfect is not enough.

Perfect, if only Poppy wasn't who She was.

Her knees bunch tight across the sofa, touching your thigh. Behind you, Poppy's tape plays on the old kind of stereo your father used to seduce girls that came before your mother. "I can't believe you're even considering this, New Guy," she says.

You shrug and swallow, the cheap red burning your throat. The song in question that started this mess when you were with her last, the song you'd stalled over and lied that you'd never heard before, for that song you suppose you rate Neil Young over Saint Etienne.

The finger rubbing circuits around the rim of Poppy's wine glass slows.

With the faded cobalt, crimson and marigold of three music-festival wristbands dangling from her wrist, she says, "There's no *comparison*. Give me one good reason why the cover isn't better."

"I could give you three." You read the logos of your own fabric wristbands like tea leaves, the evanescent colours that also match Poppy's. "But I just guess covers rarely ever live up to the expectation."

Poppy lamely punches your knee, and relaxes back into the sofa with her wine.

"Pictures paint a thousand words, but mixes . . ." She muses, lost in the bars and choruses of audio she's compiled which fill the living room and the adjacent kitchenette. "Mixes . . . mixes *feel* a *thousand* pictures . . ."

Soundscapes for any time you've imagined yourself in the music, daydreaming cinematic in the moment. Any time you've got the words in the lyrics wrong, even when the songs sounded so much better your way.

"Some of these songs" – her fingertips tracing the trim of her camisole, along the jut of her collarbone – "I could go deaf for . . . Some of these songs" – Poppy's hand now stroking her heart, the tiny pedal-kick drum beneath the swell of her breast – "I could maybe *die* for . . ."

And you nod and smile, you excellent bastard. Right now, being here, maybe so could you – but Poppy takes her tape's case from the coffee table and bullet-points the air with it.

"D-I-Y." She waves her arts 'n' crafts masterpiece: the homespun insert that's two gig-ticket stubs glued together, meeting where sides A and B should be. The track list scribbled on the back – complete with faux dropped songs crossed out, imitating an ad hoc gig set list. *Hearts* 'n' crafts.

Poppy's muddy irises peek beneath the black wedge of her fringe. "There's no mix like this."

And Poppy's right. She made it. It's one of a kind. But while you waited after buzzing her flat downstairs a whole Side A earlier, the wine you'd brought went clammy in your hand and your tape burned guiltily inside your shirt's left chest pocket.

"Come over Saturday night and I'll cook," she'd told you down the phone earlier in the week. "Just bring a bottle – and a *mix* . . ."

But then as Poppy laid down her mixtape rules, you could only think of those in dating. The futile hopes-and-hoops boys 'n' girls put each other through.

"*Cassette*," she'd said.

Two dozen songs.

Sides A *and* B.

Covers only.

"When you put it to tape, you're weeding out the wannabes," Poppy tells you now, leaning forward to top up both your wine and hers, "culling the pretenders. Any dullard can burn a CD – meaningful means *old school*. Blank discs over tabbed tapes equals song loss and drink coasters."

Her wet tipsy eyes look to the cassette wrapped inside your fingers.

"Time's up. Show us what you've got, New Guy."

You take a sip of wine and stare at the coffee table, the CD-shaped stain there – a red-wine halo tonight for all your good intentions that'll never be.

"Right now?"

You jumped at the chance to exist again, you magnificent creep, because who do you make these cassettes for now? These love letters written on plastic with the broken-bone clicks and pouring-rain hiss of track lists sequenced by hand on old tape decks.

These things of the Present, scoring the Future, yet unable to shake the Past.

"Right now." She blows hair from out her eyes.

Faking a smile, you glance over at the mock-marble kitchen counter; its sugar bowl, spice rack and knife block.

You tell Poppy you don't think she's ready yet.

"Mix*tease*." Poppy leans in, swinging an arm, and misses grabbing the cassette from you. Struggling and giggling, you play-fight in tug-of-war, letting her win for a while, until you take the tape back with clumsy brute strength and your heads collide with a dull thud. Then stay resting pressed together, temples touching.

"Ouch," Poppy sighs, letting you stroke the fragrant strands – flowers, fruits – behind her head.

And already you know, lips a first move or mistake apart, that this is a break-up.

You met Poppy at a gig where you were drunk and rinsing out your soul.

Light and sound a blurry smear, you were a wasted mess that forgot what band was playing, but not why you were there. Your pores itched with sweat as you waited in the cloakroom queue, when out of nowhere – like a flick knife – came an attractive wrist against yours – *one, two, three* matching festival wristbands.

You looked up and Her vinyl-black hair shocked you like a ghost. The stiff Polaroid of a memory slipped between your ribs, prising them apart.

You nearly said Her name.

"*Snap*." Poppy's nose wrinkled, looking to you, then to your wristbands: the coloured combo of threads that change with each year's line-up, stacked and faded the same around each of your wrists.

You thought she worked there, you were such a mess. People piling past and out of the venue, you thought this was how you gave back your cloakroom-ticket stub.

"*I love this band*," Poppy shouted on tiptoes beside your ear over the exit music, reminding you who they were, pointing to amps being cleared from the stage. She obviously couldn't hear, because she just smiled and nodded when you yelled back, "I *loved* this band . . ."

And then maybe because you hadn't searched all night for lust in all the wrong places, you and Poppy both let down by gig-ticket +1s and the drink running you on autopilot, you said enough not to put her off, and she gave you her number after taking your gnarled business card.

"Smooth." Her fingernail traced your name, written beneath the employee you'd replaced, his name struck out in fading biro more indentation than ink. "New Guy . . . "

And now here you are, inside Poppy's flat, on your third meeting.

Date.

Whatever.

Well done.

Her temple still pressed against yours, Poppy tucks her hair behind an ear, causing the festival wristbands to slide down her forearm. And exposed there, latticed inside her wrists, are delicate scars: thin beadings raised above the pale like decorative cake icing.

You haven't noticed them before.

They make you think of her kitchen's knife block.

Poppy's eyes follow yours to the marks etched beside the green-blue threads of her veins. She folds her arms, knowing you've seen them – and maybe not for the first time tonight, either. She knows *you know* they're a permanent part of her now.

"I was young." She shrugs, turning the bouquet of wristbands slowly around her forearm beneath the scars. "Everybody has a past, makes mistakes." She then covers them with the wristbands. "At least you can see mine."

Poppy doesn't mention exes. No awkward anecdotes about *friends* with careful pauses and the baggage of her past trickling out. You maybe wish she did.

But it's been one, two, three dates – enough to shut her up with kisses. So taking her hand you push back the wristbands and kiss the spider-webbed icing above her palm.

"That tickles," she purrs softly, smiling.

Then: "So what about yours?" She remembers to take back her hand, gets up, and carries the coffee table's empty wine bottle over to the kitchenette. "So what about your mistakes?"

"Not mistakes, really." You taste your lips for wine and salt, watching Poppy's back as she opens your wine. You fixate on the length of Her body, Her curves, the back of Her hair and form until they blur.

You clear your throat and ask where the bathroom is.

"Second down the hallway on the left." An arm points it out without turning, the other pouring the wine in long, red glugs. She tosses the first empty into the recycling with a heavy clunk. "Don't fall in, New Guy."

Smoothing out your jeans and intentions, you tell her, "I won't."

« ‹ □ • ▶ › »

A week and a text after Poppy first matched her wristbands to yours in the cloakroom queue, you both saw another band.

Another spare ticket +1, another welcomed distraction.

Another painful reminder.

Before the gig you kissed Poppy's cheek and hugged her, half hoping Her ghost might be torn from you. Throughout the sold-out show you felt Poppy leaning in, bass jolting your bodies, the jostling crowd manoeuvring your arm around her while stage lights carved up the darkness and your feet stuck to the floor.

"Where now?" asked Poppy after the encore's last song and people were already leaving.

You joked it was a school night, but ended up in a bar you didn't know playing jukebox songs you did. Over cocktails with straws Poppy asked about your interests, your ambitions, your job, to which she said, "*Cool*, someone I used to know always wanted to do that . . ." Both of you sat on tall barstools you always felt in danger of falling from.

And then for a while, the glowing jukebox soundtracking smiles and jokes with Poppy, you forgot about anyone else.

You forgot about Her.

So when the song started to play you fought the welling and pretended not to hear it. The piano-bass and drum-machined beats tripping over themselves during the intro, excited and with her mouth full of cocktail, Poppy grabbed your hand across the table. And again, you clocked the *one, two, three* matching festival wristbands.

"This song," Poppy said. "This. *Song.*"

She mimed the track's wavery vocal, "Only love can break your heart," and because of Her, you nearly sang them back. The same black hair and festival-mud irises, the same petite figure and paper-pale skin, the same mixtapes-for-pulse attitude that wouldn't let you forget, Her nails still ice-picked into your bones.

"Choose," Poppy said.

"Choose who?"

"Not *who*, which – *choose which version*."

You stalled because remembering meant keeping Her with you, so you opted for dumb and lied, claiming it was a song you didn't know.

"*No?*" Poppy didn't believe you. She couldn't believe you'd never heard it, this *or* the original. "*Liar.*" She nearly choked on her cocktail.

"I nearly killed you," you kidded, handing her a napkin, changing the subject.

Mouth cut in a smile, Poppy thought you were funny, but said she didn't trust you.

"How can I" – her tongue stabbed inside her cheek with mischief in her eyes – "with *your* taste in music . . . ?"

And Poppy's laughter, so much like Hers, just slayed and buried you somewhere far away in an unmarked grave.

"Prove me wrong, New Guy." Her knees brushed against yours on vertigo stools.

So you did.

You talked music – more songs, by bands, at gigs, with wristbands, during festivals, with headliners, and on mixes – until fewer and fewer people were left inside the bar. After another round, Poppy told you how she missed them, mixtapes. Missed rescuing them from deep inside her bag with the cases coated in dregs of loose make-up.

"Tapes dolled up in drag with nowhere to go," she said, and then counted mix occasions off on her fingers. From the rookie mixes compiled more from your parents' LPs than you'd care to admit, to the gooey and mortifying first-crush mistakes. All those themed tapes that outlasted boyfriends and lived inside her Walkman – Walk*men* – each replacement eventually becoming a messy tattoo of band stickers patching the perma-missing battery hatch like a band-aid.

"No one I know keeps them alive any more." She stirred and stared through her cocktail, before raising an eyebrow with mock suspicion – and interrogated your etiquette, your mix house rules: two songs by same artist, chart-hit snobbery, tone and mood sequencing, whether covers were allowed – right up until the bar staff had wiped every last table clean and unplugged the jukebox from the wall.

"Just think of all the over-priced cocktails you'd save having to buy for girls." Poppy drained hers to just a bed of ice. "The time a mix saves getting to know someone." And then the bar's houselights came up and it was time to go home – whose home? You were punk-punch-drunk, but not enough to kill the drug of misadventure.

Poppy sat upright and smacked her lips. "Let's go back to mine."

You each stared out from separate windows inside the cab, but both planned on calling in sick for work.

On her sofa you kissed, while two mugs on the coffee table lost steam, your fingers figure-skating around the small of Poppy's back while she twisted above you.

Spine butted against the broken sofa, her flatmate liable to interrupt at any moment, you kneaded Poppy's rear, light as bags of icing sugar, while her hand scaled up your chest – her fingers clawing creases in your shirt you had to iron out, all until you were reminded of the past: there, manacled on Poppy's wrist – shocking like severed skulls – the wristbands of the festivals you were with Her at.

Wandering happy-drunk through crowds to bands on different stages. The smell of sun-scorched trampled grass and dusty mud, your arms draped over Her sun-lotioned shoulders, the choruses of songs sung together as soundtracked sunsets passed in both your hearts.

Where that same space ever since has felt like the Day of the Dead, which celebrates with colour those no longer with us.

The summer festivals where you now grieve over Her like a funeral.

"New Guy," Poppy said after you broke the kiss, the tip of her tongue re-tracing your lips, her fist in your shirt weakening. "What's up?"

And then you forgot about Poppy.

You forgot about the gig you'd seen, the bar you'd drunk at, the evening you'd shared, and instead you just felt buried, trapped and alone.

You told Poppy that you had to go. That you had work. With only her honesty being 100% proof, yours was watered down like those over-priced cocktails.

"Sure." She sat up, tucking her bra back inside her vest with stiff fingers. "Fine."

Back at your flat you dug out Her shoebox. You spent the night mourning the useless keepsakes of an old time capsule broken across your bed. Swallowing hurt, rubbing your eyes until the sockets were raw and it was light outside – birdsong retching like terrible amp feedback. You wanted rid of all the songs you could no longer keep inside.

You called in sick anyway.

You stayed away until Poppy called you up. Until you came back here tonight. On this third meeting. Second date. Whatever. To paw at the knicker elastic of Poppy's trust one more time.

« ‹ □ • ▶ › »

"Vintage," she says of the dated labels and scuffed black plastic, sitting on her sofa with that tape between her fingertips, you having just flushed the toilet you didn't need for show. "*Impressive*."

You panic and frisk an empty back pocket; your temples flush hot.

The sprocket holes of the cassette Poppy holds glare empty like skull sockets.

"It's OK, we'll play yours next." Poppy fakes a frown when you snatch it back.

From talking all night it's now too late for her to make you dinner, if she ever planned to, so after this last splash of Dutch courage, you exquisite worm, there's no excuse but to tell her.

Watching you drain the wine glass, she says, with that mischief in her eyes again, "Why don't we just play it now?"

She's a complete stranger apart from the one, two, three times you've been together, but as Poppy takes your hand – her wristbands brushing against yours – she leads you towards the hallway and the door you haven't been through yet.

The mix in your other hand, you know where this is going.

You haven't lied, you just haven't told the truth. This whole evening some kind of punishment – a labour to dig your own grave with just three inches of plastic.

You try killing time by wrapping your arms around Poppy. You stare past her shoulders and around the living room: to that poster of a foreign film with its unhappy ending, the November darkness drizzling outside the window, the kitchenette she shares, your arms around her – to your shirt sleeve peaking above your wrist in the embrace. You pull at it, dragging it down over your wristbands.

You ignored colleagues who mocked you for still wearing them. You usually reaped them every autumn like a harvest, but not this summer's.

They still paralysed you, like Her mixes.

And over the years She only ever made you three, though you didn't care. But when Her heart changed, yours didn't – and the verses, choruses and melodies still rang inside the cassettes and kept time with your heart.

Poppy pulls you towards the hallway.

The first mix She made, memories dating back to when you were new like strangers, you set light to outside your flat – the transparent Sony plastic stinking, shrivelling up, ugly.

In Poppy's bedroom, a place you knew was good and safe all along, each piece of whitewashed furniture covers a past life; the wardrobe, the bedside table, the frame of her double bed.

The second mix, compiled from highlights of festival summers, cut you after you stomped it with your heel and then picked at the yellow TDK shards – the taunting tape-guts history spelling out "liar" in looping cursive.

On Poppy's vanity table are CD racks and cassette towers stacked up against the wall. Among fragrant toiletries and scattered make-up are piles of bands and songs in columns and rows you know too well to care for any more.

"Thank *you*." Poppy plucks that cassette from you, disarmed, here being somewhere you'd like be lost.

That third and last mix from Her was a black Memorex cassette of covers; the last time it played was in your car on a static road trip. With the old ghosts of dead plastic haunting your dashboard, you vexed the hours of life you'd spent being brought to your knees tabbing Pause-Play-Record on old tape decks. They'd made you naive, believing mixtapes had a power: that they could somehow mend the past and fix the future.

You spared it, unlike the others. The last of its kind. You buried it inside that shoebox within your wardrobe to somehow forget.

The same box you raided after Poppy called you up.

Poppy slots the cassette into her tape deck and clicks a chunky button. The pre-tape whirr fills the room – awkward, like a soundtrack to your own execution. Poppy then sits back on her bed and lifts up her camisole.

Up past her navel, up past her chest. Up past her neck and over her head. Her hair falls splayed around the shoulder straps of her bra, just as the first notes of the opening song kick in.

Laying back, undoing her jeans, button by button; intro then leads into first verse.

After kicking off the denim, Poppy slowly reveals to you more vulnerable skin as verse slides into chorus – all while this and every song to follow is already part of an old movie reel with Her.

"Poppy." Your voice above the music, playing in her heart but picking at your bones, her discarded bra like a fallen mourning veil. Her bare breasts blinding. You say, "You're awfully pretty."

So dreadfully lovely.

So terribly beautiful, as if it will change a thing, because you can't tell her why you were at that first gig alone. That ticket +1 you didn't sell just in case She changed Her mind.

"I know," she smiles, reclining in just black lacy briefs and navy socks – navy socks, not even realising they're still on – her face too busy smiling and on its way to aching. "I like you, New Guy." She drapes her arms across her chest while you finger the buttons on your shirt.

Letting the shirt fall to the floor, you then unbutton your jeans and curse your history.

It curses you back, as jeans follow shirt.

"I like you, too," you say, almost in apology, your blood aching and beating hot inside your ears, drowning out the songs. Her pale body cream against clean white sheets – like the colours of a wedding cake – you could stop this now but you choose to hide beneath her breasts instead.

Kissing her hips and licking her navel while blossoms burn, grateful the perfume screaming on Poppy's pulse is not the same as Hers; your teeth trace along her curves.

You worm further down to avoid her gaze turning you to stone.

Tufts of hair tickling your nose against the fog of your own breath, you busy your mouth to stop you lying any more – hiding from Her and then from Poppy, you don't want them both to see how you can't solve this – going down with a heart full of snakes, you cunning sneak. Poppy doesn't taste of victory.

But what surprises you are the freckles where you don't expect.

How she's left-handed, not right.

How much longer it takes – and all your other expectations that swallow Poppy with a past of Her that still devours you.

"Come here." She pulls at you, your mouth now on hers.

You brought this mix because you thought Poppy wouldn't call your bluff – the kisses deafening – that you didn't have the strength to make another tape. The bravery it takes to make a mix and make it well – Poppy's chest beating through yours – the spun guts that get ripped out when it all goes wrong – your jagged breathing in the silence.

Almost silence. In the background, the music's stopped.

With Her mix not playing, Poppy gasps, "Forget it," waving away the hi-fi's humming. "Doesn't matter." She grinds against you, so into you.

At least someone is, you total fake.

The tape deck whirring desperately with the fidelity of Her jammed, backing up, stuck inside while Poppy's chemistry dilutes the poison in yours. Sometimes people just have a change of heart.

An album, a band, a phase or a fad, the end of Side B; they just stop listening.

And once again, you wanted rid of all the songs you could no longer keep.

« ‹ □ • ▶ › »

In the morning, still lying in the shapes the night broke you into, Poppy uses your collarbone as her pillow – just like She used to.

The heating hasn't keyed over yet, so your warmth is hers until you sneak away and leave her to fish out the cassette jammed inside her hi-fi. The spat-out guts that Poppy will wind back on the sprocket, right around her little finger, just like She's done to you ever since.

"Your heart's so fast," Poppy says, sleepy. You didn't realise she was awake, could hear you ticking in disaster, beating in rotten time signatures. "What makes it beat so fast?"

Eyes pinched closed, you rub away last night. Working the heels of your palms into the sockets, "That perfect is not enough," you say, and, misunderstanding, Poppy hugs you tight.

Worse than a rebound, you're a car crash waiting to happen, hurtling towards the lipsticked wreckage of another girl you'll need cutting from.

"Your tape." Poppy's voice is a warm pillow, her hand taking yours across your chest so that both sets of wristbands rest together: the cobalt, crimson and marigold threads fastened by metal clasps crushed around the woven fabric – beside them her icing scars wait for your kisses. "When did you make it?" she asks.

That mix of second-hand memories now silent, you think back before Poppy, before Her, back before Everyone and to your First, as if you're only ever trying to repeat it. The One that gets away. That like songs, some people are just covers of other people; the cover over the original, the original over the cover.

Only Love Can Break Your Heart.

Neil Young and Saint Etienne.

Her and Poppy.

She purrs when you say nothing but just kiss inside her wrist. Squinting against the Sunday-morning light cutting her blinds, Poppy likes this. Already you've disarmed the one thing she'd try and hide from you.

But – a stab of nostalgia – you can't keep an open mind inside an open wound.

"Where are you going?" she says through mussed vinyl-black hair and muddy irises.

Pulling on last night's jeans, you walk out into Poppy's kitchenette, the linoleum stone cold under your feet. Light spilling in from the living-room window and onto the lino, onto the cabinets and counter top, you take from the wooden knife-block set the sharpest blade there is.

"Hey . . ." Poppy calls out from her bedroom over the thumping drum of your ribcage, the slumber chipping from her voice.

The metal hilt aching heavy in your fingers, you hope her flatmate is still away. Poppy wears her heart on her sleeve but after you, she won't do that again. It's you who hardens it. Rejects her into the arms of another boy who'll thank you and worship her until she learns in time to ruin him, too.

"New Guy . . ." Poppy calls out louder – asks if you're even listening – just as you steady the blade along your forearm. The length and tip close to wristbands, close to the thin green-blue veins inside your wrist.

The rebound you need, it's just how it is. The reverberation within your soul, the ricochet inside your heart. All your mistake-laden lifetimes you'll need to count the pieces She broke you into. Spools of chewed-up tape from Her mix you can't rewind. Every soundtrack still needs silence.

"Hey." Poppy squints beside you on the cold linoleum, cupping her free hand against her brow and autumn sun, wrapped in last night's sheets. "Morning," she says.

You look at Poppy's wrist: the scarred icing lines and architecture.

She looks at yours: the shard of steel close to it between your fingers – and then gasps, as you hack, slice and saw those *one, two, three* festival wristbands.

The threads falling to the floor, the links severed for good, before those raggedy scars slay and bury you somewhere far away in an unmarked grave any longer.

Like festival funerals.

Where only love will break your heart.

Younger
JAMIE M-RICHARDS

Sunlight falls through the arched casement window, across our double bed. I shield my eyes in the shadow of my forearm. Michael pads quietly into the room. His dressing gown drops to the floor with a dull thud. He lifts the sheet and a breath of air wafts across my thigh. The bedframe creaks as he sinks into the soft mattress beside me. I open my eyes to find him staring back at me with a now familiar intensity. Leaning over, I kiss his hair-lined chest. His skin is warm and musky. Cautiously, Michael passes me a mug of black coffee.

"It's hot and strong."

I grin.

"Like someone else," I say.

He smiles yet his attention is drawn to the newspaper resting on his legs.

Several pigeons hop and flap along a branch on the large oak in next door's garden. The sky is a cool flat blue with barely a cloud to be seen.

"It's a beautiful day. We should eat on the patio."

Michael remains transfixed by his newspaper. I place the coffee on the floor. Clenching my stomach muscles, I slowly draw the white cotton sheet down over my chest and stomach to my hips. Sliding over onto my front, as smoothly as possible, I raise my arse ever so slightly and attempt a casual yet seductive reveal, kicking the sheet off my bottom half.

It lands on Michael's newspaper. He jolts his arm backwards, sloshing the hot coffee onto his thigh.

"What are you doing?" he shouts.

He grabs the old blue T-shirt he uses to run in and quickly mops the brown tear-like rivulets running down the side of his thigh. I lift the paper off his lap; coffee mars the print, soaking through now indistinguishable text. It crumples as I press it into the rubbish bin in the corner of the room.

"Has it burnt you?" I ask.

His brow is furrowed and his top lip taut. There is a red mark on his thigh.

"I'm sorry," I say. "It was stupid."

Standing beside the bed he runs his eyes over the sheet and pillowcases. I have already checked and cannot see any stains. The silence preys on me. He doesn't meet my gaze.

"I was trying to be sexy."

"You've had kinkier moments," he replies.

He disappears into the bathroom. Each time I twist my engagement ring around my finger, the inset diamond glints as it catches the light. The pigeons on the neighbour's tree have flown away. The sun is blinding.

I sit on the edge of the bed, tracing the ridges in the thick plaited Mexican rug with my toes. Michael says the dyed wool has dulled over the years. The room is almost as sparsely decorated as the first night we lay in this bed together. The clothes I brought when I moved in are hung and stacked neatly in the large teak wardrobe. The framed photograph of us embracing on the pier last summer rests alone on top of the chest of drawers. My gaze fixes on the vacant space above the chest, where the boy's painting hung just a week ago.

The sheets rustle as he slides across the bed. He wraps tanned arms around my waist. I resist ever so slightly as he pulls me backwards, hugging me tightly.

"It didn't burn me."

His fingers glide up the inside of my thigh until my balls are clasped gently in the warm palm of his hand. His cut prick presses against the base of my spine. My cock stiffens with his slight touch.

His breath is hot on my shoulder.

"You're beautiful, Jake."

"Don't."

"You are."

I curve my head around until our lips meet. He strokes me back and forth, slowly and then speeding up. Our tongues fervently tussle, jostle for space, flick, gently curl into one another and then retreat. I lie back, stretched out on the mattress. He looms over me. His eyes are fiery with intent. The muscles in his cheeks clench as he enters and emits a deep throaty sigh. He is hot and strong.

Michael is standing at the kitchen worktop with his back to me, slicing red peppers to go into the salad.

"I bought red, white and two types of gin."

"She's not that bad," I say.

"It's for me."

Michael removes the chicken that has been marinating in the fridge. He uncorks a bottle of red wine and pours us both a large glass. "Growing up, she always knew how to get a rise out of me."

I swipe the packet of Marlboro Reds off the table and rock the wooden dining chair onto its back legs, leaning against the wall. The muscles in his shoulders are pronounced under the tight, red cotton sweater he wears over bare skin.

"Don't lean back on the chair like that."

Though there are only several flecks of ash in the glass ashtray, Michael swaps it for a new one. He plucks the cigarette from between my fingers and takes a drag.

"What did Helen say when you told her about us?"

"It's trendy to support gay marriage. Of course she was keen."

The painting now hangs above the dining table. He gazes over my head, unashamedly distracted by his own work. I vigorously stub my cigarette out. He turns and opens the patio doors. A welcome breeze drifts into the flat, quickly dissipating the smoke hanging in the air between us.

"Moving the painting in here was the right decision," he remarks. "The light is far more conducive to its dark tones."

"Yes," I respond.

I aimlessly flick through the applications on my mobile.

"I moved it here because I knew you wanted me to." His hands rest on his hips.

"You once said his image reminded you of perfection and that was why you painted it. Did you think that would make me warm to it?"

His laugh is uncomfortable. "I meant the proportions. He was just somebody who modelled for the group. I don't even recall his name."

"It's fine," I say.

"You're jealous of a picture." He shakes his head in despair. "I don't paint any more. It's one of the few relics I have from that period of my life. That is why it matters to me."

Michael returns to the counter, picks up a large knife and starts slicing a cucumber. I stand in the doorway to the patio. My eye is drawn to a small puffy cluster of clouds. How deceptive they are in their seeming lack of motion.

The boy's tanned shirtless torso fills the canvas, set against a light-blue summer sky. His blond shoulder-length curly hair rests delicately against his cheeks. A shadow falls across one side of his face. There is a solemnity to his gaze as he stares off to one side, squinting in the light of the midday sun. The boy is no doubt beautiful, but enough to warrant this apparent obsession?

Helen scoops up some hummus on the end of a cucumber baton and delicately places it in her mouth.

"You've gone to so much trouble," she says unconvincingly.

"It's good to see you," Michael lies.

"We always try and keep Sundays aside for one another," I say. I catch Michael's eye. "He makes a special effort with Sunday lunch. Things are so busy at the minute, we need to make time for each other – and family and friends of course."

Helen smiles at me. "With a wedding to plan, it'll only get busier. It can be crazy. I don't envy you."

"We've hardly talked about the details," Michael says.

"It's only been a week."

One week yesterday. Until asking if we could walk to the beach, he'd been unusually quiet all morning. There were grey skies but I was happy nonetheless. The pebble shoreline was empty, apart from one lone figure walking in the distance. Tears fell from his glossy brown eyes as he got down on one knee. Afterwards, we stripped and ran hand in hand into the bitterly cold sea. I laughed and screamed as the water rose up over my goose-pimpled skin. He continued wading deeper, dragging me in after him. Above, the seagulls cried. Eventually I locked my arms around his neck and my legs around his waist. It felt safe clinging to his stocky six-foot frame. I gave him cold salty kisses and we hugged. I kept drawing my hand out of the water to check the ring remained firmly on my finger.

"It's tough keeping up those initial good intentions," Helen says.

Her tone is tinted with sadness. She runs her thumb along the faces of the many colourful rings on her left hand. She fiddles with the tassels from her turquoise cashmere scarf. "Stuart and I started off spending every weekend together. Within a couple of years we could barely spend ten minutes in the same room."

Taking a swig of gin and tonic, she lays a spray-tanned hand on my shoulder. "You boys will be just fine." She stares pointedly in Michael's direction. "Trust and honesty – maintain that and you'll get through the rest." She pauses. "Divorce is no picnic."

"Certainly pays well," Michael adds.

Helen raises her glass.

"Sometimes."

"You make relationships sound like a trial," Michael says.

Helen shakes her head. "Forty and still not married, Mike. You wouldn't understand."

"Marriage wasn't an option. You couldn't get civil partnerships until 2005." There is a spark of irritation in his voice.

"I married my first husband after knowing him eight weeks. We did it in Vegas," Helen continues.

"Turned out to be a real arsehole," Michael says.

Surprisingly, she nods in agreement. "Alcoholic, gambler – used to give me a real hard time. Our mum was heartbroken."

"For good reason," Michael says. He shakes his head.

Helen turns to look at him. "Because you've never disappointed our parents, have you?"

He flashes her a look that I don't understand.

"Another gin?" I ask Helen.

Michael scoops her glass off the table. "Glass of water, I think. I have made lunch," he says.

Helen takes my hand and draws it up close to her face. She examines the thin platinum band, stopping to admire the diamond.

"It's classy. I'm impressed."

"I love it," I say.

Michael glances back at me and winks. As he opens the oven to check on the roasting chicken, the scent of rosemary radiates throughout the kitchen.

Michael is standing at the counter, sprinkling icing sugar over the summer pudding, coating the cherry-red breaded sides in a thin veil of white. He scatters blueberries and redcurrants across its crown, before surrounding it with their dark juices.

"Can I do anything to help?" I offer.

Helen is on the patio smoking a cigarette.

"Just relax."

"Back in a sec."

The bathroom fan whirs in the background. Having splashed water onto my face to freshen up, I dab it dry with a towel. I look in the mirror and smile. I don't remember a time I have felt happier. Raising my hand to the light cord I admire the engagement ring. Helen is right: it is classy. I pull the cord down and the light turns off; the fan peters out with it.

"You've been dropping hints all afternoon. Please don't ruin this for me." Michael's tone is fraught.

Hesitating mid-step, just out of their line of sight, I quietly rest my foot back on the large rug that covers the sitting-room floor.

"It might not be as bad as you think."

"It's none of your business."

"You need to do this, Michael," Helen continues in a barely audible whisper. "For God's sake, these things always come out in the end – didn't you learn anything?"

The traffic outside the front door seems suddenly louder. Several cars aggressively toot their horns at one another.

"He deserves to know," Helen says.

I force a cough and walk slowly into the kitchen. They are

standing beside one another in front of the sink. Michael is facing away from me.

"Can I have another glass of water?" Helen asks.

Michael removes a glass from the cupboard above the counter and twists the tap hard. Water sprays out with excessive force, rebounding off the sink and over the both of them.

"Bloody hell," he yells, turning the tap off. "We've got to get that damn thing fixed!"

His sweater is drenched. Helen simply wipes a hand through her frizzy hair. She appears distracted by something outside of the window.

"I'm going to have to change."

"I'll come with you," I say.

"I'm sure I can manage by myself. Talk to our guest," he replies.

My laughter sounds as fake as it is. Helen picks up the kitchen cloth and begins wiping surfaces that are already clean. Taking a seat on the opposite side of the table I watch her.

After several awkward moments of silence, she says, "So, have you got a date for the big day?"

"He only asked me last week." A noticeable irritation laces my tone.

"Of course."

The birds that have been chirping for much of the morning have now flown away and the breeze has subsided. Helen leans against the counter.

"Well, here we are. It feels like ages since I've been round to see you both."

"I was saying that to Michael only this morning."

The baguette's crusty end has been left in the wicker bread basket in the centre of the table. I slowly rip it into small pieces, placing them next to one another in a pile in front of me.

"I hope you've got room for Michael's summer pudding," Helen says quietly. Her face is strangely pained as she stares at the boy's painting above my head. "I didn't know Michael still had that."

"I would have liked him to paint me," I say.

"I always hated it."

I smile faintly. "Likewise."

Sitting down opposite me, she tops up both our wine glasses.

"Do you have a cigarette I could pinch?"

I offer her one from my pack.

"He was one of Michael's students."

"Who?"

"Tom." Helen gestures to the boy looking down at us. "I wondered if Michael had told you."

The summer pudding waiting on the counter will be going warm. The unwashed plates sit stacked by the sink. The window is ajar. A fly has been attracted by the smell of food; drying, congealing. Has the same fly visited our dessert?

"Tom – of course." I nod my head and mimic recognition. She knows I'm lying.

"Ask Michael about Tom." Her mouth is pinched and her eyes fall to the floor between us.

Michael stacks another plate on the draining board to dry. I do not offer to help. I rock my chair back against the wall.

"I thought lunch went pretty well," he says. "It's a shame you didn't feel like dessert. I made it especially for you."

The sun is hidden behind a cloud and there is a slight chill in the air.

"Are you all right?"

"What were you talking about when I went to the toilet?" I ask.

He removes another plate from the sink, running the dishcloth over it before angling its face under the gently running tap.

"I don't keep a tab on your loo breaks."

"I overheard you, Michael."

He wipes his rolled-up shirt sleeve across his brow and some of the soapy bubbles slip off his forearm onto the floor.

"What did Helen mean by 'he deserves to know'?"

He starts frantically wiping the surfaces.

"Know what? Don't you trust me?" I ask.

"She's talking nonsense, as bloody usual. Of course I trust you – we're getting married."

"Then tell me." I raise my voice, unable to hide the ever-growing frustration.

"Helen twists things. She needs everyone to be as miserable and screwed up as her."

I allow the chair to rock forwards, smacking its legs against the tiles as I get to my feet.

"Remind me, Michael. Who is the boy?" I nod my head in the painting's direction.

Michael pulls the plug in the sink. The dirty water gurgles as it filters through the pipes and splashes into the drain on the other side of the wall.

"I told you, he modelled for the art group."

"And his name was Tom?"

He frowns and squints as though struggling to recall. "Yes, I think that was it."

"Strange that Helen knows the boy's name and yet you have never told me it. Why would you want to keep something like that a secret?"

He walks towards me with his arms open as if to hug me. I step backwards.

"Does it really matter what his name is?" Michael says.

"You lied."

"It's only a painting."

"Helen told me you used to teach him."

He shakes his head in dismay at this revelation.

"Why is there a picture of one of your students on the wall?"

Michael walks around the table, shoves a chair out of the way and stands directly in front of the painting, with his back to me. It hangs slightly off kilter. He readjusts it to sit true.

"She must have been surprised to see it hanging up at all." There is a defeated quality to his voice. "It didn't occur to me she would use it to stir up trouble."

Michael sits down at the table and turns to face me. He lets out a long exasperated sigh. "You see . . ." He pauses. "Every time I was going to tell you – and there were many times – I kept thinking the longer I left it, the better you knew me, the more chance I had of holding onto you."

From where I am standing, with my back to the worktop, he appears smaller and more vulnerable than I have ever seen him.

"But once it reached a certain point, it also felt as though I had betrayed you by not saying anything earlier." He looks up at me and his eyes are glassy with tears. He takes a slow deep breath. "What Helen said was true. Tom was a student at Millbrook. I taught him for just over a year."

I nod and he continues. "He was one of those students teachers pray for: talented, keen to learn, paid attention in class – art wasn't just a reason to piss about for an hour. He was a good little painter – had a real eye for the figurative form."

Michael slowly runs his finger back and forth over the silver oak-leaf pendant hanging just above the neckline of his light-blue checked shirt. It had been so difficult to decide on a birthday present for his fortieth; when I came across the pendant in a jeweller's down a small street just off the promenade, I knew immediately it was perfect. Since then, I don't think a day has gone by when he hasn't worn it.

"He started spending more and more time in the studio. I realised he was being bullied. He was quite effeminate. There was name-calling: 'gayboy', 'faggot'. I had to send several boys to the Head. After that he came and spoke to me about it." Michael stares ahead with a distant look in his eye. "Looking back, I had already fallen in love. I just hadn't accepted it yet." He pauses. "Fifteen isn't as young as it sounds."

I wince.

Michael continues. "Kids mature so quickly these days. And yet I couldn't get over the age thing at first. I was conditioned to feel that it was wrong. It took time for me to realise that because this was love, and mutual, and Tom was not like other boys, the normal rules didn't apply."

This is not us. These conversations are not the kind we have. We spend Sunday afternoons at the shopping centre. Many of the shops stay open. Recently, we bought a spice rack. It's fixed on the wall between the cooker and the fridge. The rack isn't really a rack. It has a metal strip and ten glass pots, each with a magnetic base. The magnets are very strong. At the slightest touch, the jars stick to the metal strip. When we got home we realised we don't use a lot of spices. We put what we could in the jars, but half of them are still empty. It looks good though, so that's OK.

"I often wonder whether Tom still has his painting of me. We painted each other. It was romantic."

Michael looks up at me. I lower my face into my hands then push my fingers back through my hair.

"I'm sorry if this hurts you. Helen is right, though: I need to tell you."

I press my palms against my temples like my mother taught me – it relieves the pressure on your brain, she used to say.

"We were so caught up in it we took risks we shouldn't have. We were in love, and careless."

"With a fifteen-year-old?"

"Yes."

"You were his teacher. He was a boy, not a young man. A child."

Michael turns to look up at the picture. "He was so damn beautiful."

My cigarette lighter slips from my fingers. Retrieving it from the black-and-white-checked tiled floor, my eye is caught by the sunlight reflecting off the shiny metallic extractor fan above the cooker. Staring up at the grille on the underside of the fan, I am struck by the presence of numerous thin yellow stalactite-like forms. The oil we so often fry with has been carried upwards on the smoke and fumes and stuck to the grille like a wick repeatedly dipped in wax. I imagine, when it is hot enough, the grease melts and drips back into the sizzling pans of freshly cooking food.

"They found us one evening in the studio. I thought everyone had gone home." In a quiet reflective manner, Michael says, "As much as the months before were wonderful, the years to come were equally horrific." He lets out another long sigh.

It seems I've lost my voice.

He gets up and goes to the patio doors. "They charged me with statutory rape. That day was nine years ago last February 21st."

The word rape lingers in the air like a germ.

"Court was a nightmare. Helen came, and of course Tom was there with his parents. I pleaded guilty and got six years. I served four. They said I was lucky."

Michael turns to face me. His shoulders are sunken, his gaze foreign. "I'm on the sex offenders list."

I have only the painting to go on, but it is true that Tom does not look like a child. He does not yet look like a young man either. He is in that difficult transitional phase. It happened nine years ago, Michael had said. Tom was fifteen then, making him twenty-four now. Two years older than me.

I push the chairs out of the way. Slowly, I unhook the canvas from the wall. I hold it in both hands. Tom's hair probably felt soft and bouncy, unlike my short spiky cut. Would Michael prefer me to have long hair? I would have grown it.

"Jake?" There is a vague tremble in his voice. "What we have, Jake, it's something people find only a few times in their lives, if they're lucky. You know that, don't you?"

Unlike Michael, I break easily – I am not strong. Through the mist of tears, the dark pinks and light browns of Tom's tanned skin meld into shades of blue sky. The canvas is surprisingly light. It is above my head and then it is upon my knee in one violent swift movement. The canvas pops and rips. Michael cries out in shock. The wooden surround frames my kneecap and thigh, whilst ripped sections of painted canvas hang lifeless on either side.

The frame clatters as it hits the floor. Michael rushes to pick it up as I walk quickly into the sitting room. On the coffee table in front of the sofa, the roses that he bought me last week sit just as they had earlier this morning. On the wall, the black-and-white Ansel Adams framed photographs, which I remarked upon the first night I came round for dinner, hang just like they always have. Everything looks and smells the same as it has since I moved in a year ago.

I walk slowly down the hallway, towards the bathroom. Stopping just outside the bedroom door, my eyes are drawn to the vacant space where just one week ago Tom's painting had hung. Michael removed Tom's painting from our bedroom the day after he proposed. Had I not sensed there was more to this boy, who deserved such pride of place? Had I allowed Michael to brush questions away, for fear that his answers were lies?

I go into the bathroom and shut the door behind me. The darkness is comforting. The bathroom is carpeted. It's nice on your feet, but hard to keep clean. Michael says we're going to strip it out someday; we just haven't got around to it yet. There is no window in the bathroom; it is stifling. I turn the light on. I hug myself.

I watch myself in the mirror. I slowly remove my shirt, undo my belt, remove my trousers and finally my underpants. His footsteps make their way down the hallway towards me. There is a gentle knock on the bathroom door.

"Jake?"

As quietly as possible, I reach forward and slide the lock into place. Hanging my head, I close my eyes. I listen to the sound of his breathing on the other side of the door. It is heavy; he has been crying.

"It's OK that you broke the painting. I understand."

"I'm having a shower. I'll be out in a bit."

"This is everything, Jake. There's nothing else you don't know."

I examine my naked body in the bathroom mirror. Do I look young for my age? People have said that. Michael has told me I look young for twenty-two. Does he think I look schoolboy young?

"You're in shock. I understand."

The door shudders as he leans against it.

"Don't I deserve another chance at happiness? Four years I festered in that hellhole of a prison. If I thought those lads at Millbrook were bullies, I had no idea." His voice is strained.

I turn the shower on.

"When was the right time to tell you: that first night, a few months in, when I asked you to marry me? I just wanted another chance at happiness, that's why I didn't tell you. Don't I deserve it?" There is desperation to his pleas.

The warm water runs over my tense shoulders. I turn the temperature up so I can hardly bear it. I lean forwards and rest my head against the tiled wall. Jets of water propel from the stained showerhead, filtering through my hair, cascading off my brow past my face. His voice persists above the hollow drumming of droplets splashing off my body onto the cubicle walls.

"Do you remember being fifteen? Didn't you know your own mind by then? Tom certainly did."

Standing aside from the flow of water, I squeeze a pool of shower gel into my hand.

"I know it's hard to forgive."

What is Tom doing now? Aged twenty-four, how does he feel

about the whole episode? Methodically, I lather the gel over my skin.

Raising his voice, Michael shouts, "I'm not some fucking paedophile for Christ's sake."

I stop and stare at the door.

"I was in love. Tom was a beautiful young man and I was gentle and loving." Michael is crying.

I step back under the scorching water. My shoulders are heaving; tears roll down my face. When I cannot stop, I drive my fist into the wall.

"Jake?"

Dark-red blood seeps out from underneath the ring, running down my finger. It drips to my feet, dispersing in the water.

"Do you remember how you felt about us this morning, how you felt about getting married? I don't want this to ruin everything. You don't want that. I know you don't."

I sink down onto my knees and gently rock back and forth. I don't want to think about statutory rape or sex offenders or Tom. I don't want to consider whether when he looks at me, Michael wishes that I were younger.

Paul and Emma and Paul
PHOEBE BLATTON

It was dawning on Paul and Emma that approximately one hundred metres back they had taken a wrong turn.

"I think we've taken a wrong turn, Emma," said Paul. "This is some kind of dirt track. It's going to damage the car."

The car was hired.

The headlights illuminated a stone-covered path that inclined ahead of them and the branches of hedgerows that imposed from either side. The track was growing too narrow for the car.

"This is wrong," Paul repeated. "We're going to have to turn back."

As gravel rattled up under the chassis with increasing volume, Emma spotted something to their left.

"Stop," she said.

Paul cut the engine, and the air conditioning ceased. Heat from outside immediately simmered in through the car's vents.

They had reached an opening to a field that had a length of chain across it. Emma got out of the car and shut the door. The rural night was shockingly dark, and in the full glare of the headlights Emma seemed superimposed. Paul looked at her through the windscreen as she moved around the front of the car. She briefly squinted in his direction, drawing a hand up against the brightness. The back of her hair had been pushed flat by the headrest, giving her a somewhat microcephalic appearance, and she instinctively ran her fingers through it in a futile preen. Paul felt like he was watching her on television. He wanted to tap the glass between them, like a child who doesn't understand the magic of the thing. Paul watched her arm rise and point to the chain. He looked at the pale flesh that sagged slightly from her upper arm, and the practical watch she wore around her wrist. He took in the way her fingertip curved upwards like the end of a ski.

"I'm going to remove that chain so you can reverse here," she said.

Paul thought her brave to step outside. God knows where they were. He breathed in deeply. After four hours of motoring the new smell of the car no longer inspired him with excitement. Since morning they'd followed the map down ceaseless A roads. It was Paul who'd first noticed a woman, alone, on a plastic garden chair with a bottle of water and a magazine to fan herself in the harsh sun. She was just sitting there, beside the road. He'd said nothing. Emma hadn't seen her as she'd been studying the map. But soon they passed another woman, and, in quick succession, another. Sometimes Emma and Paul saw a car pulling up. One time a pack of young men on mopeds veered off the road towards a woman who'd stood up, staring at them with one hand on her hip, the other holding on to the back of her chair. Some of them were already walking towards her as the others parked their bikes. They still wore their helmets.

"They're prostitutes, aren't they," said Emma, finally.

The last woman they'd passed had, in the briefest second that the speeding car would allow, met Paul's eyes. She'd been slumped back into the shade of a free-standing parasol, her legs crossed, the top leg bouncing ever so slightly so that her high-heeled mule, barely held on by the strap across her toes, beckoned like a motioning hand.

Paul wondered where they did it. Probably some place down the B roads, or maybe the lay-bys. Emma got upset the more women they spotted. She said she hoped they had knives on them.

Emma was bent over the chain, trying to wrestle it from the post. She gave a sharp pull, and threw it aside. In the moment of turning round, her face seemed blurred by the combination of the movement and a smile breaking across it.

Suddenly a crack of gunshot ricocheted in the near distance, followed by a volley of barking.

"Get back in, Emma!"

Paul's voice boomed and instantly died in the vacuum of the car as Emma's shadow passed across the windscreen.

There was the elegant double-clunk of the central-locking system as Emma's hand grabbed for the door handle. Next came the frantic tugs of her efforts to make it open, the mechanism squeaking and springing back with a dull pop.

"Paul!" she cried. "What the hell are you doing? Open the door!"

There was a thud by Paul's side. The enormous head of a mastiff, like a tank that had been painted with a wide grinning mouth, was almost level with his own. For a moment there was just the soft noise of it sniffing along the window's edge and puffs of frustrated exhalation. Then it reared back, letting out a barrage of guttural barks, the force of which caused its head to snap round like a Catherine wheel. It sprang up against the window, and Paul felt the car shudder. It briefly took purchase, its paws firm against the glass, and Paul looked down between the braced back legs at its bulbous testicles. As the dog slipped, its claws scored lines down the glass, screeching into the paintwork as it met the door. Emma's fists banged with fierce urgency on the other window.

"Open it, open it," she sobbed, just as a torch blinked at them from up the path, and a rough voice ordered the dog away. Paul watched the dog bound towards the approaching figure, who fastened a thick leash around its neck, hauling it into submission. The figure stood in front of them with the dog straining forwards, and cut the torch.

"Open it," Emma cried. "Open it, *please*, Paul," until Paul believed that he could.

When they arrived they had to explain what had taken them so long.

"I didn't know how to operate the central locking."

Paul was telling the story.

"I'm not used to such a new car, all that newfangled technology. I'm getting old."

He paused with his wine glass aloft and gave Emma a smile,

but when she met his eyes he immediately looked down. His smile slackened off.

"I believe you meant to give Emma a scare, Paul."

Paul looked at Paul, his good friend Paul Sinnan, who was nestled into a papasan chair. The chair had been left out in all weathers, and the red upholstery had faded to a raspberry beige. Paul Sinnan picked at the splitting rattan. He looked up at his friend:

"Am I wrong?"

"Paul" – Paul cleared his throat – "that's not what happened."

"I'm only sorry," said Paul Sinnan, "that it'll cost you the deposit on the car. You won't be able to fix those scratches."

Emma went over to the wall. They were on the high terrace of Paul Sinnan's farmhouse, and beneath and before them the countryside expanded with olive trees and vineyards, lavender and the occasional sandy cluster of a hamlet set into the distant hills. But this was night, when the landscape transformed into a vast generality of black against the sky. Something rustled and grunted in the foliage below; there was boar in this region, but trying to see was futile. Emma looked up again, fixing on a sporadic glimmer of light, a far-off source of human activity, but it would blur as she tried to focus, too far away. Emma flicked one of the olive stones she had been holding in her fist over the side of the wall and didn't hear it land.

The two Pauls came and stood either side of Emma. Paul put down his glass, and rested his elbows on the ledge with his hands clasped together. His good friend suddenly laughed.

"Imagine," he said, "if we should take this opportunity to hurl Emma over the wall. You grab one arm, Paul, and I'll grab the other."

Paul looked straight ahead.

"Go on, we'll make sure it works this time!"

Paul breathed in quickly and swallowed, and in the weak light of the terrace candles Emma noticed that his eyes glistened with a surfeit of moisture.

"Make sure what works?" Emma asked, feeling Paul Sinnan's fingers circle her upper arm, like a snare that would snap tight at any moment. She dug her nails into the powdery stone bricks, and concentrated the weight of her body deep into her heels.

Paul tried to laugh, but something caught in his throat, and he began to choke. He reached for his glass and glugged the wine, but it burst from his mouth, a little escaping through his nose.

"Sorry," he spluttered, making Emma wonder if he meant for the choking, or for his inability to act on his good friend's instruction.

Paul Sinnan released Emma's arm and went to thump her husband on the back.

"You're useless, Paul."

Paul wiped his tears with his shirt sleeve and snorted.

"Absolutely useless," said his very good friend.

Emma rubbed the place where Paul Sinnan had taken her arm, although it hadn't hurt, and watched him stretch against the wall, straightening his legs back in their loose linen trousers. He'd probably had those trousers for years, wearing them in so they were just so. Everything he owned had that look. He scratched at his armpit, and she looked at the brown skin of his stomach where his shirt lifted, the fine black hair that swirled in a vortex towards his navel. Even his stomach looked perfectly worn in. Suddenly a sweat broke out all across her back. She felt dampness between her thighs, and her toes squirmed against the leather of her sandals. She wanted to take them off, and she did, stepping into a puddle of Paul's spilled wine. She pulled at the neckline of her dress, and felt it spring back against the fleshy top of her breasts.

A church bell tolled midnight. Paul Sinnan clapped his hands together and went through the French windows.

"When it's twelve o'clock," he sang, "we climb the stair. We never knock, 'cause there's nobody there."

He flung the doors wide so that Paul and Emma could hear the record he'd put on. It was Peggy Lee, a late recording, very spare and sultry, like Peggy Lee doing an impression of herself. Paul Sinnan grinned with his mouth open, letting his tongue waggle out as he rolled his head from side to side in time with the slow beat, and when the chorus came he sang along with a false breathy voice: "It's just me," he gooned, "and my" – he suddenly fixed on Paul – "shadow . . ."

He danced across the terrace towards Paul. As Peggy Lee sang

"*All alone and feeling blue,*" Paul Sinnan took a paper towel to his good friend's nose and dabbed at it like a painter. He dropped it and moved over to Emma.

"Dance?"

He pulled her in close so she could feel the bones in his chest through their thin clothes. He raised his chin away from her in an affected manner, his eyeballs rolling skywards behind the fluttering lids. He opened them directly at Emma.

"*I bet there's nobody there,*" he sang along with Peggy Lee.

"I'm very tired, Paul."

Emma slipped out of the embrace and went over to her husband.

"Perhaps we'd better turn in, eh? Call it a day. We've got another long drive tomorrow."

"I'm only sad you'll be on your way again so early," said Paul Sinnan, swaying towards them. "It's rather like you've used me as a cheap motel. A pit stop."

Emma looked at her husband for support. He'd taken to the papasan. In a tired monotone he addressed his wife.

"Emma, I'll be in shortly. I'm just going to catch up with Paul for a bit longer."

"Paul," said Paul Sinnan, grinning, "I'll bring up the brandy."

He took Emma's hand and let his lips nearly touch it.

"Goodnight, my sweet thing," he said. "I've enjoyed you, albeit briefly."

He disappeared down into the house.

Holding on to the doorframe, Emma glanced back at Paul.

"You won't be too late, will you?"

"No, no." Paul waved her away. "I'll be up soon."

Emma stepped from the shadows of the terrace into the room with the record player. The turntable was still spinning, the only sound now the rasp and beat of the needle circling repeatedly in the lock groove, and she replaced the arm back on its stand. The speakers whumped as she flipped the switch to Off. She paused very briefly, and went through the door that led to the bedrooms.

Emma lay on her back in the unfamiliar bed. Her stomach was empty. It seemed typical of Paul Sinnan to offer them a deluge of wine with nothing other than a few olives by way of food. He was the one friend of Paul's that she'd met last of all, but who'd always been there, approaching, making brief appearances, lurking in the past. Paul liked to talk about his old friend; he always met him alone but let her join in on the last throes of a rendezvous, as though providing proof that Paul Sinnan existed, but no more than that. She'd met him twice, three times perhaps, in busy places: a bar, a cinema lobby. Now they were here in Paul Sinnan's house, and Emma was unsure what that meant.

The realisation of how much land they'd covered, and how changed it was, had made the day double. The incident with the car seemed fantastically long ago. Emma had been so concerned, once safe inside, to get the hell away from there, that only when they were back on the main road had it sunk in she must confront Paul about what had happened. And then he'd snapped, and said they'd both reached their limit that day, and that if they both didn't try harder they'd never reach Paul Sinnan's place, and their bed for the night.

This was her bed for the night. She turned testily on her side and felt a spring dig into her hip. The bed linen was old but freshly laundered. She thought of Paul Sinnan making it up, tucking down the sheet and smoothing the pillowcases. She scanned the still-plump horizon of the other pillow by her head, and imagined his hands gliding across the cotton, and remembered them circling her arm. It struck Emma that her husband and his very good friend had each made a joke of her. For surely that's what it had been earlier, on the dirt track: a poor joke – so poor they'd had to pretend it hadn't happened. She contemplated how a joke and her own death could be only a fraction of a degree apart. When Emma thought of not existing, it seemed most appalling to think that this might correspond with some kind of brief entertainment. She felt her body becoming rubbery, Loony-Tuned, and then pictured the two men hurling her over the wall and doubling over, yuck-yucking with laughter. She'd appear again, screen left, black-eyed and hair in the air; "Yoo-hoo," she'd holler in a dolly falsetto, and the men's eyes would pop out on stalks, so surprised they'd leap right over the wall themselves. A diminishing circle of vision rapidly closed the scene to black.

Emma rearranged the pillows and rolled into the middle of

the bed. What a strange idea to choose one side or the other when you were alone. If she fell asleep like this, Paul would have to wake her, or try and roll her back over. She opened her limbs in a star and found the air drawing painfully in her lungs. She pictured a spear falling from above and pinning her to the mattress, a clean and simple puncture straight through the sternum. Get up, she thought, get up, and she went across the stone tiles to her handbag. In the bag was a half-eaten baguette that she'd bought in a service station. She peeled back the cellophane and bit into it. A bland mouthful of Emmental and tomato landed in her stomach as tears settled in the corner of her mouth, salting the taste. Something fizzed and crackled in her right ear, some kind of bubble trapped in her jaw, as she mournfully chewed.

She went to throw the wrapper in the wastepaper basket, but thought better of it, like it could be evidence against her. She could not rationalise why this thought gripped her, but felt a brief moment of safety as she pressed the greasy cellophane back into the depths of her handbag.

Emma lay down again, this time on her side of the bed. A burp surprised her and she rubbed her stomach with a comforting circular motion. A foreign bird cawed outside, the sound growing loud and faint as it flew away, and as she yawned and nestled and succumbed to the now deafening silence of sleep, there it hovered, just above her perception, an emanation from the terrace; the laughter of two very good friends.

At Bistro Joe's
LUCY HUME

That night the butter melted within minutes and the sweat ran from my neck down my back to where my apron tied around my waist. For once it was like an Alicante August, when we would take cold baths and hold Coke cans against our cheeks. In the kitchen the ceiling fan was only rearranging the oven heat and Michel and Bobby were taking it in turns to stand inside the fridge to cool down. As a result, the food was coming out more slowly than usual, so Joe was pissed off; occasionally the clatter of plates or a shouted expletive filtered through to front of house.

Mr Taylor arrived with the tall man as the sun was coming in under the awning. I could smell the edge of vodka on him as he removed his jacket to give to me. His shirt sleeves were rolled up and the backs of his arms were covered in black hairs that sprouted either side of his Rolex. The tall man wore tight jeans and a cream blazer. He had fair, woolly hair that looked like a circle of knitting stuck to his head.

"Table six, Sofía," Joe said as he strode past.

Mr Taylor worked nearby in Mayfair and would often bring clients in for lunch during the week, or came with his girlfriend Milena in the evenings. He had gradually become one of our most regular regulars, so even though he worked for a hedge fund and ordered his steak well done, Joe had been forced to promote him from the table next to the toilets.

Milena arrived separately a few moments later, just as Mr Taylor was sliding his belly under the table. She was wearing a low-cut purple top and had her hair pinned up. Somehow her bare neck was even worse than all the cleavage. She slid in beside Mr Taylor and they did a wet kiss hello. Usually they went in for a lot of nose rubbing and feeding each other profiteroles or whatever, so I was relieved that on this occasion there was a third member of their party.

I handed round the menus.

"The special tonight is a rack of lamb with a port wine reduction," I said. "I'm afraid we've sold out of the monkfish."

"I can't pretend to be too sorry about that," Mr Taylor said, smiling at me. He had told me once that he didn't like fishy fish. Salmon was fine, but tuna was a no-no. "Sofía and I are old friends," he told Woolly Head. "She's familiar with my little weaknesses, aren't you?"

I tried to take up the banter. "Yes: each night he comes with a different woman!"

Immediately Milena's smile dropped off her face. Mr Taylor opened his mouth, but he quickly put on a grin and said, "She's joking!"

Woolly Head said, "She has a good sense of humour." He had a Scandinavian accent. "Sofía is a comedienne," he said, studying me. "And Sofía comes from Barcelona."

"How did you guess?" I said.

He slapped the table and sat back in his chair. Milena by now was studying her menu.

"May I get you some drinks?"

"Yes, I think so," Mr Taylor said. "Well now, how do we feel about champagne?" He turned to Milena. "We've got something to celebrate this evening."

She bared her teeth at him.

It was St Clare's day, my mother's name day. I had Skyped her that morning to wish her congratulations. My brother David had set her up on the computer in his apartment, where she was looking after the baby for him and Eva. I made sure to put my violin on the bed behind me, in view of the webcam.

After all the usual news and waving Fede's fist at me for a

bit, she told me that the meetings were still going well for Daddy. The crisis was proving to be a good thing for him: now there were others in the same position – friends from the church were also out of work. Nobody bothered to ask questions any more. The jobs would come back and, when they did, firms would just think he'd been made redundant like everybody else. In the meantime he was helping out at the Oratory and she was still doing her mornings at the primary school. He had been four months sober. She had real hope this time.

I told her that I was doing OK from my music tutoring. Please would she thank Teresa Gomez for the information about the agency. Yes there were certainly many rich families in Kensington. And yes I was hoping to find a permanent job with an orchestra soon.

"So we shan't be seeing you this year, then?"

She meant the Last Night of the Proms on TV. I laughed like she wanted me to. "Not this year, no."

I said I was sorry about Fede's baptism. Next time I would be there.

"Fede won't be baptised again, darling."

Is Daddy going, I wanted to ask. But she had to say goodbye because Fede had started to throw up on her shoulder.

I went into the kitchen to inform Joe that Mr Taylor had been seated. He was bent over a plate of sea bass, balancing a blade of chive, while Bobby piped sauce around the edge. They both stepped back at the same time.

"*Ser*vice, please, Sofía," he said, ignoring my announcement.

After delivering the fish to the De Vrieses I went to collect the tray of champagne from Thomas behind the bar.

"Who is celebrating?" Joe said when he saw me with it. "Who the fuck is celebrating in my restaurant?"

I said nothing, but looked over to table six. He sighed.

"Yes of course they are," he said. "Please, continue."

After I had handed round the glasses I took my notepad out from my apron. Natalie was taking the order at the next-door table, standing back-to-back with me. She shoved me with her bum so that I stumbled into the back of Woolly Head's chair.

"Excuse me," I said.

Mr Taylor laughed. "Careful, Simon," he said. "She's taken a liking to you!"

"May I take your order?" I said.

Milena ran a copper fingernail under her choices on the menu as she read them out: the beetroot salad followed by the red mullet. Woolly Head requested the escargots and the sea bass. I didn't need to ask Mr Taylor but he told me anyway.

"I'll have the escargots as well, and then the fillet steak *bien cuit*. And we would like a wine recommendation from Joe. Just wait," he said to Woolly Head. "This guy's an expert."

Joe was sitting on the ornamental barrel outside the kitchen, proofreading the next day's menu on his paunch. His hair was even shinier than usual in the heat. When he saw me taking the order into the kitchen he took the notepad from my hand, tore the top page off and held it up to the light.

"Bobby?" he called into the kitchen.

"*Oui*, chef," Bobby called back.

"One beetroot, two escargots. One mullet, one sea bass, one steak." He paused to decipher my handwriting. "Fucked."

"OK," Bobby said.

"They would like you to please recommend a wine for them," I said to Joe.

The menu rose up on his stomach and sank back down again. He reached up, pulled a bottle from the rack above his head and held it out to me. It was one of our mid-range reds, a £95 Château Siran. I took it through and presented the label to Mr Taylor, making up some crap about a fruity bouquet and base notes of liquorice. He said yes, that sounds good, so I uncorked it and poured him a small amount to taste. He shoved his nose into the glass so that I was afraid it might get stuck on the way out, but everything was fine: after snorting violently he retrieved his nose unharmed. He nodded his approval and I filled their glasses.

It was one of those nights when Natalie and I were moving all the time, carrying plates and jugs of water or sweeping breezes past each other to get to the kitchen before the ice cream slipped off the tarte Tatin. My legs were already heavy with the pain that would later stop me from sleeping. I tried to stay away from table six as much as possible, but Woolly Head kept leaning back in his chair to get my attention whenever I walked past. One time he dropped his fork; on another occasion he stopped me to ask whether our bread was baked on the premises.

Mr Taylor may have suspected that Joe had not invested much consideration in his selection of the Siran because once they had finished their entrées he asked to see the wine list for himself. By now consonants were presenting a challenge and there were spots of saliva at each corner of his mouth. He leafed through the pages to get to the more expensive wines near the back.

His finger trawled to the bottom of the page.

"We'll try this one," he said, pointing. It was the 2004 Lafite Rothschild. We only stocked the one bottle that Joe had brought back with him two years earlier from one of his trips to Bordeaux. He had delivered a lecture to me about it one morning while I was folding napkins, describing its elegance of nose and the power of its concentration as if he were boasting about his own child. He had told me that he planned to drink it on the day he finally sold Bistro Joe's, twenty or so years from now. He must have assumed that none of our customers was rich or flashy enough to beat him to it.

Milena's eyebrows had risen into her forehead at the price marked next to Mr Taylor's index finger. She looked down at her empty plate. I acted as if there was nothing unusual in the request and took the wine list back. I carried the plates into the kitchen and stacked them on the draining board next to Aleks.

"Table six is cleared," I told Bobby, and he nodded and repeated my words back to me as he bounced a pan on the hob.

I searched the restaurant for Joe, but couldn't see him anywhere. Usually he wouldn't allow himself so much as a bog break on a busy Friday evening, but I told myself he had been working even longer days than usual, getting in at nine and staying until after midnight to help with clean-down. That morning when I arrived he had been bent over an invoice with his cheque book and an espresso beside him, a red mark on his forehead from the heel of his hand.

I realised that he had been acting oddly ever since Mr Taylor came in alone for lunch about a month ago. He ordered the duck and kept Joe talking, asking how was business, was it usually this quiet on a Thursday, what were our profit margins, overheads, turnover. I had assumed at the time that it was simply a matter of professional interest for him. It occurred to me now that since then Joe had been line checking every day, opening bills as soon as they arrived and rationing our drinks after work.

I stood on the footstool to reach the Lafite Rothschild at the top of the wine rack. The glass was black and shiny from the attentions of Joe's duster, the vintage year cast into the curve of its collar. I carried it out to Mr Taylor and presented the label to him. He put his face up close to it. His eyes were almost crossing. He nodded.

"It needs to be decanted," I said. "I'll just be a few minutes."

Milena kept her eyes on me as I took the bottle back to the bar, but then Woolly Head said something to her and she looked away.

Thomas had gone on his break, so I reached up for the decanter myself, unsettling the bottle of house red that was waiting open on top of the bar. I held it steady. It was full. There was no one around. I dropped down behind the bar and slid the Lafite Rothschild into the narrow space between the fridge and the glasswasher. I took the open bottle from the bar and tipped it on end into the decanter. Still the wine went too slowly, in big glugs. Finally I wrapped the empty bottle up in newspaper and pushed it to the bottom of the bin. I took another bottle of the same wine from the rack below the bar, unscrewed it and set it where the first one had been, with the label facing out towards the customer.

I took the decanter out to table six, holding its belly against mine. I tilted an inch into Mr Taylor's glass. This time after sniffing he took a sip. His lips grew thin and his pupils rolled up to his brow bone as he held the liquid on his tongue. He breathed in deeply through his nose. I could see the sleeve of my shirt trembling. I counted seven seconds before finally he swallowed, nodded and said, "Yes."

When I went to pour for Milena she put her hand over her glass.

"I'm fine," she said.

Mr Taylor made a sad face at her. "Moo-Moo," he said. "Why don't you drink with us?"

"I'm fine," she said again.

I figured maybe she was pregnant or something.

"Fill me up, then," he said, grinning. "I'll have hers."

I topped up his glass and poured some for Woolly Head.

"Go on and try it, Simon," Mr Taylor said. "You have to try it."

Woolly Head held his glass up to the light. He tipped it slightly to the side. He swirled the wine. He sniffed. Finally he drank.

"Well?" Mr Taylor said.

Woolly Head looked down into his glass and up at me. He said nothing.

"How good is it? It's good, isn't it?" Mr Taylor said.

"Yes," he said, putting his glass down. "Yes, yes, it's good."

I set the decanter down on the table next to his hand. The glass was marked where my fingers had been.

It was after midnight in Spain, which meant my new nephew was being baptised today. I wondered if Daddy would be playing at the ceremony, and if David would let him go to the meal afterwards. It was two years since we'd all been at Nibs together, for my going-away dinner. We had all tried not to watch him drinking. Afterwards, when it was time to say goodbye, he held me tightly, pressing my forehead into his shoulder so that my neck started to hurt. When I pulled away his face was bright pink, a grey vein like a cello string in his forehead.

By the time they had finished their desserts on table six they were all too stupid with food and drink to notice that I delivered the bill before they had requested it. It took Mr Taylor a few attempts to get his PIN right, but finally the payment went through and they got up to leave. I helped him into his jacket and he stumbled backwards slightly so that I had to push him upright to keep him off me.

"See you again," I said as I held the door open for them.

I retrieved the Lafite Rothschild from its hiding place and took it into the kitchen. Joe was sitting polishing cutlery as Michel and Bobby wiped down the work surfaces. When he saw me with the bottle he jumped up from his stool in terror as if I were manhandling the sacrament.

"What the bollocks are you doing with that?" he said.

I set it down gently on the worktable and slid it across to him. I explained how I had found out that he had been forced to sell the restaurant to Mr Taylor and that I had switched the bottles so table six had ended up drinking the house wine instead of his Château

Lafite Rothschild. Joe stared at me for about fifteen seconds without saying anything, just flaring his nostrils.

Finally he slid two fingers behind each lens of his glasses and pressed his eyes. He started to laugh, a proper laugh that made the table shake. The laugh spread to Michel and Bobby and even Aleks smiled to himself as he banged the pots around in the sink.

"You really think I would sell Bistro Joe's to that moron?" he said on a gasp, and he laughed again until tears ran down his cheeks.

When we had finished laying up at the end of the night Joe called me, Natalie and Thomas into the kitchen.

Instead of splitting the tips, he set up seven wine glasses on the worktable.

"Sofi doesn't drink," Thomas said.

"Tonight she will make an exception," Joe replied.

He rolled the bottle between his palms, swiftly twisted his corkscrew into the cork and eased it out with a succulent pop. He sniffed the end of it and closed his eyes. Next he poured the wine, a trickle at a time, between the glasses until they were all level and the bottle was empty. He passed a glass to each of us by the stem and took the last one for himself.

"*Santé*," he said.

I knew that in my hand I held a flight to Alicante but after the first taste I didn't care. Yes, it was heaven; the smell alone made me dizzy and its acid warmth sat on my tonsils and in my chest. It was difficult not to slurp: each individual taste bud in my tongue clamoured to savour the famous Château Lafite Rothschild. Bobby slapped some Gruyère on slices of bread and pushed them under the grill and we stood around the table taking the slightest of sips to make the wine last as long as possible. Joe tilted his stool and leaned on his elbows, his glasses pushed up into his hair, his eyes smaller now but sparkling still. He glanced at me occasionally, grinned and shook his head.

Every Member
a Missionary
JENN ASHWORTH

I don't normally go with Mum when she does babysitting for one of the Sisters and I should have known something was up when she said to consider it a service project, and that I'd get an extra quid in my pocket money as well as a reward in heaven if I did it without moaning. We shook on it. She had a sly look on her face but I put it down to her being able to poke around in someone else's kitchen cupboards while they were out.

After tea we put our coats on and walked. It got dark as we went along, Mum's face getting less and less visible. She had her red gloves on, and I put my hands inside my pockets and wished I'd brought my DS. Lindsey was a young investigator. A single mother. The missionaries were doing some really great work with her. She needed to feel included and valued in the Ward, so we were going to look after her baby while she went to a Stake Young Single Adults' Dance. It was important for her to make friends inside the Gospel. For her to feel like we were her family and that we cared about her. I hadn't asked, but Mum filled me in on the way. I was to count it as missionary work, and good practice for when I went on my proper mission.

When we got there I was freezing and Lindsey was standing on the pavement in front of her house holding a sparkly handbag in both hands. She waved with her whole arm, as if we were long-lost family.

"Be nice," Mum said, out of the side of her mouth. "Set a good example."

So I waved back.

"The baby?" Mum said, quickly frowning at Lindsey's battered high heels and bare legs. There was a plaster on her knee. I tried not to look.

"He's asleep upstairs. You won't get a peep out of him. I gave him a bottle and put fresh sheets in his cot, and he's tucked up all nice in there with his teddy." She laughed too loudly, with a hand cupped over her mouth as if she was ashamed of her teeth. "The house is a little bit . . ." She looked over her shoulder. "It's hard to keep things nice with the baby wanting me all the time, and no one to help. There's a bit of –"

"Don't worry about that," Mum said briskly, and looked past Lindsey through the open door and into the hallway of her house. It was dark in there – all we could see was a row of coat hooks and some cracked wood-laminate flooring. It was council, Mum had warned me, a bad area – the missionaries often worked in areas like this, because here were the Brothers and Sisters who needed our service the most. The missionaries couldn't be scared or stuck up – they had to go where the fields were whitest. And so should we.

"It's really very good of you," Lindsey said, and grinned, and I could see that her teeth were stained and crooked. "And you've brought your . . ."

"This is Anthony," Mum said, and I went forward and shook her hand. It charmed her a bit, I could see that. She put her hand on her cheek and smiled.

"Doesn't a teenage boy have anything better to do on a Friday night than come out babysitting with his mum?"

"I want to help," I said, which was a barefaced lie, but what else was I supposed to say? It wasn't her fault I'd been dragged into it.

"How old are you?" she said, still smiling. Her nails were bitten raw. There was a rim of brown blood around the bottom of her thumbnail and it made my fingers ache to see it.

"Thirteen," I said, and Mum coughed.

"Shall we go inside?" Mum said.

"Thirteen. And man of the house," Lindsey said, "just like my Jayden."

That was the name of her baby. It didn't sound like a boy's name, but I just nodded at her and didn't say anything. She smiled and pulled a lipstick out of the pocket of her coat and started painting her lips with it. I wondered how she got it so neat without even looking, but before I had chance to stare she'd smacked her lips together and put the lipstick away.

"Won't you be cold in that?" Mum said.

Lindsey looked down at herself.

"I'll be all right. It's a party. A disco, right? Everyone's going to be in their glad rags. I can't go in jeans."

"No," Mum said, slowly, and I could see her frowning. Frowning because Maggie Travers should have said something to her about appropriate dress and church standards, and frowning because very often the female investigators got themselves into pickles like this because the missionaries – well, they were just young lads themselves really, and weren't comfortable addressing matters like this with a young woman. And she was young. Three or four years older than me, tops.

"What's wrong? Is it not all right?" She looked down at herself and tugged at the belt on her coat. Her shoes were too big for her and she tiptoed out of them to look down the street for the car she knew would come.

"You look very nice," Mum said, eventually.

Lindsey sighed. "That's all right then. You made me worried." She took a set of keys out of her handbag and gave them to Mum. "Just in case," she said, "but I'll be back before you know it."

"Before midnight," Mum said.

Even I could smell the cigarette smoke on Lindsey.

"Here's my lift," she said, and laughed, and trotted away to the car that had drawn up outside her house.

We stood on the doorstep and waved Lindsey away. The car flashed its lights once, twice, three times and beeped its horn, and through the open window we could hear Lindsey shrieking and doing her loud laugh. I felt Mum's hands on my shoulders.

"Right then," she said, "let's get started."

Mum must have been clued up to the state of things before we arrived, because she didn't look surprised by the rubbish in the front room, the dirty clothes lying everywhere, the empty tins of baby milk and nappies all over the place. Cigarette ends – hundreds of them, stubbed out in mugs and in saucers, on the floor, leaving burn marks on the laminate, on polystyrene chip trays, floating in half-empty plastic bottles of Coke.

The curtains weren't attached to the poles properly and you could see that the rubbish in the room was the only thing making it look cluttered – there wasn't much furniture at all. Just a shabby sofa with a sheet on it, as if it was someone's bed as well, and a coffee table with a broken leg. There wasn't even a telly. Since Dad left and we had to move we didn't have that much either, but Mum would never have let it get like this.

"I bet you're glad you wore your old togs now," Mum said.

We walked through to the kitchen, Mum taking her gloves off and stuffing them into her handbag. The stacks of dirty plates and dishes were toppling against the walls and there was mess everywhere: baby bottles with lumpy milk sitting in the bottom of them, black burned bits stuck to the cooker and the lino all sticky. There were a few bin bags heaped against the washing machine and when Mum twitched them open with her finger and thumb we saw they weren't filled with rubbish, but with damp and dirty clothes. Lindsey had loads and loads of clothes. It smelled in there.

"Maggie Travers said she'd been having trouble keeping up," Mum said, shaking her head, "but a wash a day – I could manage that with the two of you at home and under my feet. That's all it takes. Little and often."

"Maybe she's not got much money," I said. That's all I knew about single mothers. That they didn't have much money, and found it hard to keep up with things, and that we should look after them when we came across them, for the sake of the children if nothing else.

"Soap and elbow grease doesn't cost," Mum said, and looked at the ceiling as Baby Jayden the man of the house started to cry, "and we've got plenty of both. Get started on those dishes while I see to the baby."

Even after five minutes, the water was still running cold. I looked about for an immersion heater or a boiler but it didn't feel right to be nosing around, so I filled the kettle and put two pans full of water on the hob and washed them like that. Some of the smells made me feel sick – the sour milk, bits of food gone green and sticky and gumming plates together, old scraps of fish still wrapped up in greasy, vinegary newspaper.

I wasn't that impressed to be honest. If Mum had come straight out and said that the place was in a state, and we were going to have to clean it up together, and would I help her – well, that would have been different. I didn't see how this was preparation for my own mission. I'd be spreading the Word, not scraping muck off of someone else's plates. I squirted too much washing-up liquid into the bowl and bubbles overflowed around the taps and down the front of the kitchen cupboards, but what Mum couldn't see, upstairs while she sang to Jayden, she couldn't complain about.

It was all a bit much, really. The strip light in the kitchen buzzed and I wished there was a radio. *"Give," Said the Little Stream* came floating down through the ceiling and eventually the baby gradually stopped crying.

> *I'm small, I know, but wherever I go*
> *The grass grows greener still!*

It was an hour before Mum came down the stairs.

"He's out," she said, "fast asleep. I had to give him another bottle in the end. Lindsey had made one up and left it on the windowsill." She sounded surprised, but Lindsey must not have been completely useless, because the baby was alive, and doing well, and no one had took it off her yet, had they?

I waited for her to say something about all the washing up – clean and dry and stacked up on the counters. I didn't bother putting it all back inside the cupboards like I would have done if we'd been at home, because the insides of them all were filthy.

"Let's get on with these clothes," Mum said.

Typical.

We tackled the bin bags in the kitchen. Some of the clothes had mould spots on them where they'd been washed and put in the bags damp – others were so stuck together with whatever had stained them that Mum said they weren't worth washing, and threw them away.

"Have a look at this, would you?" Mum said, and shook out a leopard-print dress. It hung from her fist. "I wonder if they make the curtains to match with that pelmet," she said, and laughed, and chucked it at the bin.

While we emptied the bags, and sorted the clothes into piles, and set the washing machine going, Mum told me a story about Lindsey.

Apparently, Sister Morrison had given a lesson in Relief Society about Preparing for Eternal Marriage, and how important it was to keep yourself pure, and develop your talents, learn home-making skills and get as much education as you can. That working was important, and supporting yourself, because then you didn't have to rush into marriage with an unworthy man. But really, no other success in life – in the world, in your career, or anywhere else – could compensate for failure in the home. Lindsey, because she hadn't been to church that much, didn't know that you were supposed to sit quiet and listen, that it wasn't supposed to be like a discussion, or a free-for-all, so she'd got up out of her chair and shouted out.

"What if you've already got a baby, and done all sorts?" she'd said.

Mum said the other women were trying to be kind, and smile and not stare, but Lindsey didn't notice them.

"What if you're already saddled with a baby you didn't want in the first place? I was only fifteen when I had him. What am I supposed to do about that, then?"

No one answered her at first. Mum said she was angry, as if she'd been taking the lesson personally, and feeling like Sister Morrison had been making pointed remarks at her, rather than just general comments about applying Gospel principles in everyday life.

"Everything in life is a choice, Anthony," she said. "You'd never catch me going on like that. Not in a million years. Your conduct is in your own hands. Always. People can choose to be offended."

I didn't say anything. Apparently Sister Morrison dealt with it like an old hand, though no one could remember anything like that happening before.

"With God," she'd said, "nothing is impossible." And everyone else had nodded and smiled and that seemed to satisfy Lindsey because she sat down and looked at her scriptures for the rest of the lesson and didn't make any more of a fuss. Though Maggie Travers had noticed, and felt sorry for her, and that's why, Mum said, we were here tonight. Maggie Travers had decided Lindsey needed to make some new friends, meet people, maybe even men, and that we could help her out by getting her home nice and straight for her before she came back from the Dance.

We had the washing machine going all night. If it wasn't me going in to empty it into the tumble drier, or fold up the dry clothes, or fill it up again, it was Mum tiptoeing up the stairs to check on Jayden. We didn't stop all evening but when it got to midnight and most of the jobs were done, we sat down on Lindsey's shabby couch listening to the tumble drier go round.

"The missionaries sorted that out for her," Mum said. "They went and asked the Bishop and he got it for her out of Ward funds."

I couldn't tell if she thought it was a good idea or not. We needed things ourselves, but she'd never ask – only wait to be offered.

"I wonder why she never ran it? All those damp clothes. Some of them were completely ruined."

"It'll be the electricity," I said. And Mum nodded and said I was a bright lad.

Lindsey was late. As well as no telly there was no radio and only a few books. The only one of them that Mum would let me read was some stupid thing about being pregnant and having a baby. There were line drawings of women sitting up in bed with their legs apart and babies' heads coming out of their hoo-haas.

"What are you staring at?" Mum said, and looked at me over the top of her glasses. I turned the page quick and did a trump.

"Whoever smelt it dealt it!"

"Anthony James!" she said, but I wouldn't look at her and she chuckled under her breath and just left it. I waited while she wasn't looking, and turned the page back.

Once it got to one, Mum was nodding, her chin on her chest and her hands limp on her knee. Then Jayden started crying. Mum always said that Heavenly Father had designed a baby's cry to work physiologically on a woman – which meant any woman, hearing any baby, would have certain things happen to her body – her boobs and stuff – and that was how it was meant to be. Women who didn't look after their babies properly had something physically wrong with them, and should be pitied and not condemned. But she didn't wake up. I waited for a bit, staring at her mouth all slack, and the bags under her eyes. Then I got up and stood at the bottom of the stairs, looking up into the dark. I didn't feel anything in my body except a tightening round the back of my neck and under my balls, like all my skin was going a size too small.

"Mum?"

Jayden was getting going now, the noise coming down the stairs like a headache, and I went up them slowly, smelling the damp and the dirty carpet and hoping Mum would wake up before I got to the top. I tried to remember the words of the song she'd been singing before, the one that settled him. The wallpaper was cold and bumpy under my hand. I pushed the door open and it scraped along the carpet because the top hinge was undone.

"All right then, Jayden," I said, but just in my ordinary voice. No baby talk, no cooing and singing. We were the men of the house, us two. I smiled a bit at the thought – me and a little brown baby. A curly top that looked like a wig. Us two, in charge of anything.

"Come on then," I said, "let's be having you. What's to do?" They were the sorts of things my dad said now and again.

I stepped forward. Mum had left the window in the baby's bedroom open. The curtain was blowing back and forth, and the light from the street lamp shone yellow into the room, and then went, and then shone yellow again. There was a black and grey mottled pattern around the window, flowing into the corner of the room and up, across the ceiling and around the light fitting.

Jayden was really going for it now, and I waited in the doorway, holding my breath in the space between his cries, not breathing when he drew breath, so that I was as still as I could be, and so I could hear Mum coming up the stairs behind me, chunnering under her breath about how we all slept through the night before we were five months, and how could a baby who'd taken a full ten ounces be up and striking less than five hours later?

But she didn't come. Between the cries was nothing but silence, and darkness – even the wind and so the curtain and so the light were moving in time with the baby's sobs.

I stepped into the room. The moving shape in the cot turned, and I saw that its arm was caught between the bars of its crib. He was in my hands, all of a sudden, his head wet and heavy against my neck and the sound had stopped. I sat his bum on my forearm, his head resting against me, my other hand rubbing against his back.

"Come on then," I said, feeling stupid for talking because it's not like he could even understand what I was saying.

"Come on then." I jiggled my arm and felt his spit on my cheek, his hot breath in my ear, the stink of milk and wee all around us, like a little cloud.

"Come on then. There's no need for that then, is there? No need for that, is there? No need for that. No need. There's no need for that. No need for that at all, is there? Is there?"

Plant Life Weekly
PAUL FLACK

I camped the first night in a mountain cave. After packing up the next morning, I smoothed away my footprints in the dust. I then ascended to the crest of a granite ridge and could see most of my route for the day ahead. I checked my bearings with my map and compass. The air was cool, the sun veiled by altostratus, a few peaks still with a white tip. I felt strong.

In terms of flora, I didn't expect to see anything more than lichen in rock crevices, though I had encountered a strange specimen the previous afternoon. I couldn't find it in *The Pocket Book of North-European Fungi*, so I took digital shots from different angles and felt excited at the prospect of forwarding it to the Puzzle Corner of *Plant Life Weekly*. I'd do anything to get into *Plant Life Weekly*.

When I stopped to check my coordinates, I felt the chill of wind curling up the valley. I put on my matching set of tri-thermal gloves and hat and thought how expert I looked, bounding along, happy in my solitude and hoping not to see anyone that day. Shafts of sunlight were striking through, hitting huge expanses of jagged cliffs. This is my church, I thought. No stained-glass windows for me. I marvelled at the changing cloud formations and the altering tincture of the rock as the light varied.

It was three-quarters up the next rise that I saw someone coming the opposite way. Instinctively, I hid. I chose a detour up a short stretch of scree and settled in the shadow of an overhang. I had to step carefully through the shale, which moved under my feet, larger plates of it sliding towards my shins, though the additional risk was well worth not having to talk to anyone.

Ten minutes later, the intruder had still not passed. I decided to work upwards towards a viewpoint. My agility was restricted by my expedition-size rucksack, but I was confident in my movements. At home during the winter evenings I sometimes put on my full mountain apparel, including rucksack and boots, and walk up the stairs, then down again, then upstairs and down again. Then I unpack and repack my rucksack at speed, learning where to find items in a hurry. Then I walk up the stairs, then down again.

After twenty minutes there was still no sight of him. I climbed out of the gloom and looked across. I scanned through my Mini-Powerlex binoculars and there he was, hiding behind a rock. How ridiculous.

I strode towards the top of the next rise and glanced back. Fifty yards away, the figure raised his walking stick. I could see a faint plume of cigarette smoke. Before I could repress it, my arm lifted in mutual acknowledgement, two parishioners of the same church.

When I turned to look again a few minutes later, he hadn't moved. I brought him into focus. His back was towards me. With one foot on a rock, he studied the panorama of the range opposite. It occurred to me that with the curl of smoke still there and his arm extended, he was one for theatrical poses. He then put up the other arm to frame the view and with the cigarette-holding hand inched his vertical palm inwards, as if he thought a particular mountain should have been placed further to the left.

I shook my head in puzzlement and continued onward. I soon felt splendidly alone. Thankfully, there were no jet trails to remind me of humanity. All I wanted that day was to savour the peaks, the sky and the purity.

As soon as I saw over the ridge, I reached for my camera instantly, but then stood there transfixed. The only sound was my breath as it left me in my astonishment. Before me was a perfect tarn: elliptical, silver, mystical. Its stillness reverberated around me. I swallowed. Having taken a couple of shots, I scrambled down the slope. As I unbuckled the rucksack, shrugged it off and stepped closer, I decided to offer the scene as a cover for *Plant Life Weekly*, except there were no plants.

I set up the tripod, composed the shot and waited for another surge of sunlight. It soon came. About to click the button, I noticed a glint in a corner of the viewfinder. There it was again. Something at the water's edge. Curious, I zoomed in, but it was still just a gash of light between the granite and water. I walked towards it, presuming it was the transitory effect of some rock and the angle of light. I saw it clearly from ten yards. I was enraged. It was glare from the silver foil of an empty cigarette pack.

Sickened, I snatched it out of the water. Before I knew it, I was running back up the slope, litter in hand. At the ridge, I saw him stepping up the incline. I raced after him. I was within a couple of minutes of him when he noticed me. It was probably the clattering shale. Even from there I could tell he was white-haired and bearded. He smiled. I didn't.

Approaching him now, I wasn't impressed by his kit: a dingy rucksack by a defunct manufacturer, a knobbly cane with an iron handle for a walking stick.

I pushed the litter into his chest.

"What's this?" I said.

Confused, he glanced back towards the ridge, the tarn beyond. He had eyes the colour of the granite. He understood.

He faced me again. "Whose is this?" he said. "Can't be mine. It's faded. Look. Been there a while."

Momentarily derailed, I examined the box for the first time. Either rain or dew had started to dissolve the lettering. A brown tinge was apparent along the edges.

"Still shouldn't be here," I said.

The granite eyes, the stare. I didn't like his manner. Didn't he appreciate I was trying to keep the mountain the way it should be? He should have been disgusted too.

Then he took the cigarette box and replayed my own action, pushing it into my chest.

"Not a peaceful gesture, is it?" he said.

He pushed hard.

There was no reasoning to be had with this man, so I hit him. Just a prod really, hardly violent. A warning pass. He tottered backwards. Then I heard him inhale. He reached for the cane, using the iron handle as a club, and swung it at head height. I parried. I countered: a hefty thump to his shoulder that should have settled things. He was down and turning on the ground, trying to wield the cane again, so I back-heeled into his stomach. The cigarette box was left on the uneven rock between us. I tapped it with my foot towards him.

From a few paces away I watched his body tighten around his winded stomach, then he spluttered garbled words and was silent. I waited for him to stand, then thought he was waiting for me to leave. The fitter man had won. Perhaps he would reduce his smoking after this.

The sight of the cigarette box still nauseated me. I should prove I was the civilised one, I thought, and went over to retrieve it. I slipped it into a pocket in my rain jacket. Possible misinterpretations of what had happened over the last ten minutes occurred to me, but I reassured myself that I had acted in self-defence after his barbaric over-reaction with the cane.

The breeze picked up a notch, as if it were from a far-off sea. His back was to me, his white hair against the rock. There was still no movement, so I walked round to see his face. The eyes were closed. From his pale temple to the granite there was a line of blood. I bent down to check for any breathing. I felt under the wrist of the hand beside the cane. A definite pulse. I stood again. In the valley below I could see the mist bulging towards us. The coldness would soon kill him. I should try to keep him warm before I look for help. I carried a silver emergency blanket in my rucksack, but that was over the ridge. I considered searching his pockets for a hat and gloves, but that could be misinterpreted too.

Ten yards away again, I dithered. He could have broken bones. Should I give him my own hat and gloves? Well, of course I should. How could I even be questioning this? I retraced my steps, took off my hat and bent down to place it on him. And then I thought, why don't I just finish him off? He must be seventy. I'll smother him with my hat.

I jumped up and away. I couldn't do it. Not yet. I should treat the wound first if I could. I pulled a pack of wipes from my pocket and tore the sachet open. About to clean the cut, I stopped in mid-movement, the tissue an inch from his temple. Was I trying to remove evidence? Was that really my reason for playing nurse? A few paces away again, I considered my options. Tentacles of mist were now drawing close. He would be feeling the cold, even if I had the foil blanket to hand, or lent him my coat and lay beside him to give him my own body warmth.

I wondered what I'd want if it were me there on the rock. I wouldn't want to end my days in a wheelchair. I wouldn't want to die of exposure either. I found myself looking into the fabric of my hat, which I still held in my hand. It wouldn't take long. It would be the kindest thing. It would take substantial bravery on my part.

I bent down to examine his face again. No breath. No movement. Pulse weaker. I leaned closer. The loudest thunderclap then exploded in my brain. Then again, louder. Half the mountain was suddenly jammed inside my head – or rather, the iron handle of his cane. It tasted of blood and tooth fillings. The sky went fuzzy, or was it the ground? The mountain wobbled. I staggered. I spun. I kicked at where I thought he was but there was only air. He was fitter than I thought. I was seeing triple of everything and nothing of him. He must have been behind me, so I threw an arm out and rotated sharply to keep him away. But he must have moved back to raise the cane for another strike. I rushed twenty yards away, tripping and lurching, at times on all fours.

As the multiplied mountains merged back into themselves, I couldn't see him anywhere. Still looking over my shoulder regularly, I made my way back to where he had been lying on the rock. There were no boulders big enough for him to hide behind and the path was clear on both the ascent and descent. He couldn't have flown off the ledge. I peeked over it. A sheer drop. Impossible.

His vanishing act had more impact on me than the metal of his cane. What about the blood? Perhaps there was a trace of it on the rock. On my knees, I examined where I thought his head had been placed. There was only the silver-flecked grey of the granite. I then realised that I did have material evidence. I stood and unzipped my pocket, but I must have put the litter into another. Doubting my own sanity, I tore off my jacket, searched every pocket and pulled at their linings. I tipped everything out onto the rock. *The Pocket Book of Fungi*, my wallet, my comb, mini-torch and knife.

No cigarette box. I definitely hadn't lost consciousness after he hit me. I definitely did fight an old man. Yet how could he have disappeared?

I ran back up the track. The tarn might have vanished too. But it was still there. I realised that my earlier surprise at seeing it was because it didn't feature on the map. My rucksack was where I had left it on the slope, my tripod and camera still positioned for the shot I didn't take.

I don't know how long I sat there, staring at the scene and listening to the silence. Even the clouds seemed totally still. Eventually, I stepped down from the ridge to collect my belongings. I already suspected what I might see through the lens, though I wouldn't need a camera to record what I would never forget.

It was all exactly as before, including the flicker from the same place across the water.

The Wilds
JULIA BELL

It was a kindness, really. Sarah could live without the interruption on her only day without the children in months, but her mother had insisted in the insinuating way she had when she wanted Sarah to do something for her.

"She's feeling very fragile," she said. "I know she needs someone to talk to and it's not like you've got the kids. And you understand what she's going through."

Sarah wondered if her mother had forgotten how exhausting it was to have two young toddlers – constantly firefighting, never any proper sleep – how precious a quiet afternoon to rest. And although she and Robin were getting divorced, she prided herself on the fact that they had kept the situation amicable. It was not the same as Peggy Marshall's predicament at all, and she resented her mother for even suggesting that it was. But Peggy Marshall had become, of late, something of a best friend to Sarah's mother and it was really for her sake that Sarah had agreed.

So here she was, walking up the back of the dunes towards the beach, the sand blasting a layer of skin from her face, the clouds threatening drizzle, with Peggy Marshall running through the litany of wrongs that had been dealt her by her feckless and unfaithful husband, who had finally revealed to her after two years that he was having an affair with Julie Sawyer, a local artist who herself had recently got divorced.

"The trouble is, the wife is always the last to know. It's so humiliating."

Sarah did not contradict this. She had known about the affair for at least a year. It was common knowledge in the pub and the village shop. In fact, it was surprising that it had taken Peggy Marshall this long to figure it out.

"It's not even like he tried to hide it."

"Oh dear," Sarah said vaguely, wondering if they would make it to the marshes and back before they got soaked.

Peggy Marshall was well known for writing crime novels, which sold in huge quantities at airports and train stations and supermarkets. Novels that told stories of women who had suffered terrible and lurid tragedies – rapes, murders, abuse – who took revenge on their oppressors. In the denouement of her best-selling and most infamous novel a rapist was served his own penis lightly cooked in cream sauce while he slowly bled to death. These novels had made Peggy Marshall a very rich woman and along with this wealth had come a certain hauteur, which made her appear in the world as if she were manifesting it – marshalling, in concert with her surname – with each flash of her expensive smile and her Platinum American Express.

She had arrived at The Wilds and loudly and publicly fallen in love with the place. She'd bought a dilapidated fisherman's cottage and renovated it to the highest specifications, with a super-luxe kitchen, a sunken living room and a designer garden and conservatory that had featured at one time or another in the style pages of most of the Sunday newspapers. This had led to an influx of copycat weekenders, Londoners with money who had muscled out the locals by inflating house prices to Kensington levels. The one pub had been remodelled as a Michelin-starred gastropub, which now served food so expensive that the locals could hardly afford to eat there.

Sarah's mother was one of the few who had stayed put. Resisting the urge to make a quick profit on her house and move inland, she had made herself unpopular with the yahoos by protesting to the local council about every planning application that threatened to spoil the unique character of the area. These included some preposterous schemes that involved Libeskindstyle glass shells or porch extensions that resembled the portals of a space station. Until recently Peggy Marshall's name had the power of a curse in Sarah's mother's house. She was usually referred to as "that bloody woman" or "that awful novelist".

So it was slightly unnerving to hear her mother now talking about Peggy Marshall with such starstruck sympathy. Although they had known of each other for years, nodded hello in the street, at the post office, they had not met formally until some protest meeting about the expansion of the nuclear power plant further up the coast when they bonded, it seems, almost instantly. Perhaps, Sarah thought, she shouldn't have been surprised. They were quite similar in character, although Peggy Marshall was some twenty years younger. Both of them had the same kind of strident English sensibility, an indomitable public face, Common Sense their moral guide. Other People's Feelings were somehow inexplicable to them, which was why Sarah had to hide just the tiniest creep of *Schadenfreude* from turning up the corners of her mouth. She wasn't unkind enough to wish disaster on anyone, but Peggy Marshall's predicament seemed like a consequence of her inability to empathise with anyone who had a conscious thought that was different from her own.

Sarah had kept out of it, as she only came to The Wilds for weekends, usually with the children, or occasionally, as now, for a twenty-four-hour respite while Robin had the kids and her mother was away, an opportunity to soak in the bath and take a walk, clear her head, making ready again for the fray.

"He's just making such a terrible fool of himself. I don't know what he sees in her. She's just a silly hippy who makes bad pottery."

Julie Sawyer's pottery was of the *faux-naïf* variety – vases and mugs decorated with cartoonishly rounded cats and squirrels or abstract shapes and squiggles. They were popular with tourists and with Sarah's mother, who seemed to have acquired a whole dinner service in gaudy blue with sunflowers painted in the middle.

"Can you imagine it? I mean I know he's had affairs over the years, but this one is just *embarrassing*. I thought there might be something going on, but I dismissed it. The very idea of them together! He's so tidy and she's such a mess – you can tell just by looking at her! All that hair and clay! I can't go anywhere without getting patronising looks from people. I don't understand why he felt the need to shit on his own doorstep. She's hardly one of *us*."

Sarah knew instinctively she was not included in this plural.

They reached the top of the dunes to face a silver-grey sea that roiled around the curve of the bay, the wind flecking the surface with spits of foam.

"Love is fickle," Sarah ventured. "It's not always possible to predict who we will fall in love with."

"Oh he's not in love!" Peggy Marshall said, dismissing the idea with a flap of her hand. "He's having a mid-life crisis."

Sarah had only seen Brian Marshall a few times, mostly behind the wheel of his muddy-green Chelsea tractor, hogging the road on the blind corner on the way into the village, forcing her into the verge, or in the pub, talking loudly about a boat that he was restoring. He had worked in banking, taken early retirement at forty-five. For a man so ostensibly wealthy he had the harried expression of someone much poorer, balding, with a creased forehead, his nose a map of drinker's veins. Sarah suspected that he was probably quite happy with Julie Sawyer: with her rainbow-knit cardigans and the mild manner of an art teacher, whatever the shortcomings of her aesthetic choices she was nice, which was probably a quality Brian Marshall had not encountered in many years.

"And it's just not fair on Lando."

Orlando Marshall. The only son. There was a daughter, but she was much older, had already left home and was rarely seen in The Wilds. Sarah had heard various stories: that she had anorexia, a rock-star boyfriend, that Peggy had fixed her up with a job on a fashion magazine. Orlando was still a child, a late afterthought, or an accident, perhaps. Sarah knew him as a shy, lanky boy who whizzed around the village on a red scooter, although more recently, she had noticed, he had swapped the scooter for a skateboard and was beginning to look like a teenager. A few weekends ago she had passed him on the beach, sat round a makeshift fire with similar-looking boys – friends from his boarding school and a few locals – giggling loudly, enveloped in a sickly cloud of marijuana smoke.

"Yes, I suppose teenagers are quite prone to rebellion," she said, vaguely.

Peggy turned and looked at her sharply. "Why, what have you heard?"

Sarah winced. "Well I –"

"Have you seen him?"

"Well no, I –"

Peggy Marshall sighed as if the air were being forced out of her. "It's the thing I can't stand about being a celeb–" She caught herself. "About being in my position. You can't do anything without someone gossiping about it. Especially round here. I hardly see him these days. He's rarely up before midday, and then when he does get up he speaks two words to me before going out with his friends or sitting in front of his Xbox shooting things. He used to be such a *good* boy. So attentive. And charming! People loved him, were drawn to him. He's Oxbridge material. But I've been called to the school *twice* in the last term to talk about his behaviour . . ."

She paused, bit her lip. "They found him smoking . . . *drugs*. I've told Brian he needs to talk to him. But he's too busy mooning over that bloody hippy to pay attention. At Lando's age boys need their fathers." She ran her hands across her face.

Sarah was surprised to hear Peggy Marshall sounding so shocked. Teenage boys drank beer and smoked pot. It was a quotidian rite of passage, just as it had been for many of Sarah's contemporaries. And Sarah had the sense that in spite of the wealth and the private education there was probably quite a lot for Orlando Marshall to be pissed off about. He would grow out of it most probably, and take up a place at university – if not Oxbridge then still somewhere good. Or he might even take advantage of his mother's connections, get a job in the media like his sister. These things were laid out for boys like Orlando, although perhaps they could not see them yet.

The beach was heavy going, her feet sinking into the wet shingle as if she were wading through mud, and the crunch of the stones and the roar of the sea made it hard to hear. She stumbled, and pressed her hand down onto the shingle to steady herself. When she was upright again she saw that her finger was bleeding. "Ow." She sucked it, tasted salt and iron. "Perhaps we could walk further up? On the dunes?"

But Peggy Marshall seemed not to hear; she was already several strides ahead up the beach. "Isn't it bracing?" she shouted, her hands pushed firmly into the pockets of her Barbour. "So wild!"

Sarah shivered.

They walked along like this for a few minutes, Peggy Marshall turning her face to the turbid sea, the wind blowing hair across her face in wispy strands. It was the kind of face into which photographers could project determination, will to power, a kind of seer's grace, as if she really could see further, deeper into the human condition than ordinary mortals. It was also the kind of face that had undergone several expensive cosmetic procedures, including regular shots of Botox, which meant that she found it hard to smile without appearing as if she were grimacing.

"So how are you coping?" she asked, suddenly turning back to face Sarah.

"With what?"

"*Your* divorce."

"Oh. Well, fine. I mean, it hasn't been easy, but things are quite well settled now. Robin's new partner is amazing. The kids really like him."

Peggy Marshall's eyes widened into two round O's. This was obviously information that Sarah's mother had neglected to pass on.

"*Him?*"

"Er, yes. Robin has a boyfriend now."

"Oh, how *fascinating*."

Sarah cringed; Peggy Marshall's expression unnerved her. There was something almost delighted in the way she arched her eyebrows.

"Well?"

Sarah shrugged.

"Weren't you *devastated*?"

"Not really," she said, staring at the mosaic of shingle beneath her feet. It seemed like a map of her head: all the millions of stones like thoughts, scattered each day by the tides then jumbled up together and beached in a different part of her mind.

Dear, kind Robin. Of course she had known. He had told her he was bisexual when they met, but he wanted to have kids and his sexual preference had been switched to override by his hormones. Their wedding had turned into the biggest, wildest party they had ever thrown, and he had expended a great deal of ecstatic attention on the details of her dress and the corsage. They did their first dance to Abba for crying out loud.

So it was not really a surprise to her, then, when he came to her one day, in tears, explaining how he had met Ben at work and how they had this intense, mercurial attraction to each other. She had let him go, almost with relief. She was never all that excited about their sex life anyway, and being with Ben meant that he happily took the boys at weekends. She wondered sometimes why people struggled along in couples at all. At how they destroyed their partners with their pathologies, their habits, until they grew into strange and distorted shapes just to accommodate each other.

"He's happy – *we're* happy, that's all that matters."

"But what about your kids?"

"What about them?"

"Well . . ." Sarah watched Peggy's frozen face as she tried to formulate the sentence. "Well . . . aren't they *disturbed*?"

"Should they be?" Sarah drew herself up to her full height, which was still several inches shorter than Peggy Marshall. She resented these kinds of underhand insinuations disguised as concern.

"Of course not. It's just that . . . it must be *hard* for you . . . being a single mum."

"Robin does more than his share." Although perhaps that wasn't *strictly* true. She'd had to bully him a bit more than she'd like to take the kids at weekends.

"But children need both parents. Don't you think?"

"Of course, but I don't see that they have to *live* together."

The sky had almost entirely closed over, the horizon suddenly drawn close by the rain. "Ugh." Sarah pulled up her hood. Another half an hour of trudging through the drizzle with Peggy Marshall – the universe owed her that bath.

"This way."

Peggy Marshall took a sharp right turn up the beach towards the marshes. It was a tradition of The Wilds that you walked along the beach for a mile and a half, and then turned inland for home across the boardwalks that criss-crossed the freshwater marshes that sat in the triangular hollow between the village and the sea. The marshes were an endangered habitat: the encroaching sea regularly punched holes in the dunes, turning the edges of the marsh brackish and spoiled. Eventually the dunes would erode altogether and the freshwater ecosystem with all its newts and caddis flies and butterflies would turn into a saltwater lagoon. Scientists had modelled the decline on computers and given reports to government: there was little point in defences, the sea would have its way, however many groynes were built. Besides, there were more important industrial sites further up the coast that needed more urgent protection.

At least the marshes afforded some shelter from the rain – the reeds had grown higher than the top of her head. The roar of the sea was suddenly muffled as they took the rough wooden steps down onto the boardwalk. They had to walk single file, Sarah, uncomfortable in front, listening to her own breathing under her hood, the scrape of their clothes against the reeds, Peggy Marshall's hefty footsteps behind her, the quick scuttle of birds.

"Isn't it quiet?" Sarah asked, interrupting the silence that had fallen between them.

Before Peggy Marshall could reply there was a shimmer in the reed bed ahead of them – bigger than a bird, perhaps a human – the shape of a hood. The gentle plosh of water. Sarah thought she heard someone say "They're coming," but she couldn't be sure. She stopped to listen. Peggy Marshall nearly bumped into her.

"What is it?"

"I don't know," Sarah whispered. "Something up ahead. I heard noises."

"Probably birdwatchers. If you'll just let me . . ." And she jostled Sarah out of the way to overtake. "Thank you . . ." Strode on ahead of her and around the corner out of sight.

Sarah was annoyed. What if it was a rare bird or animal? Whatever was there that might have been worth seeing had probably fled for its life by now. Then she heard a loud, sharp crack, which echoed across the marshes, sending a flurry of ducks into the air in a startled cloud, followed by a heavy whump, like the sound of a sack being dumped. All she could see in front of her were the reeds emerging from the water in a dense green thatch.

"Peggy?" Sarah hastened her step. "Peggy?"

The figure who confronted her was wearing combat fatigues and a balaclava printed with a green, grinning skull. Over his eyes were a pair of safety goggles and he was holding a handgun of some kind. At first Sarah could not process what she saw. This was The Wilds not some Middle Eastern combat zone. And he was considerably shorter than her.

"Where's Peggy?" she demanded, but he just looked at her. A tinny sound came from his Bluetooth headset, like the buzz of a fly.

"OK," he said curtly, then putting a finger to his skeleton chops he waved her on with the tip of his gun.

She stared at him. "You need to tell me what's going on. Now."

"We're Taliban," he said.

"*Right* . . ." she said, carefully. She recognised him. He was the son of the couple who ran the pub. He must be twelve, maybe thirteen at most, his voice still reedy, childlike. "So where did you get that gun?" she said, in her best talking-to-children voice.

"Lando gave it to me."

"Did he now? And where did he get it from?"

The boy shrugged. "Don't know."

"Can I just take a look at it?"

She stretched out her hand towards him and she sensed a hesitation, but he pulled back before she could snatch it from him. "Lando says I have to guard the frontier."

"Does he?" The boy nodded. "And where is he?" The boy pointed with the gun down the boardwalk. "Is Peggy down there too?" Another uneasy nod.

The way forward was a long corridor of green, diminishing to the next turn, which would take her out of the marshes and up onto the path that ran past the allotments and back towards the village. Sarah found her legs were suddenly watery, her brain urging them forward but she wasn't moving at any meaningful speed. She was caught between a mixture of anger and fear. She would be saying something to his parents, that was for sure. He couldn't go round pointing guns at people, even if it wasn't a real gun. The thought of it tickled her spine. It wasn't real, surely? They were just playing a game, and Peggy had rushed on and would be waiting somewhere up ahead with Orlando, full of loud comments about badly behaved youth. They needed a good old-fashioned clip round the ear.

Instead there was another figure in combat fatigues, his head wrapped in a kind of improvised turban that covered his face. At his feet Peggy lay motionless, a thick trickle of blood coming out of her nose.

"Oh my – Peggy?" She bent down to attend to her but was rewarded with a sudden and shocking kick in the face.

She yelped and fell backwards so that she was sprawled out in front of him. He took a step closer. He was so young, she thought, but his body gave off some kind of acrid, crystal smell of sweat and something else – meat, maybe.

"Now, Orlando," she said, slowly and clearly. "What are you doing?"

"I'm NOT Orlando. My name is Akhtar Mohammed Zakir," he said, his voice muffled by his scarf. "I am Taliban, and you are the infidel." He punctuated this with jabs from his gun.

She stood up, slowly, raising her hands above her head. "OK . . . but perhaps it's time to stop your game. We need to take her – your mother – to the hospital."

"She is not my mother." He kicked her prone figure.

"Orlando!"

But he just blinked. "I told you. That is NOT my name!" He pressed the gun into her stomach. "Kneel."

She did as he commanded. Then he lifted the gun and pressed it to her head. The world seemed to shrink to the cold hole of its muzzle. Her mouth went dry. She thought she might faint with the pressure. He pulled away, muttering to himself in what sounded like Arabic, walking around her, holding the gun in different positions as if he were practising. The children – oh God, the children. Please, please, don't let me die. Involuntarily, she started to whimper, and a warm trickle of pee ran down her leg.

She closed her eyes so she wouldn't have to see him and saw instead a kind of jumbled montage of scenes from her life. The children, Robin, her mother. Absurd, half-remembered things – the side of her first boyfriend's face, just the jut of his jaw; a poster of a Mayan mask that was on the wall in the anthropology department where she worked as a secretary; the riff of a song that she didn't even like. Was this what it meant to have your life flash before you? She opened her eyes just in time to see him pull the trigger.

Sarah sat on the edge of the sofa, nervously. She assumed they were going to offer her money, and there was a variety of opinions as to whether she should accept it or not. From Robin, who was utterly furious and who thought she should squeeze them for every last penny, to her mother, who brusquely pronounced that it was vulgar to take bribes, especially, she said, as the damage had been largely superficial and it was a tragedy, really, that Orlando was showing such obvious symptoms of mental illness. But although it had taken only a few weeks for the bruising to heal, she was still suffering from flashbacks and nightmares and she hadn't been for a walk across the marshes since. In fact, she had hardly been down to The Wilds.

Peggy Marshall had come out of hospital and was on the mend in some private clinic in California, somewhere especially designed to help people who had suffered traumatic shocks. She had broken her arm in the fall and a pellet had been removed from her neck. Brian had broken it off with Julie Sawyer, and moved back home. That much she knew from her mother, who, even now, was still in touch with Peggy – "She needs her friends around her now more than ever." What was to happen to Orlando seemed largely in the hands of the psychiatrists, the CPS and, as her lawyer would have it, Sarah.

Brian Marshall came back into the lounge carrying two cups of tea.

"Here." He put one on the table next to her. "You did say you wanted sugar, didn't you?"

His hands were shaking, she noticed, and she wondered if this was because he was nervous, or because he hadn't had a drink that morning.

"So," he said, smiling at her without meeting her eye, "how are you?"

"I've not been sleeping so well."

"Ah yes. Well, happens to us all as we get older. Whatever happened to that sleep we used to have as teenagers, eh? You couldn't get me out of bed with a cowpoke. I mean . . ." He trailed off.

"Does Orlando sleep like that, do you think?"

"Ah. Yes, well . . ."

As far as Sarah knew, Orlando had been sectioned. The court case was due next week, although it was just a preliminary hearing, and as Peggy was not pressing charges, the outcome of this seemed to lie entirely with Sarah's evidence and the psychiatric report.

"Well, I suppose that's why we're here."

Sarah sipped her tea. It was too weak and sugary for her. She put it back on the table, a nice-looking antique blanket box. "I suppose it is."

She looked at Brian Marshall, in his battered Italian loafers; his chinos had a grease stain on the thigh. He was scruffier than she thought he should be. With all that money he could at least afford a new pair of shoes. Or maybe that's what the poor liked to think about the rich, that if *they* were rich they would never have to wear a sock with a hole in it again, everything would be brand new, box fresh, no need to make do and mend. Whereas the reality of money was that it meant the security of knowing that you *could* buy a new pair of Italian leather loafers whenever you wanted. Whether you actualised this or not was not the point. It was the possibility that counted. This thought made her even more resolved. Whatever they were offering she would have him double it by the time she left.

"How is he?"

Brian shrugged. "Hard to tell. They've got him on so much medication . . ." He looked at the floor. "I'm sorry you got caught up in all of this."

"Me too. I haven't been able to sleep without pills since it happened. I keep bursting into tears. I've had to take time off work." It made her sound like a victim on a daytime TV show, but the real tragedy was that it was true. She had always taken for granted that she was strong and capable, that she could deal with most of the things that life threw at her, but now she found she was tremulous, nervous, jumping at sudden noises, easily moved to tears. She didn't like the sense of her own powerlessness, the realisation that an intense experience of her own fear could unseat her so utterly. And more than that, she didn't want the children to see her like this. They needed a mother who was strong and confident, who could deal with life, not one who shrieked when they dropped their toys, or cowered in the bedroom while they played hide and seek.

"The doctor thinks he was having a manic episode. Probably precipitated by the cannabis. At least it seems to have triggered a massive disconnect from reality. He thought you were soldiers.

Peggy's writing about it."

"So soon?"

He winced. "Well as you know the papers have gone mad about this one. They've been offering her silly money for her side of the story."

"She could say no." Sarah shrugged.

"You try telling her that." He laughed without humour. "So . . ." He rubbed his hands on his knees. "Obviously, we'd like to make you an offer. Some kind of *compensation*. I realise – I mean, Peggy and I realise, that this must have been a terrible ordeal."

"You could say that."

"How does fifty thousand pounds sound?"

It sounded like a fortune, though she was slow to react. "And what do I have to do for this?"

He looked surprised. "Oh, nothing. Consider it a gift. A small recompense for the trouble we've caused you. You seem like a very nice woman and Peggy has a great deal of respect for your mother. We were just wondering what you were going to say about the others . . ."

"The other boys?"

"Yes. Well here's the thing. They are both claiming that he terrorised them – that it started off innocently enough as a game, but then he started shooting them, forcing them to smoke cannabis. Kept them prisoner in the bird hide. They keep changing the story. Especially since Orlando's been sectioned. I mean, I don't have any doubts that he was being a difficult little shit but he didn't do this on his own . . ."

"I wasn't going to say that. I was going to explain what happened. As well as I can, I mean. My memory of it all is a little hazy."

"Well of course. But if you could say that, it would be a start. I mean, are you *entirely* sure it was Orlando who shot you?"

"Yes."

He sighed. "But there's sure and *sure*. You were traumatised, it was raining, their faces were disguised . . . I'm not asking you to point the finger at anyone, just to be honest about the fact that you can't be sure."

She was silent for a moment. Well here it was, the moral

dilemma. She felt as though she was on a game show – any moment the scenery would pull back to reveal an audience, banks of secret cameras. In one hand fifty grand which would pay for a new kitchen, a holiday, and the loft conversion if she was careful. Things that Peggy Marshall could probably command with the click of her fingers without even thinking about the cost. On the other hand were more intangible abstracts like justice, the truth, and the salutary triumph of standing up to the Marshalls, the fantasy that she might be the one to finally bring them to their senses by refusing to be marshalled by them. She could show them the meaning of humility, and that no amount of money in the world was going to change the fact that Orlando was mentally ill, or that if it had been a real gun instead of a souped-up BB gun, both she and Peggy Marshall would be stone-cold dead by now.

"Perhaps you were expecting . . . a little more?" She saw him reach for his chequebook. Her heart beat faster. "How about eighty thousand?"

That was a *lot* of money: she could pay off a chunk of the mortgage, take the kids abroad. But still there was something about it that stuck in her gullet. It just reconfirmed the notion that throwing money at a problem would always make things work out in their favour. Reinforce the idea that their lives had the Teflon coating of cold hard cash and family connection, which meant that unlike for the poor, nothing bad ever really stuck.

"A hundred?"

But the money meant nothing. Orlando Marshall was showing signs of a serious mental illness. This could not be changed. His mind would wander where it wanted, grow and distort and balloon in ways they hadn't even begun to dream of yet. Whatever she said in court wouldn't alter that and whatever small insult her refusal might inflict on them, the damage was already done. She nodded, and watched as Brian Marshall uncapped the lid of his fountain pen and wrote out the amount in steady circles, as if the numbers held in them the power of an ancient charm, some old capacity to turn back the sun.

Seeing Red
SUSAN GREENHILL

I knew my husband was no longer a family man when he came home one Saturday lunchtime with a brand-new Porsche. He had just celebrated his fortieth birthday.

His eyes blazed with a passion that I had not seen for a long time. Could this be the start of a mid-life crisis? Was he halfway through one? Or was this the grand finale?

"How are we going to get three kids in that, Benjamin?" I asked sourly, standing on the edge of the pavement and pointing my foot at the gleaming, bulging rear wing. I watched fascinated as my magnified shoe approached the convex shiny red surface, becoming larger and more distorted the nearer it got, and noticed his nervousness with satisfaction.

He glanced at me briefly. "They can go in your car," he said, pulling a yellow duster from the pocket of his recently purchased leather jacket and polishing the body of his tart trap with undisguised love.

I looked up at our Victorian terraced house, with its slipped tiles and peeling paintwork. I thought of the inherited stair carpet, already tired when we bought the place ten years earlier, and the sagging stained ceiling in the corner of the living room where the bath had overflowed last winter, when the dripping water had made the Christmas-tree lights fizz.

"What about the house?" I sighed.

"What do you mean?" he replied, without taking his eyes off the large headlamps. As he moved the duster gently over them, round and round, he was so close I thought he was going to lick them.

"And a summer holiday?"

"We're going to Cornwall," he whispered to the wing mirror, misting it with his hot breath.

"Camping," I said. "In a tent." I folded my arms tightly to prevent my hands escaping and throttling him. "Take the car back. Get your money refunded, and let's spend it on something we can all benefit from."

Now prone on the bonnet, his cheek pressed against the perfect bodywork, he flicked away a speck of rogue dust.

I stared down at the top of his head.

"You could get a job as a monk," I snorted.

"Want to go for a spin?" he asked, deaf to my sarcasm.

"Not really," I sniffed. "Unless you think that locking three kids in the house on their own, with the oven on high and a pan of fish fingers inside it is a good idea."

He shrugged.

"Well, if you're too busy, perhaps I'll just take her round to show Mark."

"*Her?*" I turned and stomped back into the house. I looked at the once white hall walls, now reminiscent of a Jackson Pollock, splashed by liquids, scarred and scuffed by bikes and buggies, covered in handprints, with dirty dust marks around the radiators and mapping where pictures had moved. If I dropped dead he'd be sorry, I thought, before realising that probably he wouldn't. He would most likely be delighted to get rid of a wife of twelve years without having to pay any alimony and solicitor's fees, or part with the house and children. He could just move in a younger model, for whom he'd no doubt install the latest, state-of-the-art kitchen.

A smell of burning fish fingers permeated the air. I retrieved them from the oven. Another minute and the children would have been drawing with them, not eating them. Opening a cupboard I took out the ketchup, only remembering the loose hinge when it was too late. The door crashed down into the sink. A child entered and stared open-mouthed.

"What happened?" she asked.

"Your father has bought a new car," I replied crisply, "and take those bath towels off and put them back where they belong."

"But we're playing nuns," Clementine whined.

"Find something else to do. Unless you want to play at scrubbing them clean again later. Anyway, your lunch is ready."

The child opened her mouth as if about to speak, thought better of it, closed it again, and left the room.

"Mark was really jealous," my husband laughed later, bouncing into the kitchen where I was ironing. He washed his yellow duster in the sink and smoothed it out carefully over the radiator to dry, as though it were a priceless sheet of gold leaf.

I resisted the urge to hold the iron down on the sleeve of his shirt for a full five minutes.

"Is that why you bought a Porsche? In the hope of alienating all your friends?" I hissed sweetly.

"What's got into you?" he asked. "What have I done?"

"Absolutely nothing," I replied. "Except that I rather wonder about your motive for buying such an expensive and flashy car."

"I've always wanted a Porsche, you know that. What's the problem? At last I can afford one. I work hard – my job is boring, but it pays well. The car is my reward to myself, for sticking it out day after day, year after year. What's wrong with that? You buy yourself new clothes."

"We all need clothes."

A sudden extra burst of steam from the iron froze in the air.

"I thought you would like the car."

"Why? It's not mine. You didn't even consult me before you bought it. Mine is the battered green hatchback with a dodgy fuel gauge and a radio that crackles."

"Tune it in then."

"It won't tune."

"The kids think the Porsche is great. Charlie loves it."

"He's six years old. He doesn't have to pay for anything. That car is a very expensive toy. It will eat petrol. And where are you going to park it?" I added smugly. "It'll get broken into around here."

"I've sorted out garaging for it underneath the block of flats by the shopping centre."

"So that's more money wasted," I answered, crashing the ironing board closed.

I rarely questioned the state of our marriage. I didn't have time. But suddenly I felt left behind. How can anyone feel threatened by a car? But I did. And that first night when Benjamin laid the Porsche keys down on his bedside table, and slept facing them, it was as if he had driven the car into our bed and parked it between us. Having previously been fairly relaxed about what he did and where he went when he wasn't at home, and believed whatever he told me, I now believed nothing, and became suspicious of everything.

Perhaps this was when the rot set into our marriage, or perhaps it had set in earlier and I just hadn't noticed. Things did not improve when he came home from work on Friday night two weeks later and announced that he had invited his new boss and his wife to dinner the following evening.

"I couldn't get out of it," Benjamin explained, when I complained about the short notice. "He said he wanted to talk something through with me before Monday morning. I thought we could all have dinner together, then Malcolm and I can go off to my study while you chat to his wife."

"Perhaps I'd rather spend my Saturday evening watching television or reading a book instead of cooking and being polite and then being forced to have a girlie chat with a woman I've never met," I replied, taking a swig from my glass of wine by the stove and massacring the potatoes. "And what about getting the food?" I continued. "I'm taking Clementine to a party tomorrow afternoon, halfway across London. And I never go to Waitrose on Saturdays. It's packed – you queue for hours at the checkout behind people who seem to be stocking up for the next decade. How about you doing the shopping and cooking, for a change?"

"I would be only too happy to, but I've agreed to play a men's doubles at eleven. I can't let the other guys down. And Mark managed to get us two seats for the Chelsea game in the afternoon. But don't worry about the wine, I'll get that."

On Saturday morning Benjamin collected his car from the garage, parked it outside the house, and stood by the window looking at it while he ate his breakfast.

"Your car's got a puncture," he told me. "Did you know?"

I didn't, but I was thrilled.

"You'll have to do the shopping now, Benjamin," I told him.

"Can't do that," he replied. "I haven't got time."

"OK," I said. "But in that case, as I'm ready to go to Waitrose now, I'd better take the Porsche."

"Can't you get the bus?" he asked.

"No," I answered firmly, putting on my coat. "If it's our car, I'll use it. But I'd be grateful if you could change the wheel on the hatchback before you go out, so that I have it this afternoon. You won't need a car today – you can walk to the tennis club in ten minutes."

He looked at me as if I had just told him my mother was coming to live with us, and bringing her incontinent cat.

"He is your boss. And it was you who invited them," I said, taking his car keys from the top of the fridge.

He puffed out his cheeks and eyed the ceiling as if God might be sitting somewhere in the centre light, about to perform a motoring miracle.

"Or we could order in a pizza or an Indian takeaway?" I suggested.

"I'll need to give you a lesson in how to drive it first," he said eventually.

"Why do I need a lesson?" I snapped. "I've been driving for nearly twenty years and I've hardly had any accidents."

"It's not that easy to drive. You have to be very careful. You have to concentrate. No getting carried away listening to some chat show on Radio 4, or looking in shop windows. And what are you going to do with the children?"

"They'll have to come with me," I answered.

I called the kids and marched them out of the front door. He followed, and hovered nervously around the car, banging his tennis racket against his right knee and scratching his head, as he watched us all pile in.

"Don't put your dirty shoes on the seats," he said.

I slammed the door, revved the engine hard, and roared off up the road, waving out of the window.

I was terrified. I don't like driving strange cars. The horns

are in different places and, planning to turn right, I muddled the indicator with the windscreen wipers. I wasn't used to such a big car, the bulging sides distorted my spatial awareness, and it was so low I could almost feel my bottom scraping along the tarmac. Pulling out into a main street from a side turning, I couldn't see what was coming through the windows of the surrounding parked vehicles, and was virtually in the middle of the road before I could check that the way was clear. And my concentration was shredded by the noise reverberating inside the small space, as the two younger children fought in the ashtray-size seats behind me.

Our local supermarket car park is a cavernous concrete bunker with low-slung pipes snaking across its silver insulation-clad ceiling. It is dotted liberally with large square tangerine concrete pillars, which need to be negotiated with care, like a slalom course on the flat. Parking down there is not an activity to be taken lightly. Or in a rush. Or in a bad temper. And certainly not in a car that you have never driven before, except if you are very rich. And then presumably you could get your shopping delivered by Harrods. It is obvious from the multi-coloured horizontal stripes on the orange monoliths that many drivers have misjudged them badly. Perhaps prospective shoppers should be offered free driving lessons. There must be many customers for whom the underground car park has constituted a far greater expense than the weekly shop itself.

After sitting in a queue for twenty minutes, edging slowly towards the entrance, past the optimistic five miles an hour sign, choking on toxic fumes and with the children complaining vociferously, I shuffled the great beast into a space measured out very precisely to house a medium-size vehicle and allow an anorexic driver and emaciated passenger just enough room to squeeze out through their respective side doors. I looked at the tiny gap on each side of the Porsche and contemplated climbing out through the roof. The children thought this was a splendid idea, especially if it meant they could slide down the bonnet. Taking a quick peep for anything suspicious in the glove compartment, I froze as I noticed a long blonde hair reclining on the edge of the black-leather passenger seat. I looked at my dark-haired children now bobbing up and down in the rear-view mirror, and then at myself, perhaps imagining that the anxiety of the drive might have drained the colour out of my henna-dyed hair.

"Open the doors, Mummy," Clementine yelled impatiently.

I wiped away a hot tear, and with a shaky hand took my purse out of my bag, slid out a half-empty book of first-class stamps from one of the internal sections and slipped the strand of hair inside, for possible forensic testing.

However carefully we had got out of the car, it would have been impossible for the driver's door not to come into contact with the passenger door of the car in the next bay. After we had all clambered out through the narrow gap and the children were scooting off across the car park on supermarket trolleys, my eyes were drawn to a dent and a sliver of red paint on the side of the newly registered black BMW parked on my right. I spat on a paper tissue, and looking around to see that I wasn't being watched, rubbed the red mark. The paint didn't move. Had I been on my own I would have jumped back in the car immediately, and left before the BMW driver returned. But the children had now reached the far side of the car park, climbed into a trolley and were keeping the lift doors open, much to the annoyance of the other waiting passengers.

Feeling sick and flustered I ran away from the car and towards them, their childish voices at top volume urging me on.

Inside the shop it was hot and crowded.

"Put the carrots back," I said sternly to Polly and Charlie.

"They're our swords," said Charlie, whacking his sister around the ear.

"That really hurt," she sobbed, snapping the carrot in half as she stabbed it hard into his stomach. Trumping his performance as Third Shepherd in the school nativity play, Charlie staggered across the vegetable aisle groaning loudly, and collapsed onto the broccoli and beans.

What can I do that's quick and easy? I wondered, picking up two bundles of asparagus and a bag of mixed salad, whilst trying to pretend that the children were not mine.

I looked around for the possible owner of the BMW. Was it the smart middle-aged couple in matching camel-hair coats, who looked as if they were about to juggle with three pomegranates? Or could it be the rich-looking elderly lady sniffing a tomato, who must have only just returned from wintering abroad if she felt the spring weather was cold enough for her to flaunt her mink. But it couldn't be her. She was so shrunken and small she would barely be able to see over the steering wheel.

I picked up a leg of lamb. Cooked on a bed of rosemary, it would have to do.

The children had disappeared. I found them by the confectionery, with their pockets bulging.

"Put it all back," I hissed furtively. "You'll be caught on camera and probably go to prison."

"No school then," sang Charlie delightedly, attempting a cartwheel.

I was exhausted and not yet halfway round the store, still needing cream, oranges, brown sugar, cheese – the list was endless. Reaching for a tin of coffee I caught the display with my sleeve and the contents of the shelf cascaded onto the floor. As the tins rolled from side to side they seemed to be laughing.

Charlie and Polly started hauling giant tubs of chocolate ice cream out of the frozen-food cabinet. An elderly couple stared at us open-mouthed, shaking their heads and beginning to tut. Was it my badly brought up children that they found so offensive, or had they perhaps seen me rubbing the side of the BMW with a tissue?

I felt a tap on my shoulder and swung round, ready to deny everything, but it was a neighbour.

"I've got Benjamin's bloody boss and his wife coming to dinner tonight," I told her, leaning against the pasta and rice. "My car's got a puncture, and the children are appalling. It makes me want to reach for the bleach."

"I've finished. I'm going to the checkout." She smiled. "My kids asked if yours could come and play, so why don't I take them now? You'd be doing me a favour – mine are on the point of killing each other. They need some outside interest."

Relieved of my children, I went to the dairy section. I had just picked up a pack of butter and a large chunk of strong-smelling ripe Brie, when my phone rang. It was Benjamin.

"How's the car?" he asked. "Still in one piece, I trust."

I was wondering how to answer, when he added, "I meant to tell you. My boss has a cholesterol problem and they are both vegetarians."

I hung up.

"Are you OK?" a woman asked me in an anxious voice. "Would you like some water? Or a chair? Shall I call an ambulance?"

I shook my head and thanked her. After replacing the cheese, the milk, the butter and the lamb, I joined the fish queue.

Fortunately the mark on the Porsche is on the edge of the door; perhaps Benjamin won't notice it, I told the large salmon silently, as the fishmonger slapped its silver-sequined body onto the scales. Or I could tell him it wouldn't have happened if he'd done the shopping. The glassy-eyed fish glowered. And whose hair is it? I wondered, suddenly remembering my neighbour's bouncing blonde bob. I had just given her my children. The salmon's open mouth gaped. His boss is bound to be fat and pompous, with a gold ring on his pudgy little chipolata finger. The slippery fish looked bored and seemed to shrug as it settled back on the slab. His wife will be haughty, with hair that never moves, and dressed to perfection in something stylish from Paris. The fishmonger handed me the wrapped fish. And her long drop earrings will dangle and dazzle in the candlelight.

"Candles," I shouted at the startled fishmonger.

Trundling past the sauces and spices, I spied a large, impressive, shaven-headed black guy fingering a jar of organic honey in jams and marmalades. Perhaps he is the owner of the car I have just inadvertently devalued by thousands of pounds. I remembered reading somewhere that a black BMW is the car of choice for drug dealers. He looked up and flashed me a broad grin, exposing a gold-capped incisor. I vowed to give up reading the tabloids.

Near the tills a glossy blonde smiled down at me from a shampoo-promotion display board. "Don't think you'll always look that good," I told her, banging my trolley into the soaps and shower gels. Suddenly the supermarket seemed to be swarming with an infestation of blonde shoppers. I joined the end of a long queue at the checkout and tried to distract myself by calculating how many trips around Waitrose would constitute a walk to Brighton. In front of me a middle-aged man resembling an over-fed Labrador, in his creamy-custard sweater and hairy brown jacket with the collar turned up, jangled his car keys tunefully whilst his blonde wife loaded their trolley with bulging bags. I convinced myself that he was the owner of the BMW. He glanced over his shoulder to see who I was looking at and, after realising it was him and misinterpreting my stare, he winked. Quickly leaving the line, I hid behind the cereals and waited for him to leave the shop, only rejoining the queue when I was satisfied that the parking space once occupied by the recently defaced black car would soon be empty.

But wheeling my trolley back through the car park, I saw that the BMW was still in its bay. Now with a large bunch of white lilies lying on its roof, the black car resembled a hearse. There was no sign of the driver. But just as I was reaching the Porsche a man unfolded between the cars and stood up. He was tall, smooth, and elegantly dressed in smart casual clothes. He looked straight at me.

"I've been waiting for you," he said, his greying temples glowing green under the flickering low strip light. "Where's my note?"

"What note?" I replied, clearing my throat, which had suddenly dried.

"Your note of apology. The one that I would have expected to find, under the circumstances, tucked underneath my windscreen wipers."

We stared at each other. I felt myself shrinking, like Alice. I was ten again. The whole school is in the main hall; the headmistress is asking the person who has been stealing sweets to own up. I envied Alice and her rabbit hole.

"Not much use denying it. Not with the red paint in the middle of the dent matching your car colour exactly," he said pointing.

"I'm sure I didn't do that," I lied. "I certainly didn't realise I . . ." My voice trailed off.

"I'd like to believe you, but" – he nodded towards the large circle where my paper tissue had disturbed the light layer of dust – "in that case who cleaned the door?"

My mind momentarily froze. Then I became conscious of the humming air conditioning, and wondered if the concrete underfoot had started to melt. Realising that we couldn't both stand there for ever, I sidled slowly along the opposite side of the Porsche with the intention of putting my shoulder bag on the passenger seat. He watched me. I turned the key in the lock, but when I opened the door I jumped back as the piercing sound of the car alarm ricocheted off the concrete walls and floors, and echoed through the car park. I started to shake. And we now had an audience.

I re-locked the car hurriedly. The alarm stopped. Returning to the back of the car I looked for some means of opening the boot to load the shopping. Still watching me, he breathed in loudly.

"I think you'll find the answer to what you are looking for inside the car, on the driver's side," he snorted.

With my ears still ringing from the alarm, I moved slowly between the cars again, this time towards the driver's-side door, and towards him. He stepped back a few inches without dropping his gaze. This time I used the fob to open the door and groped around on the floor. He watched and waited. I found two levers, but which was which? Suddenly the back lid of the car shot up. I smiled at him, relieved, and with a smug sense of achievement. He raised one eyebrow and looked faintly amused, as I carefully edged back to the rear of the car and picked up two bags of shopping. I was about to lift them into the boot when I noticed – the engine.

"You don't seem to be too familiar with this car. Sure you haven't stolen it?" he asked.

I was sweating. Tears pricked my eyes, but I couldn't cry; it would be too humiliating. I slammed the back shut and edged along the passenger side once more, opening the door and slinging the shopping onto the seat, then returning quickly for another load.

"I'm still waiting for an apology," he said. "And your name and address," he added coolly. "I'll be informing my insurance company of course."

Benjamin's furious face loomed up in my imagination. With his eyes narrowed to angry slits and a pouting blonde on his arm. I was about to say how sorry I was, but it wouldn't come out.

"Or shall we call it quits?" he asked, toying with his bunch of keys, carefully selecting one and holding it up to show me. The muscles in his jaw tightened and, without lowering his eyes, he dropped his hand down to door level. I stared at him across the top of the car, open-mouthed as his arm swept along the driver's side of the Porsche. I gasped. It felt as if someone had stolen my bones, while in my head a choir of castrati were holding their highest note. He began walking towards me. Thinking he was going to hit me, I grabbed the rest of the shopping, stumbled to the passenger door, opened it, threw in the bags and scrambled into the car, banging my head and bruising my arms and knees as I clambered over the piles of purchases. Falling into the driver's seat I put the Porsche into reverse and began to move before realising that the passenger-side door was still open. I braked, tugged the door closed and reversed again, at speed.

"Maniac," he shouted, jumping out of the way. As the word echoed around the car park, shoppers, like Lot's wife, turned to pillars of salt.

I didn't look at him again. I banged the Porsche into first gear and revved. The wheels squealed and spun as I shot off, lurching towards the exit, without taking the size of the vehicle into consideration when assessing the turning angle needed to avoid the concrete pillar. As the car swung to the left it juddered and there was a hideous sawing sound as the offside wing added another red stripe to the ceiling support. Fortunately the barrier was up and the ticket attendant nowhere to be seen. On the verge of hysteria, I sped up the ramp and out into the daylight, narrowly missing a bus as I hurtled towards the green traffic lights. If I killed myself now, I remember thinking, it would probably be my best option. But I didn't. I drove home and parked in the next street. I did not dare to look at the damage. Instead, averting my eyes and shaking like a road drill on speed, I removed the shopping and ran away from the car as fast as the bags bumping against my knees would allow.

The house was empty. I poured myself a large drink and curled up sobbing in the corner of the sofa. Was I really hoping that my husband wouldn't find his car? And wouldn't bother to look for it? The answer was yes to both questions. But knowing this was unrealistic and that I would have to own up some time, I dispensed with the glass, and drank straight from the bottle.

Benjamin had put the spare tyre on my hatchback, so in the early afternoon, sweating and not completely sober, I picked up the children and drove to Wandsworth, taking Clementine to her party. With two hours to kill before I had to collect her again, I took Charlie and Polly to the playground nearby. It was just getting dark when we eventually arrived home. Benjamin said I looked tense and pale and asked if the car was OK. I nodded with a brittle smile. I couldn't enlighten him before the dinner party. I decided to be especially nice, to cook the best meal ever, and be extra charming and courteous to our guests. We were so busy preparing the food, laying the table, tidying the house, pushing toys and books under the sofa, and trying out a bottle or two of the wine to make sure it was good enough, that he didn't enquire further about the car except to ask where I had parked it.

"It's just around the corner," I told him, opening the freezer door to hide my rapidly reddening face. "There wasn't a space free near the house when I got back." My skin was now generating enough heat to warm an igloo full of naked Inuits in mid-winter. The peas defrosted.

"I'll put it in the car park when they've gone," he said.

After tucking the children into bed I changed into my slinky emerald-green satin dress, in which I periodically propelled his testosterone level into the stratosphere, and covered myself in the scent he'd given me for my birthday. Perhaps if the evening was a success, by tomorrow he might forgive me for the condition of his car. There were still ten minutes to spare before our guests were due to arrive. I lit the candles. After extricating myself from Benjamin's lustful hands, I decided I had been wrong to be jealous of the Porsche, and as for the blonde hair – well, it could have come from almost anywhere.

The doorbell rang. As we walked down the hall together, I smiled at Benjamin sweetly. He put his arm around me, gave me a warm hug, and kissed my cheek. As he flung the door open he murmured, "We'll get rid of them as soon as possible. I can't wait until later when I'll have you all to myself."

A blast of cold night air blew in as a large bunch of lilies was thrust into my hands. I looked at the man standing behind them on the doorstep and, turning quickly, ran upstairs, locked myself in the bathroom, and escaped out of the window.

How to Surf
PHIL GILBERT

Finn once told me that the ocean is like a schizophrenic. In the shallows, when the water runs over you, it's like a hug from a woman after you've fucked for the first time. But if you get too far out, she can turn insane. Her tides and undercurrents will bite at you and drag you out to sea. She will beat you down with big wave punch after big wave punch.

Right now, the ocean has forgotten its medication. The waves are the biggest I've seen since getting here. It's started raining, the droplets making small, concentric circles as they collide with the surface of the sea.

"We'd better go back in," Katrina hollers, pivoting on her board to face us.

Claudia nods in agreement and they both roll onto their fronts and begin paddling back to the beach.

I turn to Finn. He's sitting on his board further out, riding the choppy waves like he doesn't notice them. He has his back to us, moodily staring out at the water that lies just beyond the second break.

Don't go there. That was all our guide said to us when he first brought us here. Don't go to the second break. That's for pros and kamikazes only.

"Come on," I shout to Finn. "It's time."

Finn turns to me and yells something inaudible across the

crashing seawater.

"What?"

He yells again. This time I make out the word "Maria". The girls are closing in on the beach. They don't hear anything.

"What?"

"I called her last night," he shouts during a momentary break in the noise. "Maria. She's pregnant."

A wave juggernauts into my side. I'm not paying attention. It knocks me off my board, into the water. That salty, disorientating slap of liquid in my eyes, nose and ears.

I clamber back onto the board, wipe my hair out of my face.

"Tell me on the beach," I yell. "The water's getting rough, mate. We need to get out of here."

I rock forward onto my board and begin the long, grinding paddle back to the shore.

Twenty minutes ago the cove was baking in the sun. Through the blue mist you could make out the mountain tops of Sanur. By the first break, where we surfed, the crayon-blue waves were about eight foot, easy and regular. The ocean had that calmness you want to stare at. Earlier, if you lay in the water, half submerged, you could hear the fizzing sound of the salt breaking around your ears, like the sea was shushing you.

Now, the waves have turned a darker blue. They're baring their teeth; a guard dog we've stepped too close to. The grey skies have arrived and they've taken the sheen off Sanur Cove. Looking around at this place I've gotten to know so well over these past weeks, it's now only vaguely familiar to me, like the face of an old friend hidden behind a newly grown beard.

As I paddle, the waves punch at me, fast and relentless, featherweight-boxer style. I use a tree on the beach as a guide, making sure I don't get beaten off course or veer with the current.

Eventually, exhausted, I reach the shore, throw down my board. I rip off my rash vest and fling it in the sand. My chest is heaving and red raw from rubbing against the mounds of grip wax on the board. I lie down and catch my breath. This is when I see Katrina's and Claudia's faces.

"What's going on?"

"He's too far out. He can't get back in."

I look out to sea and see Finn at some remote, far-off point in the water. He's struggling at the top of a cresting wave, paddling hard; long strokes, deep in the water.

"He's near the second break," says Katrina.

Shit.

Somewhere, way below him, the ocean bed is beginning to rise at a steep angle. Columns of water, pushed inland by the depths of the ocean, are hitting this rising ground and crashing in on themselves. This is where the waves form.

Big waves.

"Come on, Finn," I shout.

We watch him intently for five, ten, fifteen minutes, shouting at him like it will make a difference. His arms dig hard at each mammoth wave as they rise and fall around him. It's no use. Slowly, he's drawn into the middle of the chaos. The vortex of the second break is about to suck him in.

"Come on, Finn."

The arch of a huge wave rises high up above him and gets ready to pounce. A chill runs down my spine. Finn's board starts angling steeply downward.

"He's going to be hurt," says Claudia.

Katrina grabs hold of me, her other hand at her mouth, fearing what she's about to see.

Finn chances a look behind him just as the wave breaks above his head. It reaches around him and, for a split second, Finn is cocooned in a cavern of water.

Slam.

He's gone, submerged.

As the wave passes over, half his surfboard is left poking out of the water, like a tombstone.

I'm guessing that, underwater, he'll be somersaulting. Then, when the full body of the wave has got him, it will flick him straight, like a towel being whipped. As it passes, he'll start swimming upwards, but there'll be no surface to reach. No air to be had. He'll open his eyes and all he'll see is blue. He'll realise he doesn't know which way is up.

If he's got his wits about him, he'll grab the leash attached to his ankle. He'll follow that up to his board, and the surface.

Finn's head and shoulders launch out of the water. He clutches at his board and forces a lungful of air down into his chest, just before the second wave hits him and pounds him back under.

I'm sorry, Finn. I never did say I was sorry.

"We should call someone," Katrina says. "He's not going to make it."

"Yes he will."

"No, Leon. Look at him. He's struggling."

"He'll do it. He always does."

"We should call someone."

"Who? We're a million miles from anywhere."

This is how I remember Finn. Paddling with everything he had. Trying to make it over those waves to get back to the shore. Right, left, right, left.

Come on, Finn.

Come on, Finn.

Maria is in tears.

Finn's face is serious.

I'm holding my breath.

They're over by the departure board. Crowds of people flow between me and them, partially blocking my view of their long goodbye. They're too far away for me to hear what she's saying. He leans in, his chin nestling against her neck, putting his arms round her. Once she can't see his face he looks over at me. He rolls his eyes. A big grin flashes across his face.

I laugh, relieved.

They break and Finn's face is serious again. They take a slow walk over to me, hand in hand. I'm by the security gate, mine and Finn's luggage at my feet.

"Enjoy him," Maria says to me. Our eyes catch for a second, but then she looks back at Finn, like it never happened.

"We'll be back in two months," I say. "You'll barely notice he's gone."

"Mmm," she says.

Maria thinks I'm the bad guy here, but this trip was Finn's idea. The fact Maria's not coming: Finn's idea. I'm just the best friend, but she sees me as a bad influence. She thinks me and her have this unspoken competition for Finn's affections. Well guess what, Maria?

I win.

"I suppose we'd better get going," I say.

Maria shoots me a sideways look, her eyes blazing with anger. Once she's calmed she turns to Finn. She hugs him and says: "Come here, baby. Tell me you love me."

"I love you."

"Tell me you won't look at another woman."

"I won't look at another woman."

"You'll call me once a week."

"I'll call you once a week."

"OK, go then."

"I'll be thinking of you the whole time!" Finn says, already walking away with his bag over his shoulder.

We join the long, concertinaed queue at the security gates. A tanned woman with an amazing body resting perfectly under a summer dress stands in front of us. Finn nudges me and motions towards her arse. We both snigger. Then he turns and waves at Maria one last time.

Once we're through the gate and out of view he's grinning inanely. Finn's got his freedom.

Me, I've got my friend back.

"This is it," says Finn. "We've got two months of partying in *Indonesia*. Partying and surfing. I'm going to teach you how to surf, you're going to lose your V plates and we're going to get *laid*!"

"Timing is everything. Judge the wave. Paddle faster. Stand up quicker. Pop too early or late and you get a face full of seawater."

This was Finn's first bit of advice to me, down in Kuta Bay. Afterwards, he rolled onto his front and paddled his board out to the bigger waves, the six-, seven-footers, leaving me with the other beginners in the shallows.

He's more of a throw them in the deep end type of a guy.

The Hawaiians we took about an hour ago have started to take effect. The dusty yellow colours of the roads and the greens of the trees bleed into one another so I can't tell them apart. Restaurants and late-night market stalls are moving frenetically, like a silent earthquake has struck. Even the moon shakes back and forth like an electrical current is at it. In amongst the bustling crowds, I begin to see local people's faces growling and snarling at me.

"Finn, I'm having a bad moment."

"Me too," he says. "I don't know how to get back to the hotel."

"Let's stand by that tree. I think that tree is good."

One slow step at a time we make our way through the crowded main street of Kuta, Indonesians and tourists moving out of our way as we go. We stand by the palm tree and stare at it for a long time, hoping this moment, tinged with negativity, will pass.

A woman's heavily accented voice punches through the chaos and frenzy.

"Are you both OK?"

The woman is slim with great lengths of dark curly hair. Her eyes are wide and she has a petite nose. She is wearing a sarong. Even in my wacky state of mind I think she's hot.

"I'm Katrina," she says. I place her accent as German.

I go to speak but Finn gets in there first: "Can we tell you a secret? We took some magic mushrooms and now we're lost. Our hotel, the Green Lodge, do you know it?"

She translates to her friend, who I've only just noticed. The friend has a sharper face and is taller and spindly. They laugh.

"No," she says, "but Claudia and I can look after you until you are better. Yes?"

"That sounds amazing," says Finn, as he moves from the tree and puts his arms around her.

The girls take us to a club. Inside, the mushrooms kick in like water being added to a hot pan. This time it feels good. Really good. I'm dancing and staring. Staring at my hands, at the crowds of people, at the music.

I look over at Finn. He's staring at Katrina as she dances.

"*Magst du* Indonesia?" Claudia asks.

I'm rushing badly. I can't really handle a conversation now but I know one's coming anyway. I try to focus on her face.

"*Entschuldigung* . . . Er . . . Do . . . you . . . like . . . Indonesia?"

"Yeah, yeah, yeah. You?"

"*Es ist schön* . . . erm . . . beautiful."

I sneak a look over at Katrina, hoping she'll notice me. She's staring at Finn whilst he dances.

"Yeah. It's beautiful," I say to Claudia. "Where are you from in Germany?"

"Sorry . . . Can you repeat?"

"Where . . . in . . . Germany?"

"Ahh . . . Munich."

"Do you surf? Is that why you're here?"

"*Surfen? Ja,* I surf."

I look over at Finn and Katrina again. They're kissing, still moving in time with the music.

Claudia keeps staring at me.

I'm quickly hit with the reality that, when the Superhero pairs off, the Sidekick gets the leftovers.

I don't dwell on this for long. Its importance seems to lessen as a rush of psilocybin from the mushrooms uncorks in my head and fizzes like overflowing champagne. Colours that engulf the whole room change with the music: red then orange then yellow then back to red, and each one strikes me like it's the first time I've seen it. Energy from an unknown spring is pumping about my bloodstream. I seem to be able to dance in time with the vibes that are pulsating around the room. In a moment of clarity, I have a strong sense that everything around me and in me is connected. The proof is almost tangible to me but once I've sensed it and tried to think it it's gone again.

At around three in the morning myself, Finn, Katrina and Claudia all sit on Kuta beach facing out to the ocean. The mushrooms have worn off but we're now drinking bottles of Bintang beer we bought from the club. The air is still warm and the dark sky reaches out eternally beyond us. Lights from fishing boats bob along miles away in the water.

We're playing a game of I Have Never. The deal is you have to drink if you have.

"I have never," Katrina says, "kissed a member of the same sex."

Katrina and Claudia both drink.

"I have never," says Finn, "had sex whilst tied up or handcuffed."

Katrina and Finn both drink.

"I have never," I say, "masturbated whilst in Indonesia."

All four of us drink. We laugh at that one.

"I . . . have . . . never," Claudia says, "er . . . *nacktbaden*?" She looks at Katrina.

Katrina translates. "Skinny-dipping."

Katrina and Claudia both drink. Finn and I don't.

"Really?" says Katrina. "You guys have never been skinny-dipping? That has to change . . . tonight."

She puts her beer down, stands up and takes off her top. Her small breasts appear momentarily in the dull moonlight, before her hair falls down, covering them.

"*Los*," Katrina says to Claudia. She turns to us. "Come on."

Finn looks at me like he can't believe this is happening. He jumps up and whoops into the night air, T-shirt already half around his head.

They all strip off and run into the water. I follow. It's dark but I can make out the white glow of everybody's skin: Katrina first, Finn second, Claudia third, then me. I skip over the waves on my first few steps, water flicking into my face, until the water is deep enough to dive into. I don't turn around until I've swum far enough out so that my body is covered and my feet can only just touch the ground. The water is cool but not cold; a leftover heat from the day's sunshine. The others are closer to the shore, exposed. The waves are tall enough in the shallows so you have to jump out of the water to keep your head from going under. This is where you see one another.

Katrina's breasts.

Claudia's bush.

Finn's cock.

The phospho-plankton is out and as you run your hand through the water small dots of light, like bright blue Christmas lights, tingle for a few seconds and then fade.

"Leon, you wanker!" Finn shouts. "Get over here."

I swim over to the others and force myself to get involved in the play-fighting. Splash some water. Push Katrina over. Tip Claudia. Then Finn dunks me. During the fighting I catch my lip and it bleeds. The salty water is on the cut straightaway, hurting like a bee sting. After I wipe the water from my eyes I turn around laughing and, just ahead of me, Finn and Katrina are kissing again.

Claudia has moved to the left of me, jumping over the waves, her tall, bare frame suspended in the air briefly before the dark wall of water covers her again.

I swim over to her.

As I arrive she stands, fully naked and unashamed, and says: "Hi."

After some silent moments of indecision I stand up as well, covering myself with my hand. Claudia, she giggles and leans in and bites me on the shoulder.

Soon enough we're groping at each other. She leads me back onto the beach and pulls me down onto the sand.

Now that I'm touching her wet skin I find a hidden meaning in her paleness, her dark nipples, her elongated body. She looks at me with those sharp eyes; the whites look wet. They're speaking to me: it's time . . . but be gentle.

In amongst the flood of images spraying through my brain I think of Maria crying at the airport. Finn's face nestled in her neck. Him pulling faces at me and me laughing. My stomach is pounding with adrenalin. I can't really feel anything around my midriff. I'm not in control.

I slip my fingers into her. Claudia goes tense for a second. Then relaxes. She breathes deeper. This is a good sign.

I think.

"*Ja*," she says. "*Jetzt* . . . er . . . now."

I try.

I try again.

"*Nein?*"

"I'm almost there."

I try again.

I roll over, frustrated, and lie back on the sand and listen to the waves rolling back and forth. I pretend Claudia isn't there, tongue my cut, making it bleed again, the heavy, iron taste of blood in my mouth.

Off to my right I can hear Katrina and Finn laughing and having noisy sex.

Claudia hears it too. She lays her head on my chest, stroking my stomach. Telling me, "*Kein* problem."

We both know it is.

Today, Finn gives me his second bit of advice: "Your leash is an umbilical cord to oxygen. When you're underwater, you can be somersaulting in the middle of an exploding wave. When it's really bad, you lose your bearings and you can't tell which way is up. Now, this is important: don't panic. You find your leash and follow it back to your board and to the surface. That will save your life one day."

After a week in Kuta I'm having a go at the bigger waves with Finn. He's strong and powerful but me, I've got the next-to-nothing body weight and the agility.

We're sitting on our boards, about thirty metres out from the beach. Finn says Maria has emailed him again today, asking him to call her. He says this is typical of her: taking up his time even when she's not here.

He jokes there's a tracking device in the email.

Finn sits tall on his board. His blond hair hangs shaggy and damp around his face. He rubs the stubble that juts out from his chin as he sniggers at his own jokes.

"Maybe you should call Maria?" I offer. "I mean, you said you would."

"What? Whose side are you on anyway?"

I shrug my shoulders. "Finn, it's your call, mate."

"Look, Katrina and Claudia are heading over to Sanur in the morning," he says. "I think we should go with them."

"I dunno. We said we'd hang here for a bit. The easy water. While I get used to the surfing."

"Mate, have some faith. You need the next level. And the girls are a good bunch."

"Katrina's hot and easy you mean."

"Ha-ha, yep, that's a bonus. Claudia's all right though. She likes you. You fucked her, right?"

"Mmm," I say.

"Come on, mate. Let's go to Sanur. You'll enjoy it. I swear."

"Yeah, OK. Whatever."

*

This wave.

This is the one.

For the first time since getting to Sanur my board feels lighter. It glides gracefully across the water. Out of the corner of my eye I see Finn homing in on the same wave, his trajectory running on a crash course with mine. A momentary panic flickers and then dies inside me as I realise that somehow, for the first time, the nose of my board is out in front of his. He's pounding at the water but I'm getting more out of my relaxed strokes.

I'm riding low, trying to speed along in line with the surface tension. This board is the difference between the two worlds of under and above water. My arms are breaking the truce between the two with each stroke that I take.

I feel the wave erupt behind me. Finn knows that he has no chance of getting this one and pulls out.

I keep going.

The wave flicks up and I keep paddling in time with it. As I tip over the peak I pop and plant my feet. I ride the curve of the wave downward and angle myself so that I'm cutting in and out whilst it folds in on itself. Then I let the engine of the wave do the work. I roll five, ten, fifteen metres, wind in my face. I begin going all Hollywood on it; crouching like I'm one of the pros in the magazines. Looking at the water rushing by me makes the blood in my chest roar. I keep going: twenty, twenty-five, thirty metres before the wave begins to fade out.

I drop down onto my board so I can turn and paddle back out to where Finn is sitting in the water.

"Did you see me?"

Finn says nothing. He looks away from me, paddles past me and watches for the next wave to roll in.

We emerge from the water of Sanur Cove hours later, as the light-blue sky is merging into the metallic sheen of early evening. The girls left a long while ago, bored of watching us fight over the waves, and took the path back to town. Me and Finn lie back on the sand, our boards at our sides, not saying anything. My skin is shrivelled and there's salt on my lips.

Eventually, Finn tells me to roll a joint.

We decide that we'll have to walk back in the dark anyhow, so we may as well watch the sunset from here and then start home.

After passing the joint back and forth a few times, I try to break the moody silence he's got going on, so I say the first thing that pops into my head.

"Waves are beautiful and violent. Volcanoes and hurricanes and tornadoes are the same, but you only see them on the news in faraway places. Waves, they're most people's only experience of the Jekyll and Hyde of nature."

This is when Finn tells me he's growing tired of Katrina. He says that she's cool, she's super sexy, but he doesn't know about her.

Here we go again.

I think about how we came to Sanur because of Katrina. How she's good-looking, how she's fun, how he's not going to get much better than that. I think about how I've said the same thing about Maria to him before.

I think about Maria, crying at the airport. Finn grinning.

I don't say anything, stare at the waves and try to block out these words that grate on me. Concentrate on those waves.

"There's so much ass in Indo," Finn says. "It's off the scale! I think we need to give it a couple more days and then we need to get out of here. On to pastures new. We'll have a great time. I swear."

Somehow this seems like the right time. "I slept with Maria," I say.

I pass the joint back, hoping he'll take the news gracefully. He slaps it out of my hand and stares at me without saying anything.

I don't tell him to hear me out. I don't tell him it was, like, two months ago. Maria turned up at my place after he had left with that Beth bird. I don't tell him Maria was upset because they'd had a row. I don't tell him how I was really pissed and spent a *long* time consoling her, and that I only said she could stay over because it was late. I don't tell him how she got into my bed rather than the couch. I don't tell him how one thing led to another.

I don't tell him these things because he doesn't ask.

What Finn does do is stand up and scoop his board up under his arm.

"You got lucky today," he says. "That wave you got to first.

You got lucky."

He treads off towards the darkened path back to Sanur.

I sit there, watching the sun set behind the mountains. Watching the waves crash amongst one another until the sun is gone and I can't see where one begins and another ends.

"We should call someone," Katrina says. "He's not going to make it."

"Yes he will."

"No, Leon. Look at him. He's struggling."

"He'll do it. He always does."

"We should call someone."

"Who? We're a million miles from anywhere."

This is how I remember Finn. Paddling with everything he had. Trying to make it over those waves to get back to the shore. Right, left, right, left.

Come on, Finn.

Come on, Finn.

As the second wave passes, Finn's head emerges once more from the water and he takes another huge breath. This time he makes it onto his board and gets a few paddles in before the third and final wave hits, pulls his board out from under him and hammers his body back into the depths of the ocean.

"Maria's pregnant," I mutter, to no one in particular.

Neither Katrina nor Claudia pay me any attention. Our stares are fixed on the surfboard that is again poking out of the water, hoping to see Finn's head come bursting out of the sea.

Don't ask why, but I think about the last day before we left Kuta Bay, when we were in the water. Finn rolled forward onto his board and went to catch yet another wave. He saw my frustration after I'd just face-planted in the water for the hundredth time and he stopped, mid-stroke, turned to me and said: "Relax. Treat each wave like an individual. Ride *that* wave and nothing else. See where it takes you."

This was Finn's third, and final, bit of advice to me on how to surf.

Mangoes Indian-Style
VEENA SHARMA

"Aruna, sweetheart, you're not thinking of going out in that rain?"

Standing in the entrance hall of Graywood House, Aruna turned from the photo cabinet and looked over at the short brunette approaching her.

"Sally, I have to get to the supermarket."

"I thought your Summit had you doing that Internet shopping lark."

"He set up my weekly order, but I don't know how to add to the list . . ." Aruna shrugged her shoulders apologetically. "I'm being old-fashioned and actually going to the shops."

"Of course." Sally jerked her head over her right shoulder towards the day room. "Couple of the old boys mentioned Rea's coming home this weekend."

Aruna couldn't contain her grin. "Her flight arrives tomorrow."

"Wow, have six months flown by already?"

"Nearly seven months now."

"You must bring her over if you can. I'm sure the fellas will try and flirt – fake some palpitations, get the young doctor to examine them." Sally winked.

"They can fake away. She's an optician not a heart surgeon."

Aruna's quip elicited a staccato machine-gun cackle from Sally; the noise reverberated off the walls.

"Oh Aruna, you are lucky to have such lovely grandchildren."

Aruna glowed, giving the appearance of a woman a decade younger. "Aren't I. My Rea and Summit are very special."

"Right, let me call you a cab. It'll only take a minute or so to get here. You'll see it from the porch." Sally gave Aruna's arm a squeeze and swayed back to the office.

Aruna returned her attention to the photo she'd been staring at. It had been taken nearly two years ago, Ashok's final summer at Graywood House. Summit had persuaded some of the old men to play a game of Kabaddi in the garden. The corners of her mouth tugged up as Aruna recalled the hilarity that ensued when they failed miserably. The photo had been taken at the end of the game; arms about his fellow players, Ashok stood in the middle, wilted but beaming.

They'd been married for nearly fifty years and had expected to spend their twilight years putting their feet up. Cancer unfortunately carved up their plans. He'd beaten it but had gotten very weak, needing extra care; they made the difficult decision for him to move into Graywood House. After his passing she took to volunteering at Graywood three times a week.

Aruna trailed her fingers over the glass front of the cabinet, outlining her husband's face.

Settling herself on the age-bleached bench just inside the porch, Aruna leaned forward, extending her hand out to the elements. She felt the gentle pit pat of raindrops splashing onto her open palm and watched her weathered brown skin stain to a darker, wetter shade of nutmeg. A minute passed. Sitting back, she inserted her dry hand into her handbag and drew out a bundle of papers creased with handling. She opened them up to read. She always kept Rea's emails in her handbag; it made it feel like she was close by.

2nd January 2011

Hi Nani,

Arrived in Delhi yesterday. My sixth visit to the motherland and the bedlam still floors me. Cows sunbaking on dual carriageways I can handle but the chaos is insane. The constant noise – tuk-tuks beeping, hawkers yelling, bazaar walis arguing – can be a tad overwhelming. That strange essence of heat mingled with sweat is in my every breath.

*Talking of bazaars, spent the morning in Chandni Chowk
– plenty of tourist tat, plastic Taj Mahals and clothes. Tried to
haggle with a shopkeeper over a gorgeous shawl – got him down
to 1200 rupees from 2000 but his grin as I left was too wide.
Totally failed at haggling like a native.*

*Start work at the Mumbai cataract camp on the 16th.
Always wanted to visit Rajasthan so thought I'd use the
fortnight to do exactly that. Rang Mum and Dad, told them
about the camel safari I've just signed up for . . . They said I
should have booked a car.*

*Loving that you're finally online . . . As grannies go,
you're more hip and less hip replacement . . . lol!*

Kisses, Rea xxx

PS: 16, 8, 41, 17, 9, 6

In the supermarket, perusing the fruit aisle, Aruna's eyes fell on
the mangoes. Picking one up, she rolled its heaviness in her palm.
Usually the supermarket variety of mangoes tended to be smaller
and disappointingly tinged green. The specimen in her hand,
however, was anything but, its abundance a welcome surprise.
Aruna pressed the outer skin with her fingertips and felt the fruit
give; below the surface it was bursting with pulp. Holding it up to
her nose, she drew the scent in greedily.

The smell took her back to her childhood and a courtyard in
Punjab. A low-slung woven bed, scratching the back of her six-
year-old calves. The battered metal bucket, heavy with fruit. The
sharp intake of breath as she plunged her hand into the ice-cold
water, immersing her arm up to the elbow, rummaging to grasp a
mango. The sweet explosion in her mouth as she drew the glorious
flesh into its depths. Laughing widely as juice ran down her chin,
lush and sticky.

Eyes closed, a smile on her lips, lost in the memory, Aruna
inhaled deeply once more. Then nothing. She was sixty-eight.

The crematorium smelt of sandalwood incense.

Aruna leaned over her coffin, examining the finish. Exquisitely
constructed from solid walnut, it had four ornate gold handles

hanging from the sides. Coated in a sheen of varnish it looked stately and expensive. Like a super-sized glossy turd, it just sat there. Aruna would have preferred something light and optimistic – pine, possibly.

No doubt chosen by Sanjay, her pragmatic eldest, Rea and Summit's father. Sitting in the first row, he'd dressed perfectly in a tailored suit, starched collar and heavy cufflinks. He had been such a beautiful, affectionate child . . . How time had changed him.

Classical sitar music wafted from speakers set high on limestone pillars, serene notes undulating out over the mourning ensemble, a chequerboard of friends, family and neighbours.

The Indian women, attired in funeral white, were unrestrained in their grief. Matronly bosoms heaved with the exaggerated effort of sobbing; tissues were passed around like sweets; waves of wailing rose and fell like a drunk mermaid's song. The men conversed gravely. So unexpected . . . What a lovely lady . . . So how about the cricket?

Aruna grimaced. Bloody bunch of overactors. The non-Indian mourners in funeral black were quieter, more contained; shy in the swell of this open flood.

Grief, she mused, was an odd beast to take on such different forms. Next to Sanjay sat something in the throes of an eruption of emotion: his wife, Pinky. Throughout their twenty-six years of marriage, she had steadfastly refused to answer to anything but her childhood nickname. Pinky's pink lips were pulled back, her teeth a street of yellow houses exposed for all to see. A gaudy diamond winked from a chubby finger. Fat tears dribbled from her mascara-laden eyes, staining her white sari. Her shoulders shook as she keened. It was a wonder she hadn't dehydrated.

Aruna's daughter, Ritu, on the other hand, was the picture of composed grief. Her sari, also white, embellished with discreet embroidery, was haute couture. Marble-like, she looked straight ahead. No smudged mascara on this immaculately kept face; an efficient tissue kept such a mess at bay. The image of composure slipping only when one noticed the white knuckles gripping her husband's hand. Behind them, in the second row, sat Rea and Summit, two heads bowed and weary. Aruna rested her gaze on them, silently willing them to look up. They didn't.

The speeches began. The family priest in his orange robes started with a few words, followed by Sanjay.

But it was George McHugh's speech that struck a chord. "She brought samosas in one day. I'm looking at this triangle-shaped thing on my plate, no idea what it is. I pick up my knife and fork, thinking where do you start? She comes over and takes one look at me, says 'You're Irish, yes?' I nodded. 'It's full of potato, you'll be fine.' She picks it up with her fingers and takes a big old bite, all the while grinning ear to ear. Our little community lost a bit of sunshine today."

Aruna swallowed hard. She reached into her handbag and took out a piece of paper.

10th January 2011
Hi Nani,

Finally in Jaisalmer in an Internet café with air con. What a luxury. Just completed the camel trek across the Great Thar Desert to get here. Amazing – loved it! Although feel like I'm eighty-seven – muscles are shredded, am so sore.

The camel drivers would set up camp nightly, cook and we'd sit under the stars chatting into the small hours. Living in London, you don't really see the stars but here, the night sky is clear. It's as if a cosmic blanket of diamonds unveils itself. How insignificant we humans are.

Rang Mum to let her know I hadn't died. She's still upset with me for taking this job over the one back home.

Improved on the haggling thing. In Jaisalmer Fort I visited a traditional bazaar, twisting alleys and Aladdin-like. Found a beautiful tapestry of Mugal art. Followed the advice in your last email and when the seller refused to go any lower – I just walked out. Sure enough he followed, calling after me down the alley, and came down to my price – result (fist punching the air!!).

Lots of love, Rea xxx
PS: 18, 9, 21, 17, 46, 38

Aruna had always liked her solicitor's office. It was a homely room. Propped up against a bookcase of legal tomes, Aruna watched her children listen to her will being read. Observing their faces – to see what, she wasn't sure: perhaps a glimmer of raw grief, unvarnished, genuine emotion – anything other than the dissatisfying, controlled, B-movie melodrama that she'd seen play out at her funeral.

The family rifts had started with the arrival of Pinky back in 1982. As the newly married daughter-in-law, moving into the family home, she was welcomed with open arms. However, at twenty she was too young, too immature for what she'd signed up to. As an only child and the spoilt apple of her father's eye, she was not used to sharing her toys. Rows erupted between her and the adolescent Ritu, silly sniping nonsense: make-up, clothes, who had the right to do what – a pair of trainee lionesses circling each other, neither willing to concede. The men of the house, reluctant to take sides or incite further confrontation, said little and it was left to Aruna to play Switzerland between the two. Lines were drawn and feelings were hurt.

Once Pinky fell pregnant it was agreed for the sake of family harmony that she and Sanjay would move out, get a place of their own – which they did, 195 miles away in Leeds. Ritu, injured by what she perceived as a lack of loyalty towards her during the debacle of those petty rivalries, became bitter. The once close relationship she'd had with her brother was now eroded.

Aruna was aware of this animosity but the behaviour of her children surprised even her. When he moved to Graywood, Ashok had arranged weekend visits to and from the children. For a couple of months this worked out well, but gradually the visits were postponed, rearranged then cancelled; the fragmented contact became even more erratic. Aruna seethed but Ashok's tired body could handle only so much and he didn't want to waste what energy he had.

She and Ashok had come to England in the sixties, seeking to provide their children with opportunities and a secure future. It had worked. Sanjay and Ritu had been able to thrive financially, buy houses with ensuites and underfloor heating, drive fancy German cars, go on holidays to Dubai and Australia. But somehow, this new generation also lost their way. The quality of life became about the quality of their possessions. The core values Aruna had tried to instil in her son and daughter – family values – seemed to have been demoted.

Since her Ashok's passing the Graywood community had become a substitute family. Julia in the kitchen learned how to make Indian chai just the way Aruna liked it, Sally brought in a cake for her last birthday, and when the heating froze last winter, it was Roy the caretaker who came around to fix it.

Her son's raised voice brought Aruna's attention back into the solicitor's room.

"I don't get it."

"Which points do you need clarifying, Mr Kaur?"

"The mortgages . . ."

Looking back down at the crisp legal document between his hands, the solicitor recited, "'In reference to my two children, Sanjay Kaur and Ritu Garwal. On presentation of an official valuation by their mortgage lender of their outstanding mortgages, as at the date of my passing, my estate will pay said two mortgages off in full.'"

"That figure would come to several hundred thousand pounds! My mother wasn't exactly flush with assets."

"I'm not at liberty to divulge details, but suffice it to say, your mother's estate can provide for this clause."

Sanjay raised his eyebrows at his sister. He swung back round to the solicitor as a thought occurred to him. "What about the house?"

"If you'll allow me . . ." The solicitor indicated he had more to read. "'To my grandson, Summit Kaur, I leave my home, 16 Redcup Avenue, to do with as he wishes. However, before any of the contents of this will can be passed on to the above-stated individuals, I request that my children, Sanjay and Ritu, visit the home they grew up in, at the above-mentioned address.'"

"Why does Summit get the house?" Ritu interjected.

"What about Rea?" asked Sanjay, simultaneously.

The solicitor paused. "It's not my position to question Mrs Kaur's will, simply to read it out."

Sanjay carried on. "Well that's not fair. Rea's been left out entirely. Which is a bloody cheek given she lived with her Nani for three years."

"Summit's getting the house for God's sake, which makes no sense whatsoever." Reaching angrily for a cigarette, Ritu could not hide her frustration.

The solicitor cleared his throat. "As a courtesy I can inform you that I am, in fact, meeting with Miss Rea Kaur separately. Also, I'm afraid this is a no-smoking building."

The crumpled cigarette box hit the table and lay discarded like half-finished homework as Ritu pushed her chair back, swore audibly and stalked over to the window. She stared out moodily.

"Right." Sanjay tapped on his phone to access the calendar. "When is this appointment? I need to check if I can make it."

"You aren't required at the meeting."

"I'm her father. Of course I'm damned well required."

Intent on remaining professional, the solicitor leaned forward and stated politely, "Miss Rea Kaur is over the age of eighteen, legally an adult. Mrs Aruna Kaur specified a separate meeting with her granddaughter and I have a responsibility to my client to comply with her wishes." And with exaggerated finality he returned the document to the file and closed it firmly.

Despite herself, Aruna smiled as she reached into her handbag. Poor Sanjay. He looked rather red.

12th January 2011
Hi Nani,

Got the train to Varanasi, which was pretty unique. The hustle of a mini city contained in the one steel tin, paying travellers jostling with gypsies selling hot chilli channa in newspaper cones.

Given Varanasi is one of the most spiritual cities in India, was expecting some serious serenity but found the atmosphere more like a Mumbai shopping mall, only the clientele were less well-dressed.

In fairness the banks of the Ganges were very chilled at sunrise. Pilgrims in white kurtas offer prayers and bathe in its waters, which by the way were filthy, filthy, filthy!!! By mid-morning, everyone else and his dog arrives: those buying paan, selling flowers, and even barbers shaving on the riverside. Funeral pyres burn openly on the ghats – very graphic and rather morbid.

Randomly, sat next to a really cool Sadhu in the queue

at a mobile-phone shop. He must have been seventy-odd. We chatted about my experience as a Hindu raised abroad, the work at camp, God, kismet and one's soul. We ate mangoes Indian-style the way you taught me – he was dead impressed I didn't make a total mess of myself ;-)

Spoke to Summit. He'll swing by yours for the weekend before he goes back to uni – he'll see if he can sort out the problem with your kitchen shelves.

Ought to ring Mum but will leave it till Mumbai.

Big squeeze, Rea xxx

PS: 21, 48, 37, 25, 16, 4

15th March 2011

Hi Nani,

Consumed with work. It's rewarding but exhausting. The queues don't shrink, the supplies don't last and there aren't enough beds.

Cataracts I know how to remove, but the poverty . . . It's on such a massive scale. Things we take for granted at home – infrastructure, clean water, sanitation – are such a challenge here.

As a mini treat, I'd painted my nails red yesterday – something so simple. Working with a female patient today, I held her hand. Her nails were grimy; the dirt was embedded so far under them the skin had discoloured with infection. Even through my latex gloves the contrast between our joined hands could not have been starker. The guilt eats away at me. I had to leave the tent.

Miss you heaps, Rea

PS: 19, 27, 41, 6, 23, 44

Sitting on the worktop, leaning against her new stainless-steel fridge, Aruna couldn't decide what was more fun: the sheer indulgence of replacing her entire kitchen or the decidedly immature glee she felt now, watching her children. Ritu bent over the hob, clearly dumbfounded. Beside her, Sanjay stood hands on hips, a frown etched into his middle-aged forehead. Slowly he turned, his eyes sweeping the room, taking in the view into the lounge, where there had once been a wall, the new sofa suite, the large LCD flat screen set to one side.

"What the hell . . ." He walked up to the polished breakfast bar, and ran his hands along the surface. "Did you know she was getting this refurb done?"

Ritu shook her head haltingly trying to absorb the virgin high-gloss surfaces laid out in front of her. "I had no idea . . . This is top-of-the-range stuff."

The pair stared at each other, as if struggling to add up a very simple sum. Ritu moved to sit at the dining table. Sanjay joined her. He motioned at the now visible lounge.

"When were you last here . . . in this kitchen?"

"Why?"

"Well, it wasn't a five-minute job, knocking down walls, fitting everything. It must have taken a while."

"I came down at Christmas – brought some chocolates and a cashmere cardigan with me."

"Hmmm . . ."

"What's that supposed to bloody mean, huh? Did I bother making the effort to see her?" Ritu's eyes bulged with affront. "Well of course I did. I saw her at least twice since January."

"OK, no need to get defensive."

"When was the last time *you* saw her?" Ritu asked.

"About five months ago. She came up to Leeds with Summit one weekend. The kids saw her all the time. I thought if something important happened – she got ill or anything – they'd tell me. She was pretty active. I assumed she'd be around for another couple of decades."

"I thought the same thing. Didn't see this coming at all." Although her eyes were open, the shutters came down as Ritu lost herself in the past, childhood memories of playing in a kitchen now gone. Moments passed in silence, the warring siblings mulling over their own thoughts.

Ritu finally came back. "Do you feel bad?"

"That she died?"

"We didn't really . . . you know . . . see her . . . much."

Sanjay raised his palms up to the sky.

Arching her eyebrows, unimpressed by the dumb show, Ritu

ground on. "It's pretty damn obvious neither one of us spent any significant time with her recently . . . Do you think she felt lonely?"

"Maybe." Sanjay recovered quickly. "But for God's sake, in a recession – my business wasn't going to run itself."

"I've been in and out of hospital with the IVF treatment . . ."

"Exactly. We were just . . . you know . . . busy."

Ritu nodded slowly. "Life got in the way."

"Besides," Sanjay continued justifying, "she knew we loved her and if she was around right now, she'd hate for us to dwell on these depressing details."

Actually, Aruna thought, I'd rather you did dwell on them, and for more than a while.

Ritu blinked hard, refusing to give in to the tears that were threatening to spill. "Still . . . If I'd known, I would have liked to have seen her . . . say goodbye . . . something."

"Me too." Sanjay threw out these two words too quickly. Getting up he wandered over to inspect the kitchen some more, indicating the conversation was terminated, at least at his end. His sister remained at the table, reabsorbed in her foray into the past.

"What do you make of this?" His words came out unnaturally loud. Retrieving an item from a corner worktop, Sanjay placed it on the dining table for Ritu to see. Like amateurs in a grainy home-made video, examining an extraterrestrial being, they bent over the object: rectangular, sleek and silver with smooth edges. The familiar icon of an apple winked back at them.

"Well, Einstein, it's a laptop."

"Yes, but what's it doing here? Did she even know how to use it?" Sanjay smacked his palm on the table. "What are we missing? The kitchen, flash TV, brand-new Mac . . . Where in God's name was she getting the money for all of this?"

Ritu snapped, "Not sure what you're getting at. She left the house to your son."

Sanjay's head whipped up. "What's that got to do with anything?"

"It's unfair is what." Ritu glared at him. "We grew up here. The house surely should have gone to us."

"He's my son, for crying out loud. If you had a son, she would have left something to him."

"I can't believe you just said that!" Hand trembling she reached into her pockets, scrabbling for a cigarette. "After everything I've been through, I can't bloody believe you just said that."

"It's simple fact: I gave her grandkids, you didn't –"

"Oh God, how fucking insensitive can you be . . ."

"You damn well know it didn't come easy to us either. You have to just accept that . . ."

"Well not everyone's as bloody perfect . . ."

". . . and get over whatever hang-up you have."

". . . as your precious Pinky –"

"Don't you bring her into this. This has got nothing to do with her."

Aruna sighed. She'd seen enough. One last look at the kitchen she'd been able to use only four times, she left her children to it. Turning to go, she reached for an email.

26th May 2011
Hi Nani,

> *Can't write for long – hectic week – there's a jaundice outbreak here due to water contamination – so frustrating. Rang you twice this morning but no answer. Your last email was very cloak and dagger – is everything OK?? I'm worried. What's this big news you desperately have to tell me? I know you said you want to wait for me to return to tell me in person but I don't have any leave till July. Reply and let me know you're OK. If it's your health, just ring me!!! Texted Summit to call you too.*
> *Love – Rea x*

Aruna stood in her granddaughter's bedroom, over to one side. Rea sat before her desk, staring at the screen for some time. She pulled her hair back and expelled a long shaky breath. The blue light of the laptop revealed her swollen eyes and dark rings of fatigue. A memory came to Aruna of a little girl, forever trying to pull the red ribbons out of her unruly plaits . . . Standing in the newsagent's, hopping from foot to foot. Hurry up, Nani, let's go to the park. Just two more numbers, Rea . . . But I already gave you numbers. I know, darling, but I need six numbers and you only gave me four, so come on, you're my lucky charm – two more numbers, then we'll go . . .

As Rea began to type, Aruna read over her shoulder.

19th July 2011
Nani,

I want to scream, lash out, hurt something . . . Where are you??? They say your heart just gave out. Why??????????? Why couldn't you wait? I was one day out. I keep thinking if only I'd got my flight one day early – two bloody weeks early – a month early.

£8,220,658 . . . After all these years you finally won. I don't know whether I should laugh at God or spit at him. What's the bloody point of winning this money if He planned on taking you away weeks later???

There's a voice in my head that says I should be thrilled that you've put this in a trust for me to use at the camp. At some point I'll be incredibly grateful about the projects we can fund and the people we can help. At some point, sure. But right now, I'd burn every last penny of it to have you back here with me!!!

Sally rang, told me about the donation to Graywood House. One million pounds . . . It's got a nice ring to it. They are going to put a new bench with your name on it in the porch.

Why am I even writing to you????

Where do I go for chai and late-night philosophy now? When Mum doesn't get me, who do I speak to now? Summer's here . . . No more mango picnics in Hyde Park. I didn't get to say goodbye, no last hug, no last smile. One blasted fucking day. You couldn't even give me 24 hours . . .

Aruna smiled sadly, satisfied she'd made the right decision. Now she could go. Ashok was waiting for her.

A Gift
RACHAEL WITHERS

"I have something for the baby. Can you pop round this afternoon?"

"Not really, Mum. He was kicking all night. I need some sleep."

My mother regards sleep as an indulgence.

She's silent for a while. I can picture her, twisting the phone cord around her fingers, thinking.

She says, "Oh, maybe I can see you tomorrow, then?"

"OK, Mum, I'll be round tomorrow afternoon."

"Yes, at three thirty. Great, I'll see you then."

This is immediately followed by the aggressive hum of the dialling tone. My mother is usually excessively courteous, but not on the phone. After thirty years in the UK, her English is almost perfect, but she has never got out of the Japanese habit of just hanging up after the main body of conversation is over.

The next day I go to my mother's. I cannot slide under the steering wheel of the car any more so I have to take a taxi. I remind myself that she can't foresee these kinds of problems; that she doesn't understand the intricate limitations imposed by the new life growing inside me. For her, pregnancy remains a fairy tale.

As the taxi pulls up, she hurries out to greet me, gives me a warm hug, scolds me for not wearing a coat, then brings me inside and sits me in the comfy armchair. Tea (green) is offered, then cake (castella from Minamoto in Finchley). She regards me with a look of ill-concealed distaste as I stuff myself with a second slice of soft sponge and, absent-mindedly, she runs a hand across her own still-flat stomach. She has never weighed more than eight stone. My body is swollen, a succulent fruit. Not just my belly, but breasts, thighs, buttocks and feet. My fingers grow more sausage-like by the day. To her, I must look like a hippopotamus in earrings.

My mother used to read to me, when I was a child, from a picture book about a family of hippopotamuses; the mother hippopotamus in a shower cap, retreating to the bath for some peace and quiet. Or maybe they were elephants? Recently I find an intruder has been at my memories with a pair of scissors.

I can remember her evening perfume wrapping itself around me while she read me my bedtime story. She always wore the same scent – Anaïs Anaïs. It made her smell rich, like velvet and a big garden and treasure. I think she must have worn it for my father. Possibly he bought it for her. She stopped wearing it abruptly after he was gone.

In those childhood years I realised that my mother and I were different from other mothers and daughters. We were different from the others because we were so obviously different from each other. When I was with my father in public, we were just another parent and child. When strangers met me with my mother, they behaved as if they were owed an explanation.

I remember how, on my first day of school, my mother woke me at six in the morning with instructions to wash my face and then come to their room to greet my father.

At ten past six I went into my parents' room and bellowed "Good morning, Daddy." My father's response was muffled by the bedclothes, but it was clearly not what my mother had been expecting. She flinched momentarily, a bird considering flight, then steered me back out of the room.

When they first met at university, my father must have found her Japanese traditions exciting, but they were palling by the time I was old enough to take part in them. I don't remember him ever showing much interest in her culture.

My mother and I arrived at the school gates before anyone else. In the air was the smell of mouldering leaves and wet pavement.

A neat-looking mother and daughter were walking in our

direction. I retreated behind my mother's legs. Other mother and daughter were both red-haired – it looked like copper wire coming out of their heads – and had the very same walk. I couldn't get over how similar to each other they looked. As they came closer I could see their mouths were the exact same shape. It was unnatural, I thought. Maybe they could even read each other's minds.

Other mother smiled at my mother. I peeped my blonde head out from behind her hip. The woman looked a little confused, but just in her eyes. She kept the confusion from the rest of her face by smiling even harder.

She said, "I'm Valerie, and this is Laura."

"My name is Mika Stephens," my mother said. "This is Emma."

Other mother Valerie paused, still smiling, and looked at me, then looked at my mother for the rest of the information.

"Lovely. And where are you from, Mika?"

"Oh, we live in Caldicot Gardens."

This was not a joke, but other mother Valerie laughed as if it were, an extremely funny one. My mother looked very small next to Valerie. Then they were having a grown-up talk about how my mother was from Japan and had come to the UK and then she had met my father and they had got married. Then she found she couldn't have children so they adopted me.

"You look wonderful together," said Valerie.

This was a strange thing to say. We looked just like we normally did together. My mother said thank you, but I could see that she had given Valerie something, and that she hadn't really wanted to, and that now she was even smaller next to Valerie.

After I've finished my cake, my mother all the while taking delicate sips of tea, she says that the present for the baby is in the kitchen. She says it is from Japan. She slips out and returns with a small package in her hands, wrapped in blue and gold *washi* paper, a sliver of midnight sky spattered with fireworks.

"This is from your grandmother."

A vision of Grandmother flashes before me, a prune-like ninety-one-year-old with raisin eyes and a smile like a theatre curtain lifted on a train wreck. We used to visit her in Toyohashi once a year, but those trips fell by the wayside once I was a teenager.

My mother holds the packet, just out of my reach. I extend one arm and waggle my sausage fingers, hoping she will step closer. Getting in and out of armchairs has become a struggle of mammoth proportions. Again I remind myself that she has no experience of this and I resist the temptation to snarl at her. I heft myself forwards and up on slightly bent knees, swipe the present, then billow back into the armchair, which emits a squeak of protest.

My mother strokes some hair from off her forehead with cool, slender fingers, the nails painted a colour called Black Cherry. Her nails have always been painted like this. They are the exact same colour as the shiny skins of cherries from a supermarket.

When I was little, she would sometimes buy cherries and we would eat them together, conspiratorially, before my father came home from work. She would fetch a large blue and white striped bowl from the cabinet, and tip the cherries into it. She called this the mummy bowl. Then she would get a smaller blue and white striped bowl and set it down on the table. She called this the baby bowl. She would sit opposite me, and we would reach into the mummy bowl and each pull out a cherry, bite it in half and munch it, examining the bloody insides carefully. We would flick the stone into the baby bowl, and pop the other half of the cherry into our mouths. The juice would stain our lips, and it would often run down my fingers, and then follow the creases in my hands, down to my wrist. There, purple lines would mark the white skin.

My mother once explained that these were American cherries, and that Japanese cherries were smaller and bright red instead of black red. The flesh inside was pale pink and yellow. In Japan, the cherries were called *sakuranbo* and the blossoms on the cherry trees were called *sakura*, and they were the thing she missed most about Japan. There were so many things she missed. After my father had left us for an English woman, we both knew I was the only reason she stayed.

I examine my prize. The package is slightly smaller than my palm, the delicate pattern of the *washi* inappropriately dainty against my fleshy paw. Slipping my finger through a gap in the wrapping paper, I shell a neat box.

"Family heirloom," says my mother quietly.

I lift the lid. My eye catches something crusty that could be pus. I clap the box shut and give my mother an angry look.

"What the hell is it?"

My mother is giggling with delight at my reaction.

"It's Japanese tradition. It's my – I'm not sure how to say – it's my navel string, it joined me to my mother before I was born."

I open the box again, holding it at a distance. I can see an inch of tube-shaped scab. It looks septic.

"Umbilical cord," I say.

"Umbilical cord," she repeats carefully. "In Japan we say *heso no o*. We keep the *heso no o* for a good relationship with our child. It's lucky."

I will have a scabby cord of my own in a few weeks' time, although I don't think I will be keeping it. My mother looks at the box reverently. I suppose we put the highest value on the things we can never have.

When I get home that evening Neil is already there. He makes me a cup of tea (PG Tips with one sugar) and is suitably appalled by the contents of the wooden box.

"I'm really up for getting our child into your mother's culture, but I think we can leave this out. You don't want to end up eating placenta paté."

I laugh, and then I feel guilty when I remember the way she looked at the box, as though it were something holy, a relic from a sacrament she had never undergone. My mother once said that, although Grandmother adored *me*, she was ashamed to have a daughter that had married a foreigner, ashamed to have a daughter that needed to adopt a baby, and ashamed to have a daughter that could not keep her husband. I was thirteen when she told me this, but I had already learnt all I needed to know about family; the only family worth keeping was the family I could trust.

As I drink my tea, I keep seeing my mother's excited face as she gives me the box. Yes, we were different from each other, but we were all we had.

When Neil rises to clear away the cups, I go over to the phone and dial her number, twisting the cord again and again around my fingers.

The Thaw
ALISON MACLEOD

For Marjorie Genevieve

Wisdom after the event is a cheap enough commodity – but go back. The smoky light of a March sunrise is seeping through the winter drapes. Outside, the world is glassy; the trees on Pleasant Street, glazed with winter. Every bare branch, every dead leaf is sheathed in ice, like a fossil from another age, an antediluvian dream of blossom and green canopies. Below her bedroom window, the drifts rise up in frozen waves of white – even the sudden gusts and eddies of wind cannot disturb those peaks – while overhead, the warmth of the sun is so reluctant in its offerings, so meagre, you'd not be alone if you failed to notice the coming of the first thaw.

Above her room, a sheet of ice on the eaves gives way, smashing like a minor glacier onto the porch roof, but everyone in the house sleeps on. Marjorie – or Marjorie Genevieve as her father always called her – sleeps in what the family still call "Ethel's room", though it has been thirteen years since Ethel was taken from them by TB. Ethel, 1913. And Kathleen, just two years later. Marjorie still keeps one of Kathleen's Sunday handkerchiefs, spotted with her blood.

As for their mother, Cecelia Maud, it is true what people say. She has never recovered from the deaths of her three grown children: Ethel, Kathleen and, finally, senselessly, Murray, just two˙ months after Kathleen. Before Christmas, Marjorie found her mother sitting in the ice house with her coat unbuttoned and sawdust in her hair. Her lips were blue.

After seven daughters, Providence gave Cecelia Maud and James MacLeod a single son, a boy who would become the youngest lawyer ever admitted to the Bar in the province of Nova Scotia.

Some say the MacLeods hold themselves too high – which is perhaps why the fight broke out, behind Batterson's Dry Goods, which, everyone knew, doubled as a bootlegger's after dark on Saturdays.

No man that night would ever say who was involved or who threw the first punch. Only this was clear. Murray was laid out on a table in the store room. Concussed, they said, that was all. Come morning, he'd have a devil of a sore head, and a hard time defending himself to his mother and his wife, lawyer or no. Louis Clarke, the town's Inspector, gave them ten minutes while he turned a blind eye, stepped outside, and marvelled, as he was known to do, at the plenitude of stars in the Cape Breton sky. Two men – suddenly stark sober – heaved Murray into their arms. They took the short cut through Plant's Field; saw only the Portuguese fishermen who were camped, as ever, by the brook, their damp clothes hanging, pale as spectres, while their owners slept.

That August Sunday morning, Cecelia Maud woke early. She planned to pick a few gem lettuces from the garden before they wilted in the day's heat. But when she opened the inside door of the back porch, she found her only son slumped against the rocker, blood still seeping from his ear.

Her legs gave way. She could neither scream nor cry out.

Indeed, it was only after the clockwork of the day had begun – the stove swept (no char on a Sunday), the breakfast table laid – that Marjorie found her mother on the floor beside her brother, and for a moment she struggled to know the living from the dead.

But no charges were laid. No notice of the funeral was given in St Joseph's weekly bulletin. It was an unusually quiet gathering, family only. Murray MacLeod was the youngest lawyer ever to be called to the Bar – dead after a Saturday night at the bootlegger's – and the MacLeods, Catholics, were not unaware: they were fortunate to reside on Pleasant Street, in the enviable, Protestant district of Ward One.

Again: *Wisdom after the event is a cheap enough commodity* – but these words and the article in the *North Sydney Herald* are still unimaginable. As she wakes this Saturday morning in a frozen March, Marjorie Genevieve is enjoying the knowledge that her coat was anything but cheap.

She works Mondays and Wednesdays at the head office of Thompson's Foundry. Before her father died, he made it clear he would consent to a part-time position only. She did not *need* to work, he explained with a benign smile, and although James MacLeod is now eight years gone, no one, not even Marjorie's eldest sister May, with her fierce intelligence and heavy eyebrows, has the authority to overturn his decision.

Marjorie knew it had to be beaver, not muskrat, not even muskrat dyed to look like mink.

A three-quarter-length, wrap-round coat in unsheared beaver. She saved for two years.

In the darkness of her room, she slides it on over her nightgown and rubs her palm against the nap of the fur. The shawl collar tickles her bare neck. The silk lining is cool against her chest. When she pulls back the drapes, she can see almost nothing of the day through the bedroom window. The pane is a palimpsest of frost; the world is white. But she is radiantly warm.

She is twenty-nine, and it is only right. There has been enough grief. Thirteen years of grief. Ethel. Kathleen. Murray. Her father. And now her mother, the husk of herself.

Wearing the fur over only her nightgown, Marjorie feels nearly naked.

The furrier at Vooght Brothers had the voice of an orator. "I do not need to persuade you of the elegance of this coat. But remember, while beaver is sometimes known for being heavy to wear, it offers *exceptional* protection against the excesses of a Cape Breton winter. Notice how the long guard hairs give this coat its lustrous sheen."

She noticed.

He took the liberty of easing the coat over her shoulders. The drape felt exquisite, the weight of the fur a strange new gravity. A lining of gold dress silk flashed within. She wrapped the coat around herself, and felt the dense animal softness mould itself to her form.

"You won't find a more fashionable cut this side of Montreal."

It was the coat of a mature, stylish woman, the coat of a woman of nearly thirty.

She deposited her payment in a small metal box and watched it whiz away on an electric wire. Within moments, the box came sailing back down the line, and revealed, as if by magic, her bill of sale.

Her account was settled.

The coat would be delivered.

The dance was Saturday night.

The penalties of past mistakes cannot be remitted, but at least the lessons so solemnly and dearly learned should be taken to heart.

But not yet. Wait –

Because Charlie Thompson is pulling up next to the hitching rail outside Vooght's, where William Dooley, the funeral director, has stopped his team. Steam rises from the horses' dark flanks as a small group of men – from Dooley's, the Cable Office, the Vendome Hotel, and the Royal Albert – gather to offer, with low whistles and eagle eyes, their unreserved admiration for Charlie Thompson's new 1926 Buick Roadster.

Marjorie sees him – Mr Thompson, her employer – and nods briefly before turning right, when, in fact, she meant to turn left for home. But it's too late. Her pride in her new purchase has distracted her, and she doesn't want to walk past the group again straightaway, so she slips into the Royal Café and orders tea with a slice of Lady Baltimore cake.

Outside the gleaming window, a single, tusky icicle drips, one of a long row that hangs from the café's awning, but Marjorie is unaware.

She watches, vaguely, the gathering of men across the street. William Dooley, the funeral director, has eased himself into the driver's seat. Mr Thompson is leaning on the door of the Buick, showing him the inner sanctum, but even so, he is taller than the others. She supposes he's handsome for a man of his age: dark-haired, grey only at the temples, an easy smile. Shame about the one short leg. A birth defect, she was told.

According to Eleanor in the office, he always walks fast, trying to disguise it, and his tailor "gets hell" if the hem of his trousers doesn't hide the top of his block of a shoe. "Maybe the bad leg's the reason he likes *speed*," Eleanor murmured, leaning forward. "Well, there's that new automobile, isn't there? Plus some fine breed of horse up at the racecourse." She lowered her chin and whispered into her bosom. "Apparently, he's a *gambler*."

Maybe, thought Marjorie. But married, fifty, sober, Protestant, well off, with three children. Respectable.

She leaves two bites of cake on her plate, as May taught her. She pushes in her chair, slips on her wool coat and pays the bill. Across the street, Charlie Thompson has resumed the ordinary shape of the man who lopes unevenly past her desk each morning while the secretaries, Marjorie included, lower their heads out of courtesy.

As she slips through the door of the Royal Café, there can be no way for Marjorie to know that the man she is about to pass for the second time that day – Charlie Thompson, married, fifty, Protestant, with three children – is her future.

On Route 28, the chains on the car's tyres grip the snowy twists and bends. They hum, then clunk, with every rotation, a primitive rhythm that sends Marjorie into a world of her own. It's a sixteen-mile journey from North Sydney to Sydney, and, wrapped in her new coat, she enjoys every moment, staring through her window at the frozen expanse of Sydney Harbour, mesmerised by its white, elemental glow.

So she makes only the poorest of efforts to shout over the engine for chit-chat with Eleanor and Eleanor's brother Stan up front. The forty-minute journey passes in what seems like ten, and in no time, the flaming tower of Sydney's steelworks looms into view, spitting like a firework about to explode.

The *Herald* will assure us that, as she arrives at the Imperial Hotel on Sydney's Esplanade, Marjorie is *a young lady* whose thoughts are *centred on an evening's innocent recreation*. In the lobby, she passes her fur to the cloakroom attendant, wondering if the girl will be tempted to try it when no one's looking. *Go on*, she wants to say. *I don't mind!* But she doesn't want to presume.

"Don't forget your dance cards!" the girl calls after them, and Marjorie dashes back.

The names of the dances marked on the cards make her and

Eleanor laugh: the Turkey Trot, the Wiggle-de-Wiggle, the Shorty George, the Fuzzy Wuzzy . . . Sixteen in all. "I hope I've got a little Negro in my blood," shouts Eleanor as they sashay into the ballroom. Marjorie can only force a smile, not knowing the polite reply. Besides, the twelve-man band is already bugling and strumming, swaying and tromboning, and Marjorie knows this one – *Everything's Gonna Be Alright*.

"There must be more than five hundred people here," marvels Eleanor.

Marjorie is swapping her boots for her Mary Janes. "And half from North Sydney!"

"I told you we wouldn't be stuck with Stan all night. Besides, there are enough men from the KOC to mean that even the Pope himself would approve of our Turkey Trot. Look! Mr Thompson's here too."

Marjorie spots him, smoking near the rear door. She shrugs.

But Eleanor is still squinting. "He's here with the racecourse set."

Marjorie turns to the band. Five of the twelve men are black. Two, the darkest black. She's heard there are Negro families in Sydney who have come all the way from the Deep South.

She's only ever seen a Negro once before, a stoker from the Foundry who came into the office because his wages were overdue. She liked the sound of his voice; the lazy music of his words.

Eleanor yells over the band. "He's come on his own."

"Who has?"

"Mrs Thompson isn't here. She must be down with something again. Not that it matters! He never dances anyway with that short leg of his."

Marjorie can see Stan crossing the floor towards them, refreshments in hand. In a moment, thankfully, Eleanor will have another ear.

"Though you never know." She giggles and tugs at Marjorie's sleeve. "The Shorty George might be just the number for him!"

Marjorie knows she should, but she doesn't care enough about Mr Thompson to protest on his behalf. Besides, it's a new song now, one she's never heard – *If You Can't Land Her on the Ol' Verandah* – and beneath her satin dress, her hips are already swaying.

*

Dance after dance, time is shimmying and quickstepping away, and Marjorie has no notion of the hour. She's red-faced and giddy from laughing through all the new steps, but the room still heaves with dancers. Even Joe "Clunk" McEwan is stepdancing on a tabletop to *The Alabama Stomp*.

Someone has propped open the rear doors for a blast of cold winter air, and hip flasks of bootlegged whisky are passing from man to man, across the dance floor. The MC is starting to slur, and the twelve-man band is three men down, but the music roars on.

She plucks her dress away from her to catch any breath of air.

"Excuse me, Miss. Is there room for one more on your dance card?"

Marjorie turns. One of the Negro men from the band – the double-bass player – is standing before her, his shoulders back, his tie loose at his neck.

Eleanor's hand flies to her chest. Stan takes a step forward.

Marjorie can see the man is not drunk. His eyes are clear; his gaze, steady. For a moment, she wishes he were. She might know what to do. She extends her hand. "I'm enjoying the music."

He nods, grinning at the parquet floor. "I'm Walter. Would you like to dance, Miss?"

"Marjorie." She clasps her palms. "But I have to confess, Walter, I'm done in for the night."

He clicks his tongue. "A fine dancer like you? Why, you just need your second wind."

She risks it. "I'm sure it's none of my business, Walter, but are you one of the steelworkers from down south?" *Are the nights sultry?* she wants to ask. *Do the women carry fans?*

He nods. "From Alabama, Miss."

She wishes he would call her Marjorie. "But Sydney's your home now?"

"Not Sydney proper, Miss."

"No?"

"No." He runs a hand across his chin and searches her face. "Me and my family, we live in Cokeville."

She smiles politely. Then it comes to her: Cokeville. The area by Whitney Pier, where the filthy run-off from the coke ovens pours into the estuary.

The band strikes up a waltz, *Wistful and Blue*. Walter offers her his hand. She is surprised by the pale flash of his palms.

She can feel the eyes of many more than Stan and Eleanor now. But his hand still waits, and the truth is, she *would* like to dance.

As she takes his hand, she can feel the calluses on his fingertips. She has never met a double-bass player before. Up close, he smells of lye, like the bar her mother keeps by the set tub.

From the seating area there arises a low drone of murmurings. Couple after couple leave the dance floor.

She reaches after conversation, speaking into his ear. "So you brought your family with you to Sydney?"

He leads well. "Yes, that's right. My mamma and my sisters."

She dreads the eye of the roaming spotlight. "That must be difficult – with just you to look after them, I mean."

She can see his eyes assessing the risk: is it better to lead her into the shadows of the ballroom or to keep to the bright centre? "Yes, Miss, I do my best. But it's been especially hard since my brother was killed."

"Killed?" She stops dancing.

"'Fraid so. Just before we left Alabama. At a speakeasy in our town. Leonard was hired to wash glasses. But a fight broke out over something or another that had gone missing. The manager was drunk. Went mad as a hornet. Broke a glass – on purpose like – and cut Leonard's throat."

The shape of her brother Murray rises in Marjorie's mind's eye. Blood still seeps from his ear.

"Did they get the man, Walter, or did he get away?"

"Neither, Miss." He swallows hard. "They didn't get the man – and he didn't get away. That laid us low, my mamma especially."

Marjorie nods. *Her mother. In the ice house. Her lips blue.*

Out of the corner of her eye, she notices that several of the men from the Knights of Columbus have risen from their chairs and stand watching, their arms folded across their chests. They're wondering if Walter has offended her; if that's why she's having words. So she smiles at her partner, as if to say she is ready to dance again, and Walter waltzes her back to the centre of the floor.

On stage, the MC watches, fiddling anxiously with his cuffs and trying, without success, to catch the eye of the conductor. But

Wistful and Blue floats on into the wintery night – *one*, two, three – while the ballroom of the Imperial Hotel empties. The KOC men, Marjorie notices, still haven't sat back down in their chairs, and Walter's hand has gone cold in hers.

A voice sounds at the dark edge of the spotlight: "Excuse me."

Walter stops short. Marjorie squeezes her eyes shut. She can feel the air around her about to break.

"May I?"

She opens her eyes. Charlie Thompson is standing before them. He has tapped Walter's shoulder.

Walter nods, then smiles, blinking too much, before he thanks Marjorie for the dance. Marjorie presses his forearm. "Thank you for asking." He makes for the safety of the stage as Charlie Thompson takes her hand in his. She feels his other hand, light on the small of her back. His face tenses as he strains to pick out the beat. Then they step into the mercy of darkness, his bad leg stammering.

When he returns her to her table, Eleanor is talking to Jimmy Monaghan. She doesn't turn to acknowledge Marjorie.

Charlie Thompson hovers, his head bowed. "Thank you for the dance, Marjorie. It was kind of you to put up with my two left feet."

"Thank *you*, Mr Thompson!" She has to look away so the tears don't come.

He glances sternly at the backs of Eleanor and Jimmy Monaghan. "I'm driving back to North Sydney now, in case you need a lift."

She turns to the table and tries again. "Eleanor?"

But Eleanor pretends not to hear. So Marjorie finds her clutch on the floor and tries to smile. "Thank you. It *is* very late."

Outside, the snow that was falling earlier has turned to sleet. As she waits on the sidewalk for Mr Thompson and his Buick, she watches two men approach, their unbuttoned coats flapping. Even in the wind, she can smell the liquor on them as they pass. When one slips on a patch of ice and almost hits the ground, she turns her face away. She pretends not to hear his friend mutter that the roads everywhere are "as slick as a buttered-up bride". But everything's fine because Mr Thompson's pulling up to the kerb now. He's stepping outside to open her door, and as she bundles herself and her coat into the passenger seat, she hardly knows what possesses her. "Cokeville." She stares into her lap. "Before we go back, Mr Thompson, would you show me Cokeville?"

His hand hovers over the gearbox. He has to clear his throat. "Sure. It's not so far out of our way."

She smells it before she sees it: a stink of slag and human sewage. Under the angry candle of the steelworks tower, rows of dark bunkhouses and shacks appear in the night.

Charlie Thompson turns off the engine as she stumbles into speech. "But Bill at the Foundry said these men are skilled labourers. I thought that's why they were asked to come all this way."

"Yes."

"I thought all the steelworkers and their families lived in the Ashby area."

"Not all – sadly."

Marjorie pulls her coat tight. Charlie lights a cigarette for her, but she suspects her hand will shake if she tries to hold it.

He rubs the windshield clear of the mist of their breath. "It's after midnight, Marjorie."

"Of course. I'm keeping you, and my mother will be waiting up."

"Not to mention the fact that you'll get an earful from your big sister when she hears." In the narrow space of the two-door Buick, he turns to her for the first time – and winks. "I see her very . . . patient husband up at the track."

She lets herself laugh.

"We'll take the harbour, shall we?" he says. "Make up a bit of lost time?"

She sits up in her seat, surfacing from the depths of her coat. "Stan, Eleanor's brother, said the harbour is risky now."

Charlie casts his cigarette into the night. "I came that way. The ice was rock solid." He smiles. "You don't think I'd play fast and loose with this baby, do you?" He thumps the steering wheel, then releases the handbrake.

A gambler, Eleanor had said. "Apparently, he's a *gambler*." Of course, he'd have to be to offer her – a young, unmarried woman – a late-night lift home in the first place. Not that she had to accept. Maybe that makes them two of a kind, her and Charlie Thompson. She only knows that it's past midnight, the roads are bad – it will be a slow crawl back to North Sydney – and May will shame her come tomorrow morning. She has no idea how she'll explain: about Walter, the lateness of the hour, about Mr Thompson, married and Protestant.

At Muggah's Creek, the new 1926 Buick Roadster glides onto the ice.

But even now, there's time. Will she say it?

Shall we turn back? Everyone says you shouldn't cross after the first of March.

No.

Because what's five days to twenty inches of ice, and hasn't it been snowing most of the night? Besides, it's just eight miles across. In a quarter of an hour, they'll be landing on the sandbar at Indian Beach.

She has never crossed by night before. The swollen sky bears down on them. In the wide, dark limbo of Sydney Harbour, the Buick's headlamps seem no brighter than a pair of jack-o'-lanterns.

Every year the Council says it will provide range lights and a few bush-marked courses, but the owners of the ice-breakers protest. How will they clear the harbour's shipping lane with lights, markers and more traffic to circumnavigate?

As the car moves out across the frozen estuary, Charlie Thompson's hands are rigid on the wheel. Now and again, the car fan-tails, but he pulls it back into line and on they go.

She'll laugh on the other side. Perhaps she'll even have one of Mr Thompson's cigarettes or a swig from his flask to steady her nerves.

She would lay her head back and close her eyes – she's so tired now – but cold air blasts through the windows. Mr Thompson says they have to stay open so the windshield doesn't fog up.

And suddenly, for no reason, she remembers the old Micmac woman who came to the door selling coloured baskets. "I'm sorry," the woman said, taking Marjorie's mother's thin hand in her own.

"I am sorry about your three daughters."

How did she know?

But "No," said Marjorie, going to her mother's aid. "My mother has lost two daughters and the son of the house. *Two* daughters. Three children. But thank you for your condolences." And the woman looked at her – looked right *through* her.

She shakes herself. They are almost clear of the estuary. Another ten minutes and they'll be on *terra firma*. She tries to brighten. "All things considered," she says, turning to Charlie Thompson, "I enjoyed myself tonight."

He laughs, relieved to have conversation. "I haven't danced so much in years!"

"You danced half of one dance!"

"Exactly. My wife will never believe it."

She doesn't look at him as she says it. "You'll tell your wife then."

He leans forward, mopping the windshield with his sleeve. "Haven't decided yet. I have a policy, you might say. I try my damnedest to live in the moment."

She nods, as if his reply were neither here nor there.

"Which means," he says, winking again, "I'll think about it tomorrow when I'm sitting in church."

"Where you can calmly resolve to think about it later!"

"Bull's-eye."

She settles back into her seat, laughing. She recalls again the easy sway of her hips as she danced, and Walter's firm arm leading, and Mr Thompson bending over her, tall, close, protective. There's a tune stuck in her head, one of the big jazz numbers of the night. What was it called? The windshield wipers are going, they're lulling her to sleep, and it's only when Charlie Thompson looks over and catches her eye that she realises she's been humming the tune aloud. Her throat and cheeks go hot, but there's no need. He's not signalling for her to stop. He's *singing*. Eleanor wouldn't believe it. He's stringing together one line after the other, and it's all coming back: the deep, in-your-belly rhythm, the spell of the words, the stream in the moonlight, the honey who'll be gone by dawn. *Tonight You Belong to Me*. That's the one. Charlie Thompson has a fine voice, she thinks to herself – when the car goes through.

Her stomach drops; her spine stiffens. The hole opens like a black mouth. The Buick tips – her hands can't find the handle – and suddenly, unfathomably, the car is locked in jaws of ice.

The headlamps are out, and she can't tell if the space above her is the window that faces up or down. His or hers. There's no top, no bottom, no floor, no roof, no ocean bed, no blind hole. *Mr Thompson?* Through the open window, water and ice are rushing across her lap – *my coat, my new coat* – and her mind can't catch up.

I tell myself this.

She feels his hand grabbing at her shoulder – *thank God*, she thinks, *thank God*. He's hauling her up by the collar of her coat. She's pushing off from the passenger door with her feet, gulping air. He's going ahead, showing her the way to the surface. She's grabbing hold of the block of his shoe, an anchor in the chaos. Or is that the window frame? And is that his voice calling or the groaning of steel against ice?

But the car shifts again, a wave churns through, the world rolls and –

No.

The car is falling, juddering, through the ice. Down and down. *Mr Thompson!*

But he's nowhere.

Such darkness. Such cold.

Like she has never known.

Her coat clings, sodden. Heavy.

Unimaginably heavy.

A dead animal weight.

And the Micmac woman is beside her in the footwell – *shhh now, quiet* – as the car sinks to the bottom of the estuary.

In the article in the *Herald* entitled "Saturday Night's Tragedy", she will remain unnamed. A kindness perhaps.

There will be no obituary. No public wake. No crowd of mourners, warm and close in the kitchen.

Only talk.

Her funeral will be attended by just four, her sisters May, Laura, Alice and Ignace. As the Mass is said, her mother will close herself in "Ethel's room" and draw the drapes.

As for Charlie Thompson, he will never be able to get a song out of his head, and in the black waters of sleep, it will slow into a dirge and boom between his ears. *Tonight You Belong to Me.*

Sometimes, I tell people about my great-aunt who went under the ice.

From an Admirer
JACK WILKES

Janet liked living in Central London. It never slept, and clubs, theatres, the Opera House were within minutes of hailing a cab. Her childhood wish had been to live in a three-storey Georgian house with railings, overlooking a tree-lined square. She had fulfilled that wish without a mortgage, yet it had still come with a heavy price tag. Scaling the sales ladder, using people then dumping them, making contacts not friends, was how she became successful. As planned there were no children to get in the way; as a female it gave her the edge. Her sisters' struggles to raise their "self-inflicted injuries" had proved her right. Early retirement had come and Janet wanted to share the fruits of her success, but everyone had fallen by the wayside, unnecessary attachments on the way up. There was only her secret admirer, and tonight she was determined to unmask him.

After the rain the mid-February evening air felt fresh against her face, and there was a spring of anticipation in her step as she walked from the station to her square. The wet trees glistened around the street lights and were mirrored in the puddles, making the perfect setting for her house. Even the reflected headlights and the "Ssssssplash" of the passing cars pleased her. She walked up the steps smiling, admired her black-painted railings, the glossy red front door, and the new discreet security camera, which would film her unknown suitor. Once inside, she placed a cat's bell in the letterbox, and the trap was set.

Every Valentine's night since she moved in there had been a yellow rose "From an admirer"; tonight would be the twentieth. His identity had often intrigued her. Dismissing those whose careers she'd ruined or who'd died or married left her with brief affairs too many to recall. Whoever it was, twenty years had made him remarkable and tonight she would meet him.

The cat's bell tinkled onto the doormat. In one movement, she caught the rose and opened the door.

"Hello Mr Yellow Rose . . ."

A thin man of about fifty, his collar turned up and his hat pulled low, stared back.

"But . . . who are you?" she asked.

"But you're not . . ." He looked past her into the house. "Does Dorothy Wainwright live here?" he asked.

"Certainly not. This has been my house for twenty years."

"Twenty years! I've been putting roses through the wrong door for . . ."

He snatched the rose from her hand and went back down the steps swearing under his breath. She watched in disbelief as he crossed the road and disappeared into the darkness.

It started to rain. She closed the door slowly, sat in her favourite chair and stared at the vase containing nineteen dead roses, each now a symbol of lost hope.

The Tree of War
TANYA DATTA

I am about to nuke Hawaii.

That's right. I, Krishna the Merciless, am going to *massacre* Hawaii. Not a single thing will survive my attack. If they do, they'll soon be sorry.

"Five," I yell. The tree creaks as the boys scramble to escape. "Four . . ."

All at once my mother's voice roars out and the countdown dies in my throat. The three of us flatten down on the branches like leopards. *Geez.* She sounds like she wants to kill me. I crane my neck until she comes into view. She's standing at her bedroom window, head turning left and right as she hunts for me. No way she can see us, though. We're halfway up the tree that overlooks my back garden, hidden amongst its leaves. This is our world up here, our watchtower, where we see everyone but no one sees us.

"Krishna! Do you hear me? I'm going out. Come back home *now.*"

"Aren't you going to answer her?" Feargal whispers.

I roll my eyes. My mind's on mass murder and it's hard to shake off. Nuclear War is about the best game we've ever made up. As far as killing goes, there's no beating it. Not only could one nuclear bomb kill hundreds of thousands of people but, what with radiation and pollution, the destruction could ripple on for centuries. Imagine that! And if there were several bombs at the same time, the results would be even more catastrophic. A nuclear holocaust could wipe out the entire human race. That's what all those women on telly, the ones chaining themselves to fences, are afraid of. And why that comic book showing what radiation did to the old couple is so scary. Because nuclear war is the ultimate evil.

It makes Cowboys and Indians look like hopscotch.

As for Star Wars, who isn't fed up of making that stupid lightsabre sound?

We turned Nuclear War into a game at the start of the summer holidays and we've been playing it every day since then. By *we*, I mean the gang. That's me, ten and a quarter, Feargal, who's just turned nine, and Angus, who's eight and a half. We've all known each other for years. Feargal comes from Belfast and is as delicate as an elf. Angus is even smaller but is really brave for his size. Once he gets going, he's just like Asterix: invincible. As for me, I tower over both of them, which is good because I'm the leader.

The best thing about our game is that it has to be played in a tree. The one we call the Monkey Tree. Truth is, there's a real monkey puzzle tree a few yards away and we just stole its name. We didn't feel too guilty about it either. No monkey would touch that other tree. Why would it? Covered in spiky green needles, thin branches poking out at odd angles. It's part cactus, part reptile. Our tree couldn't be more different. With its smooth bark and soft tickly leaves, it's friendly and welcoming. At its base the trunk bends almost flat to one side before sloping upwards again. It's this small platform like the crook of a kindly giant's arm that helps us clamber into the tree. Hugging the trunk with our arms and knees, we work our way higher and higher off the ground. Soon we're swinging from branch to branch. Sometimes we even hang upside down, hands and feet wrapped tight around a branch, the blood rushing into our heads. The only thing we're missing is a tail.

"Krishnaaaaaaaaa!!!" My mother's growl of fury scatters my thoughts. I'm so close to a smacking that my skin starts tingling. OK, I think, it's after nine, long past my bedtime. But there's something important she's missing here. It isn't dark. Not even close. Instead it's weirdly bright as if the sun's refusing to budge. The sunshine reminds me of honey: deep golden and syrupy. I could almost spread it on toast and eat it. No way I could sleep in this much light. No way I'd want to. It's the sort of night when anything could happen and I don't intend to miss it when it does.

But I guess Mum doesn't see things the same way because her voice lashes out again, and this time there's no messing. "Come home this instant! Do you hear me? This instant!"

"Coming," I scream. "Back in five."

The window slams shut.

Angus explodes with laughter. "You are so dead."

It's not fair. I'm the oldest boy here, I shouldn't be going first. Besides, if I wasn't being hauled off, it'd be Angus and Feargal who'd be dead. That's mums for you – they don't care if they make you look bad. Mine, in particular, gets a kick out of being strict. She's short and scary, like a dalek on the loose. Once upon a time she used to be fun. Sometimes we'd laugh so much we'd fall off our chairs. But that was long ago.

I lower myself from the branch and jump the last bit, making sure not to catch the keys around my neck. Stay cool. I start to slouch off then swivel round. Through the camouflage of the leaves the boys watch me, motionless as lizards.

"Call round yours in the morning, then?"

"Yeah," they chorus. "Laters, Krish."

Hawaii is safe for another day.

I set off along the shady path that leads out of the park, kicking an empty can in front of me. Usually, I'd be pelting along on my BMX Burner but I broke the chain last week so I have to walk. I don't mind too much but I'm glad it's still daylight. I wouldn't want to be walking alone here in the dark. The three of us live on the same street in North London in a jam-packed row of houses that feels like a line of policemen linking arms to keep something out. From our front doors the concrete city spreads out all the way to the skyscrapers in the distance. But out back an enormous green park sweeps uphill from the end of our gardens, like a sleeping dinosaur. At the bottom of the hill a narrow strip of trees marks the edge of the park. It's here that the Monkey Tree lives. It overlooks my back garden and Angus's too. It's just about possible to climb over the high fence separating both our gardens from the park, but seeing as there is nothing but blackberry brambles and stinging nettles to fall into, we mostly use the alleyway halfway down our road.

After we came up with the game of Nuclear War we had to map out our battleground which, in our case, was no less than the entire planet.

"That's the United States of America." Angus pointed at one of the main branches.

"This is the Soviet Union." I slapped the branch that I was sitting on.

"What about Siberia?" asked Feargal, the show-off.

We looked around. Siberia was dangerous. We knew that much. People died there. Angus gestured towards the long narrow claw at the end of the Soviet Union. Too much weight and it would snap off. "There," he said coolly.

As soon as the superpowers had been sorted out, places flew out of our mouths – the ones we could remember anyway, Western Europe, Eastern Europe, India, France, South Africa, Scotland, Ireland, the Atlantic Ocean, the West Indies, Brazil, Vietnam, Greenland and Hawaii amongst them. Soon the whole tree had been assigned. Even the tree trunk became somewhere: Switzerland.

It was my job to run through the rules. "Right, so are we agreed? The winner, or whoever's turn it is, is allowed to nuke one country. You have five seconds to get out of that country, otherwise your brains boil and your insides melt into baked beans! Nothing can survive. If you're caught out at sea, you die too. Basically, you only get to live if you escape to a far-off country because, if you end up nearby, then the radiation's going to get you. If that happens, expect your skin to drop off! It's a slow painful death."

The boys cheered.

The game is simple enough. Like everything we play, it's about making us move like crazy. The only difference is that this time our playground is several feet above the ground. One small slip risks injury. Yet we never give it a second thought. In the blackened, bombed-out world we occupy, poisonous winds blow while radioactive rain pours down on our blistering skin. No mercy is shown to anyone. Our fury has no limits. We kill each other eternally and die in agony a million times.

Reaching the alleyway, I head down it past the NF graffiti sprayed in red paint, then leapfrog the concrete bollard to re-enter civilisation. Now that I've reached my road, I've got to double back from the alleyway to get home. It's a first-floor flat with old knackered windows. When Mum first bought it, I used to tell visitors that it was half hers and half mine. She says I made her laugh. Now it doesn't feel like hers or mine any more. Not since my father arrived a month ago. It feels unrecognisable. The back room has become Mum's new bedroom while my father sleeps in her old one.

When Mum first told me that my father was coming to England six years after we'd left him behind in India, I climbed into her wardrobe and stayed there while she looked for me. Squashed on top of all her saris, a bit dizzy from the smell of mothballs, I tried out the word "Dad" over and over again to see if I could get my mouth around it. My tummy felt hard and trembly all at the same time. Although I knew what my father looked like from photos, I couldn't really remember much about him. So it was annoying to see that we were practically identical. My father has skin the colour of Jaffa cakes, exactly like me. He's tall, too, the way I'm shaping up to be. Heavy drooping eyelids give his face the same sleepy look as me, although he's anything but sleepy. Under those eyelids, Mum says, lies a raging volcano.

I had spent a long time telling friends that my father had disappeared whenever they asked about him. Gradually, my tale grew to sound like he had mysteriously vanished on the flight over. I was lying, of course. I knew exactly where he was. He lived with my grandparents in India. So it was pretty embarrassing to own up to Feargal and Angus. But after they got over their surprise, they were pretty good about it. The bottom line was I hadn't actually lied about him not being around, so it was OK in their book. Dads were like that, they reckoned. A bit invisible. Angus's dad was always running away to the pub, or trying to save the miners. As for Feargal's father, he was off to Belfast so often that Angus and I figured he had to be in the IRA. Mine had simply turned out more invisible than most.

Still, having a real-life father around was weird. Odd things bothered me: the deadly silence that exploded between my parents; the way my father took over mowing the lawn. In fact, just seeing my father in the garden stirred up another garden deep inside me:

a long-forgotten, baking-hot garden, in which my mum and dad are rolling around on the grass, trying to kill each other – no joke – while I throw pieces of Lego at them to try to make them stop.

Back home, the flat feels lonely like an empty seashell. I sniff the air, Apache-style. The only things I can sense moving are particles of dust glinting in the sunlight. Great. Telling-off avoided. Mum's gone and who knows where my father might be. Kicking off my trainers, I head into the living room to sneak in some late-night telly. In my haste, I mistake the figure slumped over the dinner table for a heap of clothes waiting to be ironed. Then I freeze and start to back out. Too late. The heap sits up.

"I asked your mother for money to buy some milk and she said no. Can you believe that? She wouldn't even give me a few pence to buy some milk!" My father's voice goes funny. "No one has ever treated me like this in my whole life."

An image of a pint of milk with a silver top forms in my mind. I picture the bottle stuck in the fridge at the corner shop. Imagining the thick layer of yellow cream clogging up the top almost makes me puke. I hate milk. We're forced to drink it every day in class. One time I got caught trying to pour it out of the window. Mr Morris just stood there until I choked the rest of it down. It's good for you they say. But how can it be when it tastes so bad? Wait. Perhaps that's the reason why Mum didn't want to buy the milk? I look up but my father's eyes are darting back and forth across my face like he's scanning ancient hieroglyphs and somehow I grasp that this isn't about milk.

If I had any pocket money I'd give it to him, but I don't.

"I'm sorry," I say. And when I see his jaw tremble, I actually am.

I think about telling him how to play Nuclear War. I think about asking him what he's been doing in India all these years. But my father's no longer in the mood to talk to me. I know because he's doing that thing. That thing I suddenly remember and now I wonder how I could ever have forgotten. He is swearing at Mum in Hindi. I don't understand exactly but I can hear the madness. It sounds like a helicopter inside his chest. *Thwop thwop thwop thwop thwop thwop thwop*. It gets louder and louder until it's almost circling overhead.

"Where do you think she's gone at this time of night, eh?"

My father switches to English and staggers across the room in my direction. "Have you asked yourself where she's gone? Or are you in on the secret, you sneaky bastard? Are you covering for her? Is that it? Are you lying to your dad?"

Sunshine is still pouring in through the window but now I can't stand it, all this light, as if it's trying to trap me for ever within a never-ending day.

"She's done it before, you know. Oh yeah. She won't admit it. But I know. I know!" He bends down so close, I can smell his breath. I could even touch him if I wanted but my arms are paralysed. His eyes are looking directly into mine. And now it's all coming back. Don't say anything, Mum used to say. Don't even breathe.

"I should have known she was a bitch right from the start," my dad confides in me. "My friends warned me. But I wouldn't listen. I allowed her too much independence. We haven't even been man and wife since I came. Now I know why. No decent woman goes out at this time of night." He laughs but it comes out like a sob. "You think she has gone to a hotel? You think it's someone from her work? I'll kill her if I find out."

My eyes start to sting. Got to go. I walk out of the living room and into the hallway. My father grabs my arm and I end up falling onto the floor. The pattern on the carpet is red and orange swirls on a black background. I pull myself up quickly so that I'm sitting. My father squats down in front of me and puts his hand on my shoulder as if we're old comrades. Father and son having a pow-wow in the middle of the hallway as if it was the most normal place in the world. As if it was *our* place, but we don't have a place.

"Can't you help?" he asks after a long pause.

"Help what?" My voice is a whisper.

"Help me and your mother stay together."

I stare at my feet.

"You're *supposed* to help, Krishna. You're our son. You're supposed to want us to stay together. It's only natural."

There's no way he can lay this on me, I think furiously, and the tears I have been holding back for ever drip down my face onto the stormy swirls below. Help them stay together so we can carry on living like this? He must be joking. Even if I wanted to, which I don't, it'd be no use. Because I've cracked why my mum won't buy him milk, see. But my father doesn't get it.

I take a deep breath and think of the Monkey Tree, waiting patiently, on the other side of our garden fence. I love that tree. No matter what, it's always there for me, always within reach, and as I imagine myself clinging onto its branches, I feel something surge through me. It's clear what I must do. There is no other solution. It's the only way to make the madness stop.

This is war and war means taking sides.

Closing my eyes, I begin the countdown. See, what no one gets about Nuclear War is the silence. There's no dumb explosion sounds after the missile is launched like in Battleship. It's not about scoring a hit – that's never in any doubt. Instead, there's just a red button. An imaginary red button and, once you press it, there's no going back. *That's* what the game's really about. That decision. That awful moment when you choose total destruction over everything else. That moment when you just want to kill.

"Why did you have to come, Dad? Mum and me were so happy before you appeared. You've spoiled everything. You just sit at home all day. You can't even get a job. Don't you get it? No one wants you here. No one loves you any more."

Somehow, without me realising it, night has stolen in while we have been sitting here. Darkness gobbles us up like a monstrous fog. How could I have thought it would never come? Night always comes. When I eventually look up at my father, we are already fading into shadows. For a moment, I almost miss the microscopic white explosions in his eyes. Then I catch sight of them and gasp. Two minuscule mushroom clouds billow against his inky-black pupils.

What I can't see is how they're reflected back in mine.

Broke
ERINN KINDIG

Carl rubbed the top of the dog's black head, scratched him behind the ears, thumped his ribs. The hound looked up at him expectantly and barked once. The tail beat a steady rhythm against the cold morning air and he panted a white fog through his open mouth. He was a good dog. Carl put the aluminium mixing bowl of kibble on the ground in front of him and left him where he was, chained to the plastic, igloo-shaped doghouse near the pond.

Frosted grass glittered in the morning sun and crunched under the weight of Carl's work boots as he made his way back up to the house. He passed the ticking furnace and the two trees that had adapted to the hollow steel pipe that his dad, Dick, had put up for Carl's daughter so she could practise gymnastics. Back then, Carl was usually either too tired or too loaded to drive his kid to the YMCA for her classes. Dick hadn't driven her either but when he put that bar up, it was like he was drawing a line, making Amber pick favourites. He'd always been a miserable old prick.

The screen door complained when Carl pulled it open and it sighed as it slowly closed. He'd barely shut the front door behind him when the old man said, "You ain't done it yet."

"Nope," Carl said and poured a cup of coffee from the percolator on the stove.

"Steve called for you. Says he's comin' by in a little while. Gonna drop off some Sunbeam for your pigs and then take me to the senior centre for some pinochle." He pronounced it *pee-nickel*. "I want it done by the time I get back."

Carl grunted and took his cup to his bedroom. It was the same room he'd had when he was a boy. The clothes in the closet were bigger but that was about the only change. The same blue paint clung to the walls. The same twin-sized bed was pushed up in the corner.

The rest of the house wasn't any different either. There had been some small alterations, but not enough to count. The brown shag carpet had been torn up and replaced with a low-pile, indoor-outdoor when Dick complained about his cane getting tangled up. A raised seat was put on the commode in the bathroom, a safety seat in the tub. Other than that, everything was pretty much the same – just older and shabbier.

Carl should have been grateful that Dick had taken him in but it depressed him to be back in this house, in this bedroom. In return for the roof over his head, he cooked the old man his meals, scheduled his doctor's appointments, reminded him to take his medications and, when the time came, he would wipe his ass, get him dressed, and change his sheets when he shit himself in the night. Carl considered pouring a slug of bourbon into his coffee but decided against it.

The dog's barking pierced the air. Steve was pulling into the drive and Carl went out to help him unload the crates of mouldy bread from the back of his delivery truck. By the time they had finished setting them up on the porch, there were two stacks, four feet tall each.

"I'll get them crates when I drop Dick back off. That work for you?"

Carl nodded and watched Steve help the old man down the cracked cement porch steps and hoist him into the truck. Then he went back inside and poured another cup of coffee. The electric burners around the stove were littered with cigarette ash and the carpet needed a good vacuuming. One of the cousins would be by later to clean for them. One of the cousins came every week. Sometimes they even brought food.

The handle of the tin pail cut into his bare hand and he was careful not to slosh the mix of mouldy bread and leftover stew as he walked down the hill behind the house. The dog caught sight of him, his front feet bouncing up off the ground each time he barked. The chain strained against his collar, against the doghouse. Carl ignored him. He'd settle down shortly.

The pigs garbled at him. They liked Carl and Carl liked them but it was getting about time to say goodbye. There was a lot to do before he could send them off for slaughter. He had to get their ear tags in. He had to de-worm them and that meant getting someone to take him down to the Agway for more turpentine; he'd used up the last of it when he'd castrated them. All the work made him tired just thinking about it and he only had five of the animals this year. He put down the pail and held open a big enough gap in the barbed-wire fence to climb through. The pigs snuffled and he patted their heads and scratched them behind their ears. He would miss them when they were gone and he hoped they were smart enough to know it; that it wasn't anything personal.

Carl's neck and back ached and he felt the cold bite through his arthritic joints. He'd have to get some bear fat to rub on his muscles but he'd need turpentine to mix in. If the old man had some methylated spirits tucked away somewhere, he could use that instead.

He'd heard there was a small brown bear up on the crest a few days ago. Now wasn't a good time to go hunting for it, but maybe tomorrow or even later in the evening he could head up there if he had time.

Carl gently shooed the pigs away from his legs and then again with more force. The pigs scattered back, curious if this was a game. He reached between the wires and got hold of the pail and brought it through. They came back and Carl moved around them. When he was a couple of feet from the fence, he emptied the slop on the ground and watched awhile as they slurped and jostled each other.

It was noon when Carl sat down, tired and hurting, in the orange-velour lazy chair. The fabric at the arms was worn threadbare and dotted with cigarette burns. The chair had been Dick's but nowadays the old man had such a hard time getting out of it that he'd lately took to favouring the straight-backed rocker and Carl took over the recliner.

He pressed the remote and the TV hummed to life. Lines of static dripped down the screen but he could still make out the picture. Reception had never been good and no amount of tin foil on the antenna was going to change that. Besides, Carl didn't care much about what was on anyway. He reached into the cooler he kept next to the chair and pulled out a Yuengling. It wasn't very cold but it was cold enough. He popped the tab and, slurping, caught the foam that wrestled out.

The dog was kicking up a racket again and Carl craned his neck as best he could to look out the front window. He was stiff all over from having sat so long and he thought again about the bear on the hill, knowing it would be more effort than it was worth. He waited a minute more and was rewarded by a couple of kids on four-wheelers barrelling down the road. They went by pretty fast and he didn't think he recognised them. He watched after them for as long as it took them to turn down the rough dirt track that led down the holler to Carl's old house. Dalton Hess and his mom lived in Carl's house now and Carl could tell that neither of the boys who rode by was Dalton. He didn't know who they were. Once they were out of sight, the dog quieted down and Carl went back to watching the TV. A rerun of *The Daily Show* was just coming on when Ronnie pulled up and set the dog barking again. She banged into the house with a bucket full of cleaning supplies and a cellophane-wrapped bouquet of pink carnations.

"Holy hell, Carl," she said, "if I'd known you took the afternoon off to lounge around, I woulda stayed home myself."

The TV was still drawing lines and Carl wasn't paying it any attention. He reached for the remote and turned it off.

"Here." Ronnie tossed the flowers onto his lap. "I was the tenth customer at the bank today, or some such shit," she said and gave him one of her big-gummed smiles.

"They give you flowers for that?" Carl asked.

"I know. 'Stead of giving me a bunch of damn flowers I wish they'd stop charging me all 'em fees."

Carl eased himself out of the chair and carried the flowers into the kitchen. He didn't have a vase so he stuck them in the sink and ran a little water.

"I was just gonna make some lunch. You want me to fix you a

sandwich or somethin'?" he asked, opening the fridge and taking out some bread, a plastic bag of sliced ham and a block of white American cheese.

"Make me one for later?" she said.

Ronnie was struggling with the vacuum cleaner. The woven-nylon-covered power cord was badly frayed and patched in places with black electrical tape.

"You really should get a new one a these 'fore I get electrocuted."

Carl didn't answer. There were a lot of things that needed replacing. A new mower and a washing machine for a start, but those things would have to wait until he got the pigs butchered and sold off. Even then they'd likely come up short.

"Where's Dick at, anyway?" she said, finally getting the cord to catch so she could plug it into the socket.

"Over at the senior centre."

"Breaking hearts and stealing money?" Ronnie grinned, her toe poised over the switch on the vacuum canister.

"Stealing money, anyway," Carl said.

"Yeah," she said, "I always thought he cheated."

"He does," Carl said.

The kids on the four-wheelers came racing back up the road. This time, Dalton was with them. The dog was barking so hard he could practically be in the house. Carl went out on the porch and called for him to shut up just as the boys passed by. The boys looked at Carl, Carl looked at them. He thought about waving to Dalton but didn't. Dalton was a good kid. Carl liked him. He noticed the boys had rifles strapped to the backs of their vehicles. They weren't dressed for hunting and only turkey was in season anyway. Carl hoped they were just shooting targets but figured that was unlikely; the boys he didn't know looked like they were after trouble.

It was just coming on five o'clock and the sun had dropped low in the sky. Ronnie started restocking her cleaning bucket and said, "I'm about finished up here. How 'bout a drink before I go?"

Carl went to his room and fetched the bottle of Jim Beam from the back of his closet. Since Carl's accident, Dick didn't approve of him drinking anything stronger than beer, but that was asking too much. Ronnie got two jam jars from the cupboard and he cracked the seal on the fresh bottle. They sat at the clean kitchen table and Ronnie poured two fingers each. Carl kept the bottle close.

"You been real quiet today," Ronnie said and clinked her jar against Carl's in a silent toast.

"Dad wants me to shoot the dog."

"Amber's dog?" she asked and Carl thought she looked surprised. "That's a new low, even for him." She sat silent a minute then asked, "You gonna do it?"

Carl took a swallow of the bourbon. The hound was getting old and he didn't hunt – never had – but he was loyal. But there was more to it than that. He knew it was stupid but he half hoped that one day his kid might come back for him.

"I don't know."

Carl and Ronnie knocked back another glass. The boys roared by again. Carl thought they must be freezing their asses off, riding around like that all day. Soon it would be full dark and they still didn't show any signs of slowing down. Carl wished they would call it a night if only to stop tormenting the dog. At least he hadn't heard any shots popped off yet.

"You know them boys out there?" he asked.

"Yeah," Ronnie said. "Bad news. They're Mavis's."

"I heard something about them getting sent up awhile back but I never did hear what for. Figured it had to do with drugs or dogs, knowing Mavis," Carl said.

Ronnie reached into her coat pocket and pulled out a pack of cigarettes. "You figured right," she said and lit one. "Anyway, I been meaning to ask you, when are them pigs of yours gonna be ready?" She reached for the bottle and poured.

Carl saw that her eyes were bright under the fluorescent light that hung over the table. "Pretty soon. Good to go now but I haven't called over to the processor yet. You gonna want some?"

"If you have extra," she said.

Carl nodded. "I should. After I stock the deep-freeze, I'll set some chops and bacon aside for you?"

It wasn't enough having just a handful of pigs to slaughter and sell, especially after giving Steve his cut for the bread he brought over for them and Ronnie some for her help around the house.

"Mind if I take one of these?" Carl asked and picked up the pack of smokes.

Ronnie slid her lighter across the table towards him.

"Store-bought," he said and fingered the pre-rolled cigarettes.

Ronnie poured them each some more bourbon; it was nearing empty. Carl knew his dad would be back soon but he didn't care. He didn't care there was a bottle of Beam in full view on the table or that it was more than three-quarters gone. He didn't care that Dick would lay into him the minute he walked in the door while the dog barked at the sound of Steve's truck.

"I better head out," Ronnie said, and took a couple of cigarettes out of the pack for him. She pocketed the rest.

A pair of truck lights swung around into the drive and filled the front room with watery light. Carl could hear the pea gravel crunch under the tyres and the sound of doors slamming shut. The porch light came on and Ronnie bundled herself into her puffer coat.

"Hi Uncle Dick," she said, going over to kiss him.

"Hang on there a minute, honey. Help me get out of this coat first," he wheezed, and propped his cane against the wall. Dick's voice had the phlegmy rasp of a lifetime of cigarette smoking. He shrugged out of his coat and draped it over the back of the lazy chair. His flannel shirt hung against his thin frame. He offered Ronnie a broken-toothed smile and waited for his kiss.

Carl heard the clatter of the crates as Steve took them from the porch to the truck. He went to go help load them up but Dick turned his attention on him.

"I see you have supper on the table," he said and limped over to the bottle. "Why don't you take this on home with you, honey," he told Ronnie.

She cast a glance at Carl; he shrugged. She took the bottle.

"So what've you been doing all day? Drinking whiskey and skinning your pecker?" Dick asked once Ronnie had left.

Carl poured the remainder of Ronnie's bourbon into his own glass and sat back down at the table. Dick picked up one of the cigarettes that Ronnie had left for Carl and lit it off the stovetop before easing himself into the chair at the head of the table. He looked old, Carl thought. The collar of his shirt was loose and the tendons in his throat stuck out, cratering a hollow in his throat; pulling sevens, it looked like.

"You want to know the difference between you and me?" Dick asked, exhaling a stream of grey. "The difference is that I'm a winner and you're not. The difference is that I got a free lunch today *and* my wallet's thirty dollars heavier while you, you can't take care of anything so you lose everything." Dick warmed to his subject. "You ain't got no wife. Your kid won't talk to you. You ain't got nothing at all – not even balls enough to stand up to me."

Carl went to bed early. He was too drunk to stay up without the help of more beer or bourbon to keep him going. He lay in his dark room and listened to the sounds of the old man moving around the house. Then, around nine thirty, the line of light that crept in from under his bedroom door went out. Carl stared into the dark and thought about what his old man had said. He knew Dick was right and he hated him for it. Finally, he closed his eyes and sleep came.

Carl woke in the cold darkness of early morning. His head ached and his tongue was thick and furry. He threw back the tangle of blankets and sat on the edge of his bed and tried to get his bearings. The moon was bright and filled his room through the uncurtained window. On stiff legs, he stood and walked to the kitchen for a glass of water. He turned on the small light above the stove and sat at the table drinking from a tall Bugs Bunny glass. His back was to the window and he heard the four-wheeler before he saw it. The headlights dimmed and then pulled into the drive. The clock on the wall showed it was four thirty in the morning. The old man had locked the front door before he'd gone to bed. Carl went over to the coat closet where they kept the gun safe. Quietly, he slid the doors open and pushed the coats aside. He twirled the combination and the heavy steel door clicked open. The combination was easy to remember. It was his mother's birthday, though she'd never much cared for guns. Carl pulled out his Mossberg and pocketed a box of shells, then went to the front door.

The porch light had come on and Dalton was knocking softly. Carl's face reflected back at him in the window and he put the gun down just inside the door jamb.

"It's late, Dalton. Is everything OK? Your mama OK?"

Dalton nodded.

"What do you need then, boy?" Carl asked.

"It's your dog," Dalton answered.

Carl opened the door wider to let the boy in. He put his finger to his lips and nodded towards Dick's room. The boy followed Carl to the kitchen.

"Now, what about my dog?" Carl asked and it dawned on him that he wasn't barking.

The boy sat in Dick's chair and blew into his hands, warming them. His hair was lank, separated into greasy clumps around his head. He wasn't dressed for the weather but it was probably the best he had.

"Well," Dalton said slowly, warmer now but unsure how to start, "Del and Marlon come up here a couple of hours ago with Mavis's car and got your dog. I told 'em not to – to find another one – but they said they wanted yours 'cause he's so old. I just thought you should know."

"I didn't hear nothing. The dog would have barked if they came anywhere near," he said.

The boy shrugged. "Them two got a way with animals."

"OK," Carl said, "what'd they want my dog for?" He didn't expect an answer. He was more or less awake but he was having trouble keeping up.

"You had that dog since longer than me and Mama started rentin' your house. I figure you're attached to it so if I were you, I'd go on up to Mavis's soon and get 'im."

Carl nodded but Dalton could see he still didn't get it.

"Mavis got them a new pit bull pup for when they come out. They need a dog for him to train on."

Carl finally understood what Dalton was telling him and his rage tasted like burnt tyres. "Can you take me up there on that four-wheeler?"

Dalton pulled back in his chair. "Nah. I ain't gettin' involved," he said and stood up to leave. "Like I said, I just thought you should know."

Carl watched the headlights disappear into the holler. He got up from the table and went over to where the telephone hung on the wall. He dialled Ronnie's number. She answered on the third ring, her voice thick with sleep at quarter past five in the morning but she said she'd be right over. It would take her at least twenty minutes to get to him and Carl figured he'd use the time; feed the pigs at least. Walking down the hill he was met with clear air and silence. The dog didn't bark his welcome, the pigs were still sleeping.

He was just coming back towards the house when Ronnie pulled up. The car idled in the drive and she rolled down the window when Carl approached.

"Give me a second," he told her and set the feed pail on the porch and went inside the house for his twelve-gauge.

Ronnie passed him the thermos of coffee she'd brought and he poured a swallow in the lid.

"You know where we're going?" he asked and she nodded.

They drove for a good fifteen minutes past desiccated corn and hay fields. The road was smoothly paved for a long stretch before it gave way to rougher tracks that were riddled with potholes and narrowed by eroded shoulders. The sun was just beginning to come up; the sky red with warning.

"You sure you want to do this?" Ronnie asked, keeping her eyes on the road.

Carl took a minute. "You asked me before if I was gonna put the dog down and I told you I didn't know. I guess the answer is no."

Ronnie turned right onto a hard-packed road. A weather-beaten sign that read, "The End is Near: You must *PERSONALLY* accept Jesus Christ as your Saviour" was tilted precariously in the fork. The sign made Carl laugh. He took the box of shells out of his pocket and loaded one in the chamber. He checked that the safety was on. The road turned into a rocky track lined with weeds and vines that threatened to overtake them. As the track climbed and the pitch grew steeper, Carl felt himself leaning into his cousin as though to counterbalance the car in case it tipped over. Finally, Mavis's double-wide trailer came into sight. The yard was littered with an old trampoline, empty gas cans, a cold burn-barrel. A Ford Escort was up on blocks, its rims gone, the hood open revealing an empty cavity where the engine had been. The four-wheelers were parked neatly under the carport next to what Carl figured was Mavis's car.

Ronnie stopped the car a few feet away and left the engine running. Woodsmoke drifted through a makeshift chimney and they stood in the damp, chilled morning air, listening for signs of movement. Satisfied, Ronnie crept around one side of the trailer and Carl went around the other. They met in the back by a cinderblock shed. It was about as big as two good-sized chicken coops. The door was padlocked and it occurred to Carl that this was probably where Mavis cooked her meth. He listened hard and thought he could hear whimpering inside.

Ronnie heard it too and said, "Sonofabitch. Now what?"

Carl lifted the shotgun to his shoulder and aimed at the padlock. "I'm gonna get my dog."

Picturing Her
THADDEUS HICKMAN

George regretted answering the phone as soon as he heard her voice. He'd now have to wait for her to stop talking before he could hang up.

"You remember my friend Stacey?" she said.

"No," he said.

"Oh, I'm sure you do. She used to come round the house all the time. Anyway, she works at this insurance company in town . . ."

As Belinda droned on, George opened his mouth and cautiously took hold of his front teeth. He winced in expectation of pain and then, with a wet suction sound, pulled out four teeth attached to a gum-pink plate. It was difficult to imagine that he'd liked the dentist at first and his educated way of talking. George had only gone in for a check-up, but before he knew it he was heading back home on the 78 bus, feeling gummy and humiliated.

"And the thing is," she was now saying, speaking like those sales people who phone when dinner's on the table, "it's this afternoon and what with it being half-term . . ."

George put his dentures back in his mouth and leaned close to the hallway mirror. He watched his lips draw apart to display a jumble of teeth. The new ones looked too white and too perfect for the face that scowled back at him.

"Dad?"

He brought the phone closer to his ear. "So you've got an

interview?" he said.

"Yeah, at two thirty," she said, her voice now less sure of itself. "And what with me not being able to get a babysitter . . ."

He knew she wanted him to make soothing sounds, like her mother used to make. To say everything would be fine. But he wasn't her mother.

"You can bring the boy over," he said. "Just make sure you pick him up on your way back."

Then he hung up.

The young couple from Number 24 were pulling IKEA bags out of their car. This was the second time in a week. They seemed addicted, thought George, as if they needed those bulging blue bags just to keep going.

He was standing at his front window feeling anxious. He'd already finished Task Two on his To Do list: *sort recycling*. He'd had to skip Task One as there wouldn't be enough time to complete it before Belinda arrived. And he couldn't start another task until they got here. So all he could do was stand at the window and wait.

The young wife from Number 24 was staring at him, like he was doing something wrong. She tapped her husband on the shoulder and he turned around too, with his fat head and scrunched-up face, trying to give a territorial stare. It made George feel like he was some kind of neighbourhood pervert. "Fuckers," he said to the window. He puffed his chest out, put his hands behind his back and stared resolutely beyond them.

Finally a red car came into view, making its slow way towards him.

He was standing on the doorstep as she parked upfront with a jolt. She gave a quick wave and went to the back seat to get Stevie. She was having trouble unstrapping him from the safety seat that at seven he was obviously too old for. George considered going to help but didn't want to encourage Belinda's knack of getting other people to do her work for her.

"Hello, Dad," she said, pulling Stevie up the drive. She was wearing a grey suit, which looked smart and professional. Though, with her having put on weight in recent years, it was unflatteringly tight around her thighs and hips. Her hair looked newly dyed and unnaturally dark.

She pecked him on the cheek. "Like I said on the phone, it's really good of you. If it's a problem, I'll just take him with me . . ."

"Don't talk nonsense, Belinda. How can you take him with you?"

"Well, I don't know . . ." she said, looking at Stevie, as if he might know the answer. She laughed nervously.

George stood to one side. "Come in," he said.

They both stepped in over the threshold. Belinda put down the large bag she was carrying. "There," she said, like she'd achieved something.

"What's that?"

"For Stevie," she said, pointing, as if George hadn't seen the boy come in with her. "To keep him off your back."

"Well," he said, "that sounds a good idea."

"Hello, Granddad," said Stevie, stepping forward like a cadet on parade. Someone had made a poor attempt at brushing control into his thick, unruly hair.

"So what do you think?" said Belinda, pulling at the lapels of her suit jacket. "Do I get the part?"

"Sure," he said. "You look smart enough. Why not?"

"Mum used to say I looked 'sparky'," she said in a childish voice, as if her doting mother was back in the room. He was about to tell her that she wasn't a child any more but he thought he heard something in the kitchen, like pans being moved on the hob. He stopped to listen for a moment. But no, it was nothing.

"You haven't told me about the dentist. How did it go?" asked Belinda, trying to make conversation.

He thought about the mauling of his gums, the callous dentist, how his new dentures were surely designed to cause him suffering. But what did any of that have to do with her?

"Routine stuff," he said casually. "But it's getting on. You'd better be making tracks."

She looked distracted, like she was waiting for something.

"Do you know how to get there?" he asked. "To the interview?"

"Sure," she said. "I've got it all written down in the car."

But just to be sure, he gave her exact directions. The most direct route. With each road, each junction and turning, the speed cameras to watch out for.

"You've got that?"

"Right. Got it," she said. But he knew it wasn't true. She rummaged in her bag, dug out her mobile. "God, I'm going to be late." And in a flurry, she kissed Stevie on the crown of his head, waved and ran down the drive. George watched her tinny car go back up the road until it was out of sight, then he shut the door.

"Bloody warm in here," he said, and headed off towards the kitchen.

He pressed buttons on the boiler controls and tried to follow the instructions on the tiny digital display. Even though he'd had it installed two years ago it was still impossible to use.

"Granddad?" said a voice behind him.

He turned to see Stevie standing there.

"Yes?" he said.

"Granddad, what are we going to play?"

The boy's face was full of expectation, as if George's role was to come up with endless forms of entertainment. Learned straight from his mother no doubt, thought George. But there was also something different about him too. He had a direct way of looking that was almost insolent and made George feel uncomfortable.

"I like to do cooking with Granny," said Stevie, as if it was something that they still did together.

George looked around the room. The years he'd seen her moving about this very kitchen. Over by the sink washing up. Or by the oven, putting on her glasses and bending down to read the dials. He could almost hear her voice now.

"Can we do cooking, Granddad?"

George looked down at the boy as if for the first time. "She's gone," he said. "And that's all there is to it."

"I know that," said Stevie, like his Granddad was being silly even saying it. "But when I cook with Mummy she says that Granny still likes to help."

"Best to cook when you get home, then," said George. He'd had enough of the boy already. "Come with me," he said, and walked into the hallway. He picked up the bag that Belinda had left behind, stopped for a moment to make sure Stevie was still following, then continued on into the lounge.

Stevie entered the room warily, as if looking for signs of a trap. He stopped in the middle and turned slowly until he was facing the wall with the photos. "Wow," he said, his eyes and mouth stupidly open. "Look at all those!" He stepped closer, suddenly engrossed, looking from one photo to another. He seemed small standing there, in front of all those pictures.

George thought about those first few months, when all that he had known had gone, and all that was left felt hollow and unsteady. Others offered help – out of politeness and pity, no doubt. But he didn't want anyone around, so he did everything alone. And that's when he found the photos. They were everywhere – in shoe boxes, in albums, loose in drawers. So many moments of her. All so nearly forgotten. Suddenly so important. He couldn't put enough of them on the wall, trying to find just the right place for each one.

"Where are the pictures of me and Mummy?" said Stevie, looking up at his granddad.

George looked from Stevie to the wall. Yes, she was in all of these photographs, but it still didn't feel enough. Bent double laughing in their first-ever kitchen; dressed to the nines for a summery barbecue; caught in thought looking at something out of shot. And then the two of them: leaning over the railings on Brighton pier, in black and white . . .

"Is that baby Mummy?" said Stevie, reaching out.

"Leave it alone!" ordered George.

Stevie jumped back and snapped his arms to his side.

"Don't touch anything," said George. He put down the bag. "You can play in here. You've got more toys than you'll ever need. But don't touch anything. Right?"

Stevie didn't say anything.

"Right?" said George.

Stevie nodded.

"If you want something, come and ask," said George, shutting the door as he left.

In the kitchen, he switched on the kettle and waited for it to boil. Trying to ignore the hard edges of the dentures against his raw gums, he folded the newspaper shut, placed it to one side and put the pad with his To Do list in front of him. Task Two was already crossed off – the deeply scored horizontal line made him feel better somehow. He poured hot water into a mug and watched the tea bag bob. He had five other tasks which he hadn't even started yet. At least Belinda would take the boy away in an hour or two. He looked down at the task he'd missed. Task One: *sand down back door*. He'd need to go to the garage to get his tools – the only reason he ever went out back these days. He looked out the window at the garden. Her garden. Where she'd busy herself until she'd used up all the daylight. Strange to think that the overgrown lump in the middle of the patio was her rockery. He thought of the rough sketch she'd given him to work with. And how, when he switched on the water and it trickled down the rocks to the tiny pool at the bottom, she'd applauded.

The sound of the lounge door opening made George jump. It was the boy again.

"What do you want?" said George.

Stevie looked from George to the window and his face lit up with excitement. "Granddad," he said, "we can play in the garden!"

"No," said George. "You're staying put in the other room. Until your mother gets back –"

But Stevie laughed with delight and ran across the kitchen towards the back door. George tried to grab him but a sharp stab in his gums made him stop and put a hand uselessly to his mouth. The back door banged against the wall outside and George heard footsteps running down the side path.

He stood there cursing his teeth and Belinda, and just cursing. Then he went out to the garden with his slippers still on. He stood at the edge of the lawn as if he was afraid to go any further. He scanned the overgrown contours for signs of movement.

The sound of Stevie giggling made him look towards the far end. There he could see the boy's dark shape just visible behind a partially covered trellis.

"Come in now!" bellowed George.

Stevie stepped out from his hiding place. He looked like he thought it was all a game, wiggling and bouncing on the spot. "Granddad! Granddad!" he called out.

"Stevie," said George, "I'm warning you."

Stevie ran to the patio in the centre of the garden and stood at the far side of the hidden rockery.

"Get out of there!" yelled George as anger surged through him. He ran at the boy and for a moment Stevie froze, looking too scared to move. But just as George got close, his hands reaching out, Stevie shrieked and ran off in the other direction. Round the circular patio he went, round and round, calling for George to catch him, taunting. George kept getting closer and closer, stamping down the undergrowth that got in his way. Until he stumbled and fell, his knees landing on a damp mossy clump. His breathing rasped and struggled. He sat down heavily, one leg awkwardly underneath him. His vision blurred. The sound of Stevie running round him, of his goading and laughing, receded. Then there was silence.

She came into view, lying on her side, head resting on an outstretched arm, as if taking a nap. She looked so peaceful, he didn't want to wake her. Some rosemary clippings were in her extended hand, like an offered gift. Scissors glinted in the grass near her other hand. He touched her shoulder and said her name quietly. He gave her a gentle shake and she rolled onto her back, her head lolling to one side at a strange angle. He froze for a moment, not understanding what it meant. But then he knew and he leaned forward, placing his fingers on her upturned wrist. It was shockingly cold. He snatched his hand away. Then he was shaking her and shaking her. He heard his voice moaning, telling her to wake up. It was all wrong. Everything was all wrong.

A voice called out to him.

"Are you OK?" George was being shaken. He opened his eyes. "Are you OK, Granddad?" It was the boy, Stevie. George unbent his legs, breathed air deeply in and out of his lungs. Then, as he slowly got to his feet, Stevie stepped back several paces. When George reached the back door, Stevie was at his side. George grabbed him hard by the arm and dragged him inside, his tiny body no heavier than a bag for the bins. Stevie yelled out but it would make no difference now.

George kicked the door shut and Stevie clawed at his grip, trying to pull free.

"Stop!" ordered George, but Stevie struggled all the harder.

"Fucking stop!" shouted George and shook Stevie violently from side to side. Then Stevie bit into George's hand. And in one angry flash George grabbed him by the front of his shirt and with one arm raised him high into the air. Stevie hung there without moving, slack with fear. Then he kicked George in the stomach and George dropped him back to the floor. As George's hand rose to strike, Stevie cowered, covering his head with his arms, twisting this way and that. So George locked his arm around the boy's middle instead and lifted him off the ground and held him there. He grabbed one of the boy's flailing hands and squeezed the wrist tight, making him squeal. George could feel his power and strength over the boy. He looked with curiosity at the little fingers that stuck out the top of his large fist and wriggled feebly. How small the wrist felt, so easy to snap. And the skin so warm. Hot, even. How different from her skin. From which the heat had already gone. Everything left cold and still. While he read and dozed in the lounge . . .

George felt a blow to his mouth, making him wince and groan with pain. He dropped the boy to the floor but kept a tight grip of his arm. He shut his eyes for a moment, waiting for the pain to subside, then opened them to see the boy staring at him.

He spat his dentures into his free hand and put them in his pocket. The boy's fast, shallow panting made George look at him. He was little more than a wild cornered animal.

As George pulled him down the hall, he felt sure that he now knew what to do. With one hard shove, he sent Stevie flying into the lounge where he fell to the floor. The boy looked up with a desperate, hunted look. George slammed the door and turned the key in the lock.

There was instant pounding on the door.

"Be quiet!" yelled George, and the pounding stopped. "It's best you stay there for now." He turned and made his way up the stairs.

He closed the door to the bathroom with care, removed his shirt and hung it over the chair in the corner. From his pocket he took his dentures and put them on the shelf. He turned on the tap and splashed water onto his face. He squirted a ball of dense foam into his hand, and smoothed it over his stubble. He did all this very slowly and methodically. While the sink filled with steaming water, he put a new head on his razor. He wanted it fresh and sharp. With each deliberate, downward stroke he watched a streak of smooth, clean-shaven skin appear. He then rinsed the razor in the hot water before continuing. With each new strip of skin revealed, George felt order returning to his day, as if he were beginning it all over again. Once his face was towelled dry, he picked up his dentures and held them under the cold tap. As he turned them, to make sure they were perfectly clean, he felt the constant movement of water cool and soothe his skin. And he could hear the trickling of water down the rockery, passing over the stones he'd put in place for her, pouring into the little pool at the bottom that never overfilled. Just the way he'd designed it. He watched his mouth open in the mirror and a hand put his dentures back in. There, he thought. Not so bad.

Downstairs again, he flicked on the kettle and reviewed his list. He circled Task One and put down the pen. He went down the hall and unlocked the lounge door.

He was already back in the kitchen and sitting at the table when he heard the door cautiously open and movement in the hall.

"It's OK, Stevie," he said. "You can come in."

Stevie appeared in the doorway looking nervous.

"It's all right," said George and pulled out a chair next to him.

Stevie crept in looking guilty and suspicious. He sat on the chair and kept his eyes downcast.

George poured milk into a glass and placed it in front of Stevie. He pointed to a cheese sandwich on a blue plate. "That's for you too," he said.

"But . . ." said Stevie, his gaze not leaving the table. "I'm sorry, Granddad. I . . . didn't mean to . . ."

"No," said George, shaking his head. "Things just got out of control, that's all, Stevie."

Stevie looked as if he couldn't understand what his Granddad was saying.

"Soon your mother will arrive. She might even have a new job, you never know. But for sure she'll be taking you home, and things will be back as they were. OK?"

Stevie drank his milk, his eyes staring at George over the top of the glass.

George poured out some more. "Drink up," he said.

Stevie wiped his mouth and shook his head.

"Well," said George, "just make sure you eat some of that sandwich –"

A car horn beeped twice out front.

"Well, that's good timing," he said.

When George opened the front door Belinda was already coming up the drive. He stood aside for her to come in.

She shook her head. "Sorry," she said. "I've really got to get going."

"How did it go?"

She waggled her head and puffed out her cheeks. "Hard to say," she said.

George turned around to look for Stevie, but he wasn't there.

"You must have some idea, surely?" he said. "Anyway, come in. We're letting all the heat out."

But she just shook her head and kept saying that she was late and had a million things to do.

Stevie suddenly appeared between them, dragging his bag of toys.

"Ah," said George, "there you are."

He bent down to take the bag but Belinda already had it. She took Stevie by the hand and led him down the drive. George watched from the doorstep as she put the bag on the back seat and started strapping Stevie in. Then George found himself walking down the drive, though he didn't know why. Belinda looked up with a surprised expression.

"I hope he wasn't too much trouble," she said, her eyes searching his face.

"No," said George, "not too much."

He followed her gaze to his legs. He had dried mud on his knees.

"Jobs around the house," he said, though it sounded more like a question.

Her forehead tightened but she didn't say anything. She got into her car, said thanks through the open window, and drove off.

George closed the front door and locked it for the night. The silence in the house was familiar and reassuring. He noticed that Stevie had shut the door of the lounge, trying to be tidy no doubt, to make amends. Opening the door to its normal position, George saw marks in crayon and pen on the wall. He stepped quickly into the room and stopped. He turned slowly on the spot, trying to take it all in. His eyes followed multi-coloured scribbles as they snaked around the room from wall to wall. Whirling here and there into dense angry spirals and swirls. Until finally, George was facing the wall with the photos. But now there were no photos. Except for a few high up, they had all been removed and thrown to the floor in a sprawling heap. In their place was a four-foot drawing within a black-scribbled frame. It was a wonky crayon portrait of three people. A woman with blue hair and red lipstick stood next to an oven, where large pots steamed. A second woman, with black furious hair that floated above her head, held hands with a small boy. Both the women had crazy, oversized smiles. But the boy wasn't smiling. He was looking out from the picture, with his large teeth bared like a snarling animal.

Tryin' to Hit It, Chic-a-Tah
CHRIS LILLY

"**M**oms U R brilliantastic," she'd messaged, and "Luv U lodes," which was good, and sitting through God-awful Madonna movies was a small price to pay, it was, even if she'd really wanted to take Ells to the premiere but couldn't get tickets. How do you get tickets for premieres? No idea. Was that actually how Ells communicated, how she spoke with her mates? How she texted. Txtd. She was teasing her old vowel-dependent mother, wasn't she. Wasn't she? Anyway it had been a good thing to do, a thing to make the first vacation a bit special, to send her back to Norwich happy. Which was the important thing. Now she was back at uni and reconnecting with all her bestest Norwich friends, friends she'd known for about ten weeks off and on not counting the family-sized hole caused by coming home for Christmas. And Becky was back to being on her own. Not so brilliantastic, that. Not so brilliantastic at all.

Somebody once said that the best thing about gin was how well it thinned mascara. More panda-eyed evenings in front of David Attenborough on the digibox, nursing a tall gin and tonic, wishing there was someone else there other than the bloody cat. Kylie was a lovely cat but a rubbish conversationalist. Good for cuddles sometimes, when in the mood. And then the bloody mother polar bear sets off across the tundra with three babies and arrives with two, and Becky's in bits again. Ridiculous. Stop it. You are a senior manager in a local authority that had been voted "Best in London 2009", you are not someone who blubs over bereaved polar bears. Look, the mother doesn't care, she's hopping across ice floes happy as a sandboy with the two cubs she's got left, she isn't getting sniffly and red-nosed. But Becky had discovered that, actually, she was someone who mourned polar-bear bereavement now, so she turned it off. She didn't have any cubs left, not one. Maybe if she read something? That little book that won the Booker, Jan had said it was good. And short. First all the kids went off to uni, which she didn't like at all, then one of them killed himself. Quarter of the way in to a very short book, and there's misery and despair wherever you look. Thanks Jan. No books then.

Music? Ella had left an Adele disc in the player, no cover, the cover was in Norwich with Ells, just the disc. *19*, like Ells. That Adele, she put such a lot of work into naming her albums: *19*, *21*, if it took her two years to make her next multi-platinum platter, would anyone care to guess what she'd call that one? But Adele did cover Dylan, even if it was crappy post-God Dylan. And that made her well up and overflow, too. Bugger. Make her feel her love indeed. Coffee, then. A cup of coffee in the back garden, looking out across frosty Hackney Downs and thinking that Hackney wasn't so bad, really. Pretty, on a night like this. Only occasionally set on fire by resident hoolies, generally quite pleasant, a good place for a little girl to grow up, really, whatever her mother thought. "You can't raise a child in Hackney, darling. Where will she go to school?" Hackney. "Where will she learn to ride a bicycle?" Again, Hackney. "She won't have any friends. Any English friends." God, Mum. Weren't you a hippy once? Didn't you believe in peace, love and understanding, and get off with a sexy French rioter in Paris in May '68? What happened to all that? No English friends? She has dozens of English friends, and some Jamaican friends, and a bunch of Indian friends, and a really good mate called Sabisha who was Turkish though possibly actually from Azerbaijan, anyway loads and loads and loads of friends. More friends than you bloody have after forty years in Welwyn Garden bloody City, that's for certain sure. Come to that, Ells had more friends in Hackney than she did. Jan. Trisha. Split-a-bottle-of-wine friends. Go-to-*Sex in the City*-at-the-Rio-and-shout-at-the-screen friends. Come round and weep together over lost men, lost looks, lost earrings. But Trisha and Jan didn't have children. No weeping together over lost children, that she did on her own. All on her own.

When Ella was eleven she wanted, really wanted, really really wanted Britney's new album. Please it's nearly Christmas please. It's called *In the Zone* and it's awesome, please please please. But it's hyper-sexualised twaddle sung by a pitiable young woman abused by fame and media hype, switching between declarations of abstinence till marriage and shrill promises to shag everyone in the building because she was in a mood to party all night long. How can you like that? It's grotesque nonsense. It's not Mum, it's awesome. And anyway Amy's got it and she'll burn it for me if you don't buy it for me, and that's just stealing royalties from working musicians and you say you don't like that, Mum you're such a hypocrite. So she got *In the Zone* and played it non-stop for three weeks, and then decided she liked Madonna better. Did Becky like Madonna better? Not really. Though if there was going to be a lot of talk about shagging, it sounded better from the mouth, the dirty mouth, of a forty-something woman with a few miles on the clock than from a raddled ex-Mouseketeer who was only a year or two older than her teeny daughter. Eleven isn't teeny, Mum. Eleven is quite grown-up. And what's a Mouseketeer?

When Becky was eleven, she was listening to J. D. Souther, and Manassas, and Chris Hillman's band, what was it? Desert something. Rose. Desert Rose. Because she was a lonely child and Welwyn Garden City didn't offer her all that much, so her mum's record collection was her comfort and her company until she was old enough to get paid work at the Wheatsheaf and buy her own records at Record World in the High Street. She decided to like Frankie Goes to Hollywood, and Queen, and Culture Club. Then David Evans pointed out that all the bands she liked were really gay, so she'd hurried back to her mum's records, which were made by real men, or anyway David Crosby, who she fancied a bit. And Gram Parsons. Oh God, Gram Parsons. No one had ever been quite so gorgeous, so doomily heart-meltingly gorgeous as Gram. Tim Buckley, he was gorgeous. And Jeff. So like his father. Becky had spent quite a lot of 1997 mourning the tragically short life of the Buckley boy, no space for concern about over-privileged young women copping it so that fluffy-headed twerps who thought they knew her could feel miserable. Jeff had rare talent, rare chops, rare beauty. Doe-eyed Sloanes? Do us a favour. And Ells liked him too. Play that sad song Mum. *Hallelujah.* They'd sat on the bed being sad together, then Ells would say "Lilac wine!" and they'd giggle because that was silly, you couldn't make wine out of lilacs that grew at the bottom of the garden, buddleia wine, silly, ivy wine, grass wine, giggle giggle giggle. Together, giggling together. And she'd grown up and grown into Britney and grown out of Britney and grown into Madonna. Madonna was cool. Amy Winehouse was cool. Adele was a bit too round to be cool but she had an amazing voice. And off she went to UEA with her new iPod full of Madonna and Amy and Adele, off to learn about French and drama and boys and being her own girl, her own woman, and being away. So far away, much further than Hackney to Norwich.

Becky went back inside, because it was a bit chilly. Half past nine, time for bed? She went to turn off the CD player. She ejected Adele and stood there with her finger through the hole in the disc, wondering where the cover was, remembering where the cover was. She wasn't going to cry any more, she wasn't. She looked through the stack of CDs to find an empty box. They were all the discs Ella had ripped onto the iPod her dad had sent her for Christmas, and top of the pile was *In the Zone.* Becky put it on, track one, *Me Against the Music.* It's me against the music, says Britney, just me. And me, says Madonna, and me. If you really want to battle, saddle up and get your rhythm, tryin' to hit it. Chic-a-tah. People passing a terraced house in Hackney Downs on a brisk January evening might have heard, if they'd listened hard, the sound of a woman doing Britney's part, doing Madonna's part, whipping her hair, to hell with stares. Getting her rhythm, trying to hit it, trying to hit it. Chic-a-tah.

One Man's Poison
NICK ALEXANDER

As I walk towards Caffè Nero, my stomach feels knotted with nerves.

Of course "dates" are always slightly nerve-wracking, but more worrying than whether Mike will look the same as his photo on Grindr, and even more worrying than wondering if Mike will fancy me, are my own reactions if this should all go wrong.

Because the truth is that "dating" hasn't been working particularly well for me. And my feelings of desperation about being single have not only pushed me to what feels like the edge of a breakdown, but are now being matched by weariness of the experience of modern dating. So I have promised myself that this, today, is my last attempt. And I'm not sure where that leaves me if it all goes tits up yet again. Do I have to resign myself to being celibate until the end of days?

The problem is that in the ten years during which I was with Rob ('99 to '09), the world moved on. In fact I'm coming to see that the world not only moved on, but left me way, way behind.

Since we split up I have tried bars, nightclubs, and the Internet.

The bars are full of kids, of course – kids who don't even notice a forty-nine-year-old codger like myself – and "chatting", which, last time I looked, was what you did when you wanted to meet a cute guy in a bar, seems to be a lost art. When I have tried to talk to someone they have just looked vaguely embarrassed and shuffled away. Chatting, it would seem, now equals not speech, but typing messages into a computer, and the kids in the bars actually do seem to spend more time typing on their phones than talking to each other these days. The music makes real talking difficult, I suppose.

I worry sometimes that it's just me getting slower, but everything really does seem faster now. TV has a presenter on screen telling you one bit of news and a scrolling banner (or two) telling you something entirely different. Driving is no longer enough – you have to be able to look out for speed traps and scan for red-light cameras and follow the signs and read the GPS and talk on the phone at the same time. Everyone on the Tube of an evening is travelling and reading and listening to music. Some of them have one earbud removed so that they can talk to a friend at the same time.

People multi-task all of the time, and even when it comes to dating, everyone seems to be chatting to everyone else all at once. It's like the entire world is suffering from attention deficit disorder. Even guys in relationships, judging by my contacts on Gaydar, seem to spend as much time looking for extras to fill the gaps between meals as they do eating at home with their husbands. It's all faster, faster, faster, and more, more, more, and having spent ten years of calm evenings and weekend-length cuddles, I'm honestly worried that I'm maybe just too old for it all. I'm starting to think that I'm the only gay man left on planet Earth whose brain hasn't been turned, by the Internet, into mush.

As I round the corner, I can see Mike sitting outside. He's texting on his phone, and because I assume that he's texting me to see where I am, I speed up to save him the trouble.

"Mike?" I say, when I reach the table.

He glances up at me, raises one finger, then returns his attention to his phone and continues to type. So not to me, then.

I stand for a few seconds, waiting for him to acknowledge my presence, and then, deciding that whatever he's doing, it must be important, I fix a (probably stupid-looking) smile on my face and sit down.

The good news is that Mike looks even better in the flesh than he did in the photo. He is about my age, or more probably a couple of years younger. He looks fit and sporty and has cropped black hair, full, somehow tasty-looking lips and some rugged stubble covering his chin. He's wearing jeans and a blue Fred Perry top. His arms bulge slightly where the short sleeves end.

I watch his thumbs zipping across the tiny screen as he texts and then decide to go and get myself a drink instead. When I return five minutes later, he's still at it.

"So, are you writing a novel?" I ask, an admittedly lame attempt at humour.

"Uh?" Mike says without looking up.

"Something important?" I ask, nodding at the phone.

"Hang on," he says, and proceeds to type a few more words. He then puts the phone down on the table, spins it so that he can see the screen all the same, and then, finally, looks up at me. "So," he says, "Jim62, right?"

"James," I say.

"James62?"

"Just James is fine," I say.

"That's right though, isn't it?"

I nod. "It is. So!" I say.

"So," Mike says, unconsciously stroking his iPhone with one finger.

"Beautiful day for it," I comment, looking up at the stunning blue sky, the first such sky we have had in London for over a month.

"Um," Mike says, and when I lower my gaze, I see that he has returned to his texting operation.

"Work?" I ask.

"Um?" Mike says.

"Is that work? What did you say you do again?"

Mike frowns at the screen and then looks up at me. "I'm sorry?"

"What do you do?"

"What, work-wise?"

"Yes!"

"IT. I'm in IT."

"So are you working there?"

Mike frowns and shakes his head indicating non-comprehension.

I nod at his iPhone. "Is that work?" I mime his thumb-typing.

Mike laughs. "Oh!" he says. "No! No, I'm chatting to this guy. Hang on . . ." He swipes at the phone screen and then points it at me. The screen shows a muscle-bound bear with thick chest hair and a full beard. He's wearing leather jeans and one of those diagonal military belts. He is incredibly sexy, but in an entirely virtual kind of way. I doubt personally that people who look like that really exist – well, not outside of the porn industry at any rate.

"You know him?" Mike asks.

I peer in at the screen as if to ponder the question. "Hum," I say. "Leather Bear Stockwell. No, I don't think so." As if I would know Leather Bear Stockwell. It's an attempt at irony, but I don't think Mike gets it.

"Right," he says.

"Is he a porn star?" I ask.

"Dunno," Mike says. "But I intend to find out."

I sip my coffee and watch Mike as he continues to frantically exchange messages with the leather bear. I watch people wandering up and down Compton Street enjoying the sunshine and try to remain calm. Is this how one knows a date isn't going well in 2011, I wonder. When your "date" continues to browse right in front of you, is that how you know it's not going to work out?

"Mike!" I eventually say, unable to bear the constant clicking emanating from his phone as he types.

"Um?" he asks, glancing at me, and then, apparently finally twigging, "Oh!" he says, laying the phone down. "Sorry, he's just very hot."

"But I'm here."

"Yeah," Mike says. He doesn't sound enthusiastic.

"Maybe you'd rather go and meet him," I offer in the flattest tone of voice I can muster.

Mike nods and sips his Coke. "Yeah, probably tomorrow," he says. "He seems busy today."

I cover my mouth with one hand and stare at him, barely able to believe my ears. "So why am I here?" I ask eventually.

"I'm sorry?" Mike asks, propping the phone up against his glass so that he can see the screen and me at the same time.

"Why have I just travelled in from Walthamstow to meet you?" I ask.

Mike raises one eyebrow and grins at me lopsidedly, saucily even. "I don't know," he says. "Why have you come in from Walthamstow?"

I'm confused now. Having been ignored for the last ten minutes I'm now surprised to see that I'm being given what can only be described as a come-on.

"Look, Mike," I say with a sigh. "Let's cut the crap. If you're into . . ." I reach for his phone (he looks a bit panicked about this) and then having checked the screen, I put it back where it was. "If you're into Leather Bear Stockwell," I continue, "then there's not a lot of point to this, is there?"

Mike shrugs. His eyes flick up and down as he gives me the once-over. "You're OK," he says. "You look pretty fit to me."

"Oh," I say, irritated at the sensation of flattery I feel despite everything else that is happening here.

"Which gym do you go to?"

"I don't."

"You look like you do."

"I swim."

"Right. You said you're a top, yeah?" Mike says.

"I'm sorry?"

"On Grindr. You said you were top? Active."

"Oh, I don't think we discussed it actually," I say.

"So are you?"

"Well yeah, but frankly . . ."

At that moment, Mike's phone chirrups again. He leans down and peers at it and groans. "Oh Jesus!" he says.

As he picks it up and starts jabbing at the screen again, my irritation swells to anger, then fury, and then, surprisingly, thankfully, crosses some invisible boundary, and slips over the other side into amusement. This guy is beyond rude. He's insane.

"Bad news from Leather Bear?" I ask, trying to stifle the laughter now creeping into my voice. "Can't he make it tomorrow after all? Has he got a porn movie to make?"

"What? Oh . . . No . . ." Mike says, vaguely. "No, it's this other guy. Fucking lunatic."

He points the phone at me. This time the image is of an astoundingly ordinary, but not unattractive-looking guy in an

Aran sweater. "You have been warned," Mike says with a laugh. "Steer clear!"

I lick my lips and wonder what kind of guy Mike would consider to be a lunatic. "So what's up with him?" I ask.

"Won't shag unless he's in love," Mike says. "I mean . . . love." He rolls his eyes. "Like anyone still believes in that!"

I struggle to control my eyebrows, which I fear are making their way to the top of my forehead.

Mike jabs at the phone. "There. Blocked."

"You met him?"

"Yeah," Mike says. "Right here in fact. He said he was a bit old-fashioned. I thought he just meant the jumper, ha ha! But no. Prehistoric is more like it. Into, um, opera and reading books and going on dates." Mike makes a silly geeky voice and pulls a face as he says "books" and "dates". He shakes his head. "Oh and love, of course."

"God!" I say. "How awful. What did you do?"

Mike types another brief message on his phone, and then smiles wryly, so I assume that things are still going well with Leather Bear Stockwell.

"So yeah," he says, returning his attention briefly to me. "Umh . . . stay away from funny boiler."

"Funny boiler? Is that his handle?"

"No, bunny boiler," Mike says. "With a B. And no, it isn't, but it should be."

"What *is* his handle?"

"Um . . ." Mike pulls a face signifying lack of interest. "Um, Brian Irving or something."

"Right, well . . ." I drink the last of my coffee and clap my hands preparing to leave. Surprisingly this seems to get Mike's attention.

"So!" he says, downing the dregs of his Coke with a flourish. "Fancy a trip to Sauna Bar?"

"Sauna Bar?"

"The sauna," Mike says, "in Covent Garden."

I laugh. "You want me to go to the sauna with you?"

Mike nods exaggeratedly. "Yeah," he says. "It's just around the corner. Can't have you coming all that way from Wapping for nothing, can we?"

"Walthamstow."

"Right."

I shake my head and struggle to hide my smile.

"Come on," Mike says, mistaking my smirk for coy embarrassment. "You know you want to."

I laugh again, a short gasp of a laugh – almost a snort.

"What?" Mike asks.

I wrinkle my nose and shake my head. "No," I say. "No, actually, I don't, Mike. This um . . . well . . . It isn't happening."

Mike shrugs and turns his attention back to his phone again. "Oh!" he says. "This one's cute." He points it at me. "D'you know this guy?"

I glance at the headless picture of a guy in leather chaps and a posing pouch. "Hard to know . . ." I say with irony which, again, Mike misses. "But no, I don't know any of them."

Mike types a new message on his iPhone and pushes his lips out into a pout. "Wish I could say the same," he says, still texting. When his phone chirrups again, he swipes at the screen and says, "Oh my lord!"

He flashes the screen at me and I catch a glimpse of a purple-headed penis. In close-up.

"Oh my," I say. "You're right. He is gorgeous." And then I add, "See you Mike," and I stand to leave.

As I walk away, I'm not sure if Mike has even noticed, so I glance back to check. He seems unaffected. He is too busy typing to care.

By the time I get back home, my amusement has faded and I'm actually feeling irrecoverably depressed. It seems an unavoidable truth that I don't fit into this brave new world, and increasingly probable that I'm the only person left on the planet who requires a date, a one-to-one chat, and perhaps even a romantic dinner before moving on to that first kiss. Tonight, the future really does feel hopeless. And yet having had the joy and the passion and the pain and struggle of a ten-year relationship, I'm simply not able to sign up for these short stories that pass for "fun" nowadays. Everything Rob and I had – the laughter, the shared memories of foreign beaches and leaky tents, the intimacy with friends and relatives, and even the fights and the heartache at the end – I want it all over again. I like that intensity. Maybe I'm just that kind of guy. I never did like short stories much, I suppose – always preferred to invest my time in a whopping novel that made the backpack way too heavy but at least left me with a profound sense of loss once it was over. Maybe it's the same genes doing their stuff here.

I put some music on and slump onto the sofa. I stare at the mantelpiece where a photo of Rob and me on Bondi Beach still takes pride of place. Ten years. Ten years! I should probably remove it. That would probably be for the best. But then why would trying to forget the best ten years of my life be the healthy thing to do?

I wonder if Rob is finding this dating game as difficult as I am. If he's still with Giles – the twenty-seven-year-old he left me for – then probably not. But despite the whole Giles business, out of all the people I know, Rob is probably the only person I could talk to about this. That's what happens when you spend ten years with someone. And yet, of course, being my ex, he's the only person I can't talk to about this.

I take my new phone from my pocket and switch it on. I stare at the little orange Grindr icon. My Grindr date hasn't been much more successful than my Gaydar or Gayromeo dates.

I suppose the problem is one of probability. With guys like Mike meeting three or four guys a day, and guys like me meeting one a quarter, the probability of meeting someone like Mike rather than someone like me, is – I work it out in my head – one in three hundred and sixty. Today was the first time I have ever gone to meet someone from Grindr though, and it's unfair, I suppose, to judge the whole concept on a single date, but all the same, isn't Grindr just the whole faster/more/faster concept pushed to its limit? Can relationships between men get any more immediate, any more superficial than this?

I launch Grindr and look at Mike's smiling face. He's still online. He's probably still sitting outside Caffè Nero.

My phone chirrups with a message from him. It says, "Whappen?"

I think for a moment about replying, but if he doesn't "get it" by now, how could I ever explain?

Another message from Mike: "In sauna bar. Coming?" and I

wonder how he manages to use his phone in the sauna without damaging it. And I wonder why he would want to go to a place where men are waiting for sex and still continue searching through cyberspace. I think he probably has some major (but common) personality disorder. I should probably remove him from my favourites. Or delete the app altogether.

But then another icon catches my eye further down the page: the guy in the Aran sweater.

I click on it. The title is "Bill Erling" – his name, presumably. I stare at the photo for a while. A normal bloke called Bill Erling, hiding in a big jumper that his mother probably made.

Bill looks vaguely embarrassed about something. About having his photo taken perhaps. Or the jumper. Or being on Grindr maybe. Or perhaps, like me, suddenly finding himself in cyberspace in 2011 and not quite knowing how to cope with it.

His text reads, "Is it hopeless out there? Or are you going to prove me wrong?"

I sigh and think, "OK. One last try. But this really is the last one."

"Hi," I type. "I'm James. A little bird tells me that you and I have lots in common. Fancy a coffee somewhere sometime?"

I nod to myself and absent-mindedly stroke my iPhone as I wait for him to reply.

My phone chirrups. I click on the message. "You and I?" it says, then: "OMG! He's literate! Hello!"

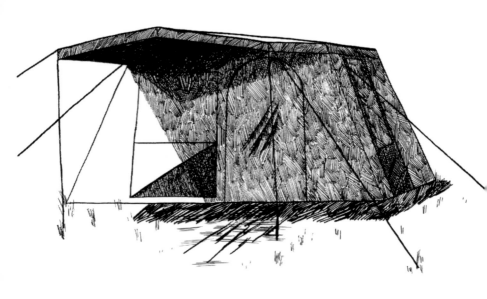

Glittery Insides
VICTORIA GRIGG

In Mum's wash bag, there are two packets of pills. She takes one at night, and the other in the morning when she wakes up. Throws a pill in her mouth. Throws a gulp of water in. Tilts her head back, eyes screwed shut. When she's taken them, she always stares straight ahead for a couple of seconds before she says or does anything. It's like she's thinking about something she can't believe.

Mum and Dad are sitting at the folding table inside the tent, and Mum is fiddling with the handle of her plastic mug.

"What do I have to do?" Dad says. "Fucking prostrate myself?"

Mum looks round at me. Her face is all orange in the strange light. "Alice. Go outside and play, darling," she says, and I notice that her body is slunk in the chair, like it's full of sand.

"Well, I'm sorry," I hear Dad say when I'm outside. I bat the ball round the pole a few times, and it keeps swinging round too fast, like it's going to smack me in the face.

It's all weird and quiet around the tent then, so I go out to the woods. Ferns everywhere, knee-high, all around the trees. And there's no one else here.

I find a twig covered in this crazy white fungus, like a dead person's skin. I scratch at the ground with it, and this little beetle, like a drop of blood, is crawling on the twig.

I look up at the big old trees growing high above me. And it's as though nothing will ever happen again. I won't sleep tonight. I won't wake up tomorrow. I'll just be walking around these woods for hours and hours and more and more hours for ever.

Light flickering, glinting through the tree trunks. A clearing. I walk towards it, and then – I see someone. Some kids. There are three of them jumping into a river – off a bridge. I see a boy swimming, sleek-headed, then he wades out at the bank, and water streams off his body. They can't see me, I don't think. I hope they can't see me.

They're so bright in the light. I can see every tiny bit of them. An ankle in the air, an elastic waistband, shoulder blades like wings. And their voices. Their voices are bright too, like cracked glass. These are the kinds of kids who sometimes sit somewhere totally different in History – for no reason. Yeah, it's these kinds of kids who paint those deformed pictures in Art, with red and blue and green, and the teacher puts them up next to the whiteboard. In the most prominent place. And you don't know why their picture is better than yours. But it is. And I want to be friends with these kinds of kids, I think, don't I?

I go back under the trees, my green guardians. All quiet in here again. It's better here under the trees. I feel safer. Don't I?

We're at the pub again. Mum says she's going out to the car to fetch something, and Dad looks across at me. He's squeezing ketchup on his chips. "You're really growing up, aren't you, Alice?" he says, smiling at me, twinkly-eyed, chewing. But his eyes are narrow and strange. I cut into my lasagne and watch the mince swelling out the sides. "Do you like your watch, darling?" he says. I look at it there on my wrist – see the stars and the moon on the face, and the diamanté crystals round the edge. I think of Charlotte at school. "Wow, I love your watch!" she'd said. "That's gorgeous!" and she'd pulled me by the forearm across to Emma's table, and like four of them had stood around my arm, grasping at the watch face as though it belonged to them or something.

I look up at Dad, ready to smile, say thanks for the watch, but his long eyelashes are lowered, and his attention is on his plate again. I watch him cut another piece of salmon en croûte and mash some peas onto the forkful. He eats with his mouth open, making big physical bites like an animal. I can see the food moving around in there with his muscly tongue. He's wearing a white shirt open at the throat and rolled up at the sleeves – like a prince, I'm thinking. Neither of us says anything, and I wait for the moment when he'll look up at me again. Finally, he does, and his pupils are super-small and his irises are so blue. And I have this feeling. I have this feeling like he sees everything there is to see about me.

Mum comes back from the car and settles in her chair. She places the white napkin on her knees and doesn't even look up at me or Dad. She just carries on eating her food. The music is loud now and people are starting to dance near us. Someone jigs into my shoulder, and I'm kind of laughing, but I'm sort of annoyed as well. A fake Elvis has taken to the stage – all sunglasses and sideburns. His silver jumpsuit is stained at the armpits where he's sweating. He stands in a star shape and swings his hips and points his crotch at different corners of the bar. The music's battering my eardrums – "Why can't ya see? What you're doin' to me?" – so I slip out to the loo and look in the mirror. I don't feel right. Like everything I know is kind of trembling. I chill my hands in the tap water until they hurt.

It's another dazzling day and the kids are back at the river, ripping the air up with their shouts. As I come out into the light where they'll be able to see me, it's as though I'm naked. I say, "Hello," to the girl. She's just climbing up the muddy bank, and her long wet hair looks like dark ribbons hanging from her head.

She says, "Hi," and squints at me.

"Are you staying at the campsite?" I say. If I can just keep my voice even, it'll be OK.

One of the boys calls "Yeah!" from the bridge. The girl looks over her shoulder at him.

She turns back to me. "Are *you* staying at the campsite?" she says, and the boy's body slaps into the river behind her. The other one leaps in immediately afterwards.

"Yeah," I say.

"My name's Skye, by the way." She doesn't smile. Her hands are on her hips. "What's yours?"

"Alice."

I watch the two boys slink out of the water. Their bodies are glistening with strings of light. They waddle around Skye, holding their arms away from their torsos and hunching their shoulders. One of them glares at me. "Have you got your swimming costume?"

"No, I'll just jump in in my clothes."

And Skye says, "That'll be a nightmare. Jump in your knickers. It's the same as a bikini anyway."

"No, I'll be all right." And I see Skye shrugging and walking back onto the bridge. I sit on the ground and take my sandals off. "How deep is it?" I call over to them, but no one hears me. The boys are launching in again. I see the blond one fixed for a second in high space, limbs stuck out at angles, nose pinched, running in mid-air. The wind surges and drags ripples along the surface of the water. The trees are rustling massively, like they know all there is to know.

When I'm on the bridge, I squeeze through the metal railings and stand with my toes sticking over the edge. The concrete's all pebbly and sharp under the soles of my feet. Below me, the water's shifting around as though it's waiting. And it's shivering like it's alive. I can see bits of me down there, blurred and broken up, the colours of myself flickering. "Is it deep?" I say again, maybe just to myself. But still no one answers.

I let go of the chilly rail and I raise my arms over my head as though I'm at some kind of special ceremony. I step into nothing.

Totally free for a second. The weight in me – in my chest, my shoulders, my face – is pulling up. And my lower body pulls down. I'm taking a breath, slowly, inward. It takes an aeon. I will be here for ever.

Then crack. I break through the terrible surface, deafening, and it's like I'm wrapped in plastic. I'm lumbering and stupid. I heave my arms and legs in the chaos, and seal my mouth tight against all the swarming forces. Maybe I can't get back to the normal world. Maybe. Maybe. My clothes pull at me like greedy hands. I press my arms out wide in breaststroke, but I'm still not up there, safe. There's the surface above me – tilting – and I can't get there! I can't get there. I try to punch out again, but my arms won't move properly, like I'm some kind of slug thing. Then I feel the water parting over the top of my head and pulling my hair down smooth. I grab breaths and the banks are swinging like they're drunk. And the bushes too. And the clouds. Swinging. It's so cold. I can't breathe properly. But then I can – and I see the round heads of the others twinkling in the light, over there. "Ha!" I'm waving at them. "That was great!" I shout, and I'm swimming towards them in this like elegant kind of way. And it's as though my bones are firmer. And when I get to Skye and the boys, we all bob in a circle.

"How was that?" Skye asks. She's smiling at me now.

"Cool!" I say.

Then the blond boy says, "*Fucking* cool, you should say," and swims off back towards the bridge.

"We've got to go soon, actually," Skye says then, and the other boy smiles at me and swims off as well. "We're going to Stowbridge Castle this afternoon."

"Oh, I think I'm going there tomorrow," I say. I realise I'm shaking.

"Yeah, they've got like armour and stuff and you can try it on," she tells me as we tread water. My trousers are making it harder than it needs to be. "You can try on like a gauntlet or something. And you can try and lift the sword, but they're so heavy. Only guys can do it. How old are you, by the way?"

"Twelve."

"I'm gonna be thirteen in three weeks," she says. "Feels weird."

"Yeah, and twelve is weird anyway," I say. "Wonder what it feels like to be sixteen or something?"

"I can't wait to be sixteen," she says.

They've gone off and I'm alone again. It's like they weren't even here. And the whole place seems bigger somehow. Too big. I sit on the shore and look at the way the sun lights up the inner parts of the water. I don't want to go back to the tent yet, so I go up on the bridge again, slip through the railings and grip them behind me. I lean out forward over the water, feeling the stretch in my muscles. Would I be able to get to the bottom? I want to grab one of the smooth round pebbles that's been assaulted by centuries of water currents.

And I jump.

In the water, I keep my eyes open and strain down through the mad pressures, reaching reaching for a pebble. I can see so many of them huddled. I clutch one painfully in my fingers, then struggle through the ropes of water to the shore.

I wade out, heavy, and place my prize on the gravel. It's elephant grey and speckled. Thinking to itself. I wrestle myself out of my soaking combats. My legs are white and goose-pimply. I step up again onto the bridge. And I'm shivering so much, kind of jerking. And it's not even cold. I clench my jaw.

The trees look like they're watching. I can see them all along the sides of the river as it curves round ahead of me like a road. I place my feet on the rough bridge edge again. And fly out, feeling the air push against my chest.

I smash into the waters and steady myself more quickly this time. I power down to reach another stone, a precious caramel one, then battle out of the water again and place it next to the elephant one. I'm lurching and giddy, but there's something solid in the core of me. I'm going in again.

The sun slides low in the sky, melting like butter. So many times I've broken through the water, and slowly my spiral of stones uncurls on the bank. As I walk out at the shore again, I feel faint. It's like I can still feel the river surging on my skin, even when I'm standing on the dirt.

A bird makes a panicked sound high up in the trees. I think of Mum cooking pasta outside our tent, the steam rising in the gloom. The woods are quietly collecting their dark. I should go back.

Wriggling into my wet trousers, I admire my artwork. I want to keep it with me somehow. I brush soil from the elephant stone at the centre of my pattern, and pocket it. I enter the woods and feel my way along the cavernous path, like I'm floating. Near my feet, I can see tiny star-shaped flowers making their own light. The pebble is banging loosely against the front of my thigh. It hurts. There'll be a bruise there later on, I think, but I don't really care.

Mum's been at the toilet block for ages this morning, making herself beautiful. I like the way she dresses – she's always very careful about it and everything's coordinated.

"Come and give your dad a hug." He's lying on the blow-up mattress in their inner cubicle and the light glows in lemon-coloured through all the walls. I crawl in over the silky sleeping bags and go to him. The top half of his body is bare where I can see it out of the covers. "Let's have a hug," and he reaches out to me. I back into the crook of his arm and he rests it, heavy, over my shoulders. It's hot in here. I can only breathe lightly. He seems weird. He isn't saying much. "You're growing, aren't you?" he says and, reaching over with the other hand, he touches the fleshy tip of my right breast through my T-shirt. I look down at his hand. His arm is greenish in the light and so are my legs stretched out before me on the blow-up bed. I see the neat hairs on his forearm, and his wide thumbnail. I see the tendons under the skin of the hand, and the capable fingers feeling around. He sighs and grabs my breast roughly for a few seconds, then takes his hand away. I look at his head. He's turned his face away in the other direction and his chest is heaving up and down. He takes his arm off my shoulders. I can't move. I feel as though I'm a doll fixed in a pose. When he turns his face back to me, his eyes are glistening. They dart all round my face, and the corners of his mouth squirm down as he says, "You know I love you."

As though shoving off a great weight, I scramble out of the tent, feeling like a dog with its tail between its legs. I stand outside in the clean white air and hear the voices scattered through the campsite. To my right, a woman in purple shorts is pegging towels to a guy rope, and I can smell sizzling bacon on the breeze. I run, left, into the green shadow of the woods. A couple with two large dogs come towards me. Their dogs lope ahead of them and jog round me as though I don't really exist. My breath is coming too fast, so I sit down on a rotten tree and try to slow it down. The couple smile at me and walk briskly past. In and out. In and out. The ferns breathe in and out. The high canopy breathes in and out. "Aa-lice! Aaaa-lice!" I hear her voice ringing into the woods as if she's calling from another planet. "We're going! A-lice!"

At the castle with Mum and Dad, I feel strange and wobbly as if I've been running a long way. I stick close to Mum. She's looking carefully at every exhibit and reading all the signs. We stroll through a stone room, and peer in at a rusted dagger lit up in a Perspex case and a faded tapestry dress that a lady must have worn somehow, even though it looks so stiff and constricting. I look down at the small empty shoes staring up from the bottom of the cabinet.

"Mum?" I say. "Are we going home on Sunday?"

"Yes," she says, finally gazing down at me. Her eyes are brown and liquidy, very pretty, like Bambi eyes, and it isn't like they're vacant. I can tell she's in there, she's just stiller or something. I take her hand and move my body in close. I remember when her hair used to be messier than it tends to be these days, now she's got the straighteners.

We drift around without talking, and I see Dad on the other side of the room being told off for taking a photo of a red-plumed helmet with his phone. "We don't allow photography in here, sir," the guard says.

Still holding the phone high, Dad turns fully to the guide who's stooped over and blinking at him.

"Why is that?" he says.

"The exhibits – many of the exhibits are light-sensitive, so we ask –"

"But this one's not, is it?"

The guide's hands hover away from his body. "Sir," he says. "It's one of our rules, so I do ask –"

"No. Sorry. This doesn't make any sense. I'm sorry, but this is ridiculous." Dad faces the helmet again and moves the phone close to the visor.

Sunlight sweeps across the car park as a cloud unblocks the sun. Mum stands in front of Dad, shuddering. "Get over yourself," she says, through a tight mouth. Dad is swaying his hips, one hand in his pocket, like a restless child who's been told to stay put. His hand swings up towards Mum's face as though he's going to slap her, but it slows and rests on her cheek instead. And she looks across at him, under the hand. It's like she's dissolving, breaking up. They just stand like that – for ages. With Dad's palm stuck to her face.

I'm lying in absolute darkness, hearing Mum murmuring and whining quietly in their compartment. Bodies slide against fabric.

There's a sudden low squeal as a zip unzips. The torch switches on, and I see a fuzzy disc of light bobbing around on the pretend wall. Then the bang of the car door. Who's gone out to the car? There's a slow grunt near me and I realise I'm alone in the tent with Dad. I lie here tense as wood in my zipped-up sleeping bag, holding the stone in my hand.

Then, just blackness all around. I've been asleep. Has anything happened? I listen out for the sounds of him near me. Then I make out the rise and fall of his breath – the small rasp as he lets it out through his mouth with each exhalation. He can't be more than a metre away from my ear. I listen for ages and ages, and the stone feels cold in my hand.

It's dawn now and I creep out and sit in the driver's seat next to Mum, who is lying with her eyes half open on the reclined passenger seat.

I go with her over to the toilet block. The grass is saturated with dew, and birds are singing from all the secret places around us. There's an empty space where Skye's family's tent was – only a square of pale grass left there now.

In the ladies', I scrub my teeth. I don't feel sure about anything. Mum is stroking expensive cream over her face. *Refine Perfect Protect*, it says on the jar. "You want some, Alice?" she says to me, offering the tub of delicate, egg-white stuff. But, I don't know. I don't want anything today. I dab my finger into the coolness and touch it to my face. *Melts into your skin*, it says. It vanishes under my fingertip.

My hands feel fluttery and weak. I find the stone in my sleeping bag – unbury it.

I walk in circles round the woods. A goose egg. It feels smooth and heavier than it should do in my palm. Should I throw it in the river? Should I break it? Somehow, I am going to have to break it. I want to see it cleanly split in two, showing its glittery insides. My foot tangles in roots, and trees shove my shoulders. It's like the whole wood is turning beneath me, slowly spinning apart.

I press it against my cheek. And pictures fill my mind. Dad seeing himself in the mirror, hair spiked wet – those eyes clear as a cat's, but his face like an old man's. And Mum sliding her hand along her skirt – no creases at all.

Ants are crawling in my arm hairs. Could I hurl my stone on the rock at the river, crack it open? Could I bash a tent peg down into the centre, split it that way? What would it be like to hold the two halves, one in each hand? Then I see a crop of rocks at the base of a tree, and run over there to smack my stone into them. I bash it hard and feel the jolt in my arm, a metallic shock which runs through the bones. I bash it again. And again. It slithers along the rock. And each time I hit it down it makes a hollow sound which echoes around the tree trunks. There's a white-hot throbbing in my forearm. I look at the side I've been hitting against the rock. No change yet except a small powdery area where a part of it has chipped off. I bash it again. And again. It's not breaking. And my whole arm is lit up with pain and my fingers are numb. I tighten all the muscles in my arm. Screw my eyes tight shut. Throw it down as hard as I can.

And, in my mind, I'm walking back along the nettle track. Like I'm growing. Tall. Towering. Will I grow as high as the trees? And I see Mum in my head again. I'm telling her. Telling her everything. The way I feel. The way I feel. And I think she's listening. What's that expression on her face? She leans in close to the mirror. Sweeps mascara on her lashes. Pulls a burgundy high-heel onto her foot.

I smash it down again. I smash it again. I smash it again.

The Tale of Lordywens
M. J. WHISTLER

I'm in my bed, and Asha says that I should call her Mother, Asha-mother, though I know we have different blood. I beg her to tell me the tale of my name again – I never tire of hearing it – but she says after everything that has happened it is I who should tell it. She says that one day people will relate the story of Lordywens in the same way they tell fairy tales. She says, too, that it shows why we should honour our birth-stars because they guide the paths we take and give story to our life.

"It is time for you to tell your own tale, Lordywens," she says.

So I start, where it all started.

In our village, when a child is to be born, the women crowd into the hut of the mother-to-be as she goes through labour and begin to chant names. One after the other they make their suggestions and in between softly wail as they watch for the birth, which occurs when the child recognises its name.

"This one doesn't know itself," the women said after they had called out all the names they knew, when my birth was due. Old Asha said I must be afraid to enter the world. The chanting started again: Anindo, Hanuni, Radha, Bahati, but my mother struggled to part with me. I was her firstborn, she herself scarcely a woman; she had now been in labour for nearly two days and was weak with exhaustion. "The baby is stuck," one of the women said finally, and they paused in their name-calling. Then Asha, who had eight children of her own, wiped the sweat from my poor mother's face and said: "Lordy, when's the child –" and out I popped, into the world, before Asha could finish, "going to be born."

Asha cut the cord and handed me to my mother, who, I am told, kissed me and breathed her last as I lay crying on her breast.

My father was not from the village. When he heard his wife-child had died, and that I was not a boy-infant, he left in the night. Some said his grief was too hard to bear, but others knew he did not want a girl-baby to tend to. People said I would be cursed if they changed my name, so they called me Lordywens, and though I had no family of my own, the village women looked after me, especially Asha, who had named me. They fed me and clothed me, and in return, as soon as I was old enough, I did chores for them and ran errands.

In the centre of the village where I was born there was a two-pronged birch tree and all the houses looked out onto it. The villagers said I was like a cat the way I could climb, or like a bird when I nestled in its branches. I loved this tree with its peeling, pale-yellow bark. I decided to make a house for myself in the birch tree, for although there was a place for me in Asha's hut, I did not like to sleep with the dogs on the floor, and her own eight children took up all the bed-space. From my place in this tree I looked down on the little houses of my birth-village, with its warm red earth, deep in the Mweusi-wazee district.

We call it Africa's heart.

Sometimes visitors came to our village. One was a medicine man who said the sap of the birch tree was good to drink for it took away pain and cured all manner of ailments; I wished this had been known when I was born, for maybe it could have saved my mother.

Another visitor said it was good that the birch tree stood in the village centre, for it would protect the houses all around from evil spirits. He spoke of lands far away, where their winter days were always dark, and in summer there was never night, where the birch tree was sacred to Thor, and how Thor was an important god, the god of thunder.

I didn't need the visitors to tell me it had special powers. I knew my birch tree looked after me, protected me. I would sing to it at dawn when the early birds started to wake us, and I would make offerings to it when we had feast days. From here I would hear the village women shouting.

"Lordywens, go and fetch the water from the well."

"Lordywens, come and peel the potatoes."

"Lordywens! Sweep the yard."

"Lordywens, wash the dishes!"

All day long they would call me, and all day long I would run from family to family to do the chores, while the other village children attended classes. I would hear them chanting prayers, like "Two times two are four, four times four are sixteen," and I would chant these too, in the hope it would keep the bad spirits away. Sometimes, I would listen to the stories they were told. Crouching under the window outside the classroom, I'd hear tales of people who lived far, far away, of princes who wore crowns and rode white horses. There was even a mother-orphan who danced with a prince, though she wore only rags and slept by the ashes of the fire. I longed to meet a prince. But Asha would wave her stick at me, shouting, "Lordywens, get on with your chores," and I would scuttle off without hearing the end of the tale.

That's how my days were filled. The sun would come up and the sun would go down, and the nights were always cold. But it was a good life and I longed, one day, to do something special for my village and the women who looked after me – though I longed, too, to be like the other children.

One day Asha summoned me to say a special visitor was coming to Mweusi-wazee. How her big eyes rolled with awe as she said this.

"Is it a prince?" I asked.

"He must be, for he has already sent us money and food." She rolled her eyes some more. "His coming will bring honours and opportunities for the children of the village."

"Then why are you crying, Asha?"

"He says all great opportunities come with sacrifice. He will take the chosen ones away so they can receive their privileges."

"Will I be chosen?"

"You!" Asha shook with laughter. "Lordywens, no. You know

nothing. You have no fine clothes to impress him. You won't be in the procession. But you can sweep the yard, and help prepare the feast for him and dress the hair of the other children. Then, when he comes, you must keep from sight, for with your rags you would bring disgrace upon our village. We must do everything to make his visit a success."

That night when I climbed up to my branch in the tree in the cool starlit air I told the birch all the things that Asha had said. That night the tree swayed its branches, and a leaf fell on my face. Through the gap it left among the twigs I saw the crescent moon smiling at me. That was when I decided: when the prince-visitor came, I would hide here and watch.

The younger children practised their dances until they were perfect and the older ones made music with their pipes, while I swept and swept and hummed the tunes I heard. I helped Asha and the villagers prepare the feast: we sliced the mango and the pawpaw and I sucked the sweet juice from my fingers. We collected and arranged leaves and flowers, decorated the chair to make it a throne for our esteemed visitor. Never had I seen my village so fine.

The day had arrived. I did my chores as quickly as I could and scurried up the smooth cracked bark, to hide and have a clear view. Here I sat nestled among the leaves, directly above the seat for the prince.

In the distance I saw a dust-cloud announcing his arrival and I became veiled in fine sand as they drew up nearby. Then with surprise I saw he had come not on horseback, or driving a grand car, but in a shabby bus. It was like the one those priests brought when they came that time with beads and crosses and told me to read some holy book; I'd said I could not read and Asha clipped me round the ear and sent me to my work.

Our awaited visitor stepped out of the bus, and now I was even more surprised, for there was nothing that marked him as fine: his features were coarse, his clothes strained around his fat body. Another man stepped out, and he looked even less like a prince. The elders of our village seemed far more distinguished than either of these visitors.

However the two men were royally greeted. My village family bowed to them and hurriedly arranged another seat beneath my tree for the second man. Then a breeze began to blow. The leaves flapped against my face as I struggled to keep out of sight and the branches whispered, "Thor." It troubled me to hear this, yet I stayed as still as I could, for below me the men sat, shaded by my waving tree. The ceremony started, with the dancing and the chanting, and none of them put a foot wrong, though all the time the wind grew stronger.

Afterwards the children were presented, one after the other, bowing, curtseying, and I felt so proud of them, with their oiled, beautiful bodies, all smiling their best smiles. The prince asked some of them their names, and the other man wrote these down in a book. Then Asha announced the table was ready. Even in the wind I could smell the goat stew, and my tummy rumbled at the thought of dipping the ungali into it, biting open the plantain balls. Everyone excitedly hurried over. Everyone except the two men for whom the feast had been arranged. They stood beneath me, talking. They seemed displeased. I strained to listen.

"Was hoping for a bigger pull."

"Three, maybe five have potential."

"But they'll need grooming."

"Lordywens. Lordywens!" I heard Asha calling. "When's the child going to answer?"

I could not. The two men were below. Now they were walking to their bus.

"You reckon the cases are strong enough to hold them?"

"Yes. But I'm glad we won't have the job of cleaning them up when they get to Belgium."

"Let's get this mud-pie meal over with then, and split."

I watched them go into their bus but they came out almost at once and wandered towards the feast we had prepared for them. If that was what princes were like, I was glad I would not be among the chosen ones. I would not want to go away with them. Yet maybe the red bus was special inside, like the pumpkin that turned into a coach. If I went and had a look, maybe I would also discover who they had chosen, for I could see they had left their notebook on the driver's seat. Quickly I slipped down the trunk of my tree, some of the peeling bark clinging to me, my ragged skirt swirling from the wind that pushed against me as I ran to the bus. I tugged at the door to open it and stepped in. But there was nothing special inside. It was dark, still and cold, and it smelled of stale plastic. The windows whistled with the wind.

The notebook on the seat was black. I opened it, but I could not understand the writing. There was also an attaché case, with many papers inside. I did not need to be able to read these, for there were photographs on each sheet. They were pictures of girls who looked not unlike the girls of my village. They were naked. It was not unusual for us girls to be without clothes, yet something about the girls in these pictures made my eyes open wide, and a chill ran down my back. Something told me I must show this to Asha. I folded some pages and hid them inside my skirt-rags. Then a noise startled me. And suddenly it was as if I were being stung by a hundred killer bees, or lying on a bed of bullet ants. My skin turned both hot and cold, my mouth went dry. The man, not the prince-driver but the other, his face like a storm, was hitting me and slapping me. I tried to scream, but he silenced my mouth with one hand and with the other snatched both my wrists together. I wriggled and twisted and kicked, until I managed to bite him.

"You little wild cat, you're in big trouble."

He knocked me to the ground. I shouted to Asha but my voice was as nothing in the hubbub of the rising storm. I was powerless. I was going to die. I was afraid. For the first time in my life, I felt truly afraid. He gagged me and got out some rope, and it tore my skin as he yanked it tight. Then he threw me to the back of his bus, and I heard him shut the door. Never had I known an animal treated like this. I rolled over, feeling my hair wet as I lay on it. Maybe now, if I died, I would meet my mother. Through the dusty windows of the bus, from my place on the floor, I looked up at my birch tree, silently wishing for help. But my beloved tree waved its branches as if saying farewell. I saw a leaf fall, like the one the night before, but this time it fell to the ground. I blinked. I missed my tree, I missed my village and all the people who had looked after me. I loved them. I started crying and I heard rain begin to fall onto the roof of the bus. The patter became louder and louder, until it was beating down, thrashing the bus like the man had struck me. The wind called out, "Whoah!" and it rocked the bus like a baby.

The door burst open as the two men returned, hurriedly

climbing in. They sat at the front, swearing and cursing that they would have to wait until the storm subsided.

"What about her?"

I shut my eyes. I felt their attention bear down on me as they looked along the aisle. Through half-closed eyes I looked at my birch and with every breath implored it to protect me from them, to protect us all. Suddenly there was a flash of light and a violent hammering. It was the drumroll of thunder. It was Thor: my birch tree had summoned its god. Then I heard a deafening crack, and from my place on the floor I felt the bus jump about and I tried to wedge myself under a seat. I heard screams and the bus sharply jolted. It sent me flying along the aisle. I hit something, and my world went dark.

"She's alive."

There were many hands around me, pulling at me. I coughed, for my mouth was full of sand. I started choking. I was being held, but not by ropes – by safe, strong hands. I tried to open my eyes, but it hurt for they were coated in dust. Someone wiped my face.

"What a miracle, she is unhurt."

"Lordywens. Lord be praised!"

It was Asha. I knew it from her voice and from her smell, with its homely mix of milk and earth and sweat. I opened my eyes and smiled at her. I looked around, but though I could see it was my village, I knew at once something was different. The birch tree, my birch tree, was no longer standing. It now lay flat, across the remains of the red bus. Then Asha told me about the storm, and how the two visitors had been crushed by the tree, and how everyone had nearly despaired of finding me, until she spotted me lightly covered by leaves, under a red plastic seat.

"Why did they tie you up?"

I started to tell her what I had heard and how I had called to her, and prayed and prayed to my birch tree and to its god to save us. From inside my skirt I brought out the folded pictures of the naked girls.

"Lordy, lordy," she said, but almost silently. "Truly you have saved our village." Then she hugged me, and promised me a bed in her house now my tree home was no more. And as I hugged her

I looked at my fallen birch, saddened it had died, but silently too I gave thanks, to Thor.

"You told it well, my child."

Asha-mother reaches over, to kiss me goodnight.

Asha-mother says tomorrow I can start school with the other children. Tomorrow they shall hear my tale.

"Truly your ancestors will be proud of you, Lordywens," says Asha-mother. Then she bustles away.

From my bed under the little window I look out at the ceiling above the earth and I see her, my real mother, tiny and silver. She is there in the sky, sitting on the branches of my birch tree, shining down on me.

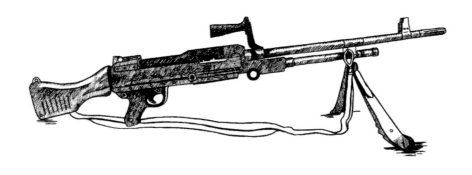

Roar
NADIM SAFDAR

MAGAZINE.
Magazine. Still warm from the ammo pocket. Check. In my hand.

LOAD.

Clip it in nicely. Remember not to fumble. The sun was in my eyes but I wasn't fumbling. My magazine was reaching for the well and I was nearly there.

CAN'T FIND THE WELL? STORY OF YOUR LIFE YOU FUCKING PAKI CUNT. FIND THE FUCKING HOLE. FIND THE FUCKING HOLE. NOW.

The Corporal screamed in my face. His breath stank of beer and fags and I got his spit in my eye. He had his thumbs hooked in the straps of his webbing, like a schoolteacher playing with the elastic on his braces, and his head stuck out like a pecking hen as he paced back and forth along the line.

AHH, AKRAM. FOUND THE FUCKING HOLE? BOYS, THE PAKI HAS FOUND THE FUCKING HOLE.

They all cheered, but not as much as last night, when my elbow accidentally knocked a pint out of the Corporal's hands. They were serious now. Pumped up for a Live Fire Exercise.

SAFETY OFF.

I reached down but the switch wasn't in the horizontal position where my fingers remembered it and then I felt a sharp ache in my shoulder as my rifle was wrenched out of my hands.

YOU FUCKING IDIOT, IT WAS ALREADY OFF. WHAT THE FUCK ARE YOU DOING WITH YOUR SAFETY OFF BEFORE INSTRUCTED TO DO SO? YOU'RE A FUCKING DISASTER. A FUCKING DANGER TO EVERYBODY.

He blew a whistle and everybody stopped.

SIT DOWN YOU LITTLE FUCKER. SIT DOWN.

I sat on the warm grass and as he laid into me everybody pointed with fingers like rifle tips. Two kicks to my chest and then a lecture. I had heard it all before.

YOU NEVER, NEVER, NEVER LET YOUR SAFETY OFF UNTIL INSTRUCTED TO DO SO BY THE COMMANDING NCO.

Unless the Russians invaded and were approaching into range – then the Corporal wouldn't be saying that. I mean, he wouldn't want me to wait for his order. Of course, I'd have to be certain it was the Soviets, but I had seen them in the manual; they were grey and square and always stooping. In the blink of an eye I'd switch the lever to the off position and fire like crazy. Bum. Bum. Bum. Bum. There you go you fucking Ruskies. Take that red-hot 7.62 up your red Commie ass. How does that feel?

GET UP. EVERYBODY BACK INTO POSITION. YOU WILL REMAIN THERE UNTIL I GIVE THE ORDER.

The wind started up as we waited and he took out his cock right there next to our line and then he stood and chatted to the Sergeant who carried on nodding and laughing like the hot piss wasn't blowing at an angle and sloshing with the mud on his boots. I saw the Corporal point to me and braced myself for a shout, but none came. I would have been OK today. I had gone over it again and again in my mind. But I hadn't got any sleep, and now that we were here and I was so much colder than I had thought it was possible to be, I couldn't think properly.

ROAR. I WANT TO HEAR YOUR WAR VOICE. ROAR. LOUDER. ROAR, YOU PUSSIES.

I was roaring but it didn't sound very soldierly. It was hard to do that at the top of your voice for very long. It hurt your throat.

I SWEAR I'LL JAM MY COCK IN YOUR THROAT IF YOU CAN'T DO BETTER THAN THAT. ROAR, AKRAM. PRETEND SOMEONE'S TAKEN AWAY YOUR CHAPATTI AND RAMMED

IT UP YOUR MOTHER.

I roared because I knew he was watching, but it got harder and harder and I ended up just roaring when he didn't have his back to me. I must have looked like C Company last night, with their big open mouths, after I had accidentally elbowed the pint. I was on the floor and there was blood running down my nose and the Corporal had got out his cock and was pissing all over me, and I knew if I tried to get up I might cut my hands on the broken pint glass, and the others were enjoying it with their big open mouths, and then they all started to unzip their trousers too, and it was only the shout from the NAAFI manager behind the bar that had stopped them, but it was too late because I was already soaked with the hot piss that smoked off the fabric of my civvies.

After that I was made to sit outside next to a toilet like I was on guard duty, but I knew that wasn't right because we were staying at barracks and there was already a proper guard in a guard house with a jail next to the gates. I didn't dry at all; it didn't rain but I still didn't dry. It was like there was wet in the air. I sat on the bench and rocked back and forth and thought about how I could be a better soldier and how I could show them all that I was just as good as they were. But I had always known that I had to be better than them if they were ever going to accept me. I had to be something special like the SAS. I had to pretend I was hiding out in a dugout, like for the entire six weeks of basic training, and because the Corporal and the others were the enemy it didn't matter what they did to me. It couldn't be any worse than being captured by the Ruskies and hanging out in a POW camp in Siberia, and that was something that really could happen.

I was good at running. It didn't matter what they loaded me up with, I could outrun them all. On my first day, doing the annual CBT, I ran so far out ahead I lost my way and ended up in Richmond town centre. A nice lady showed me a road map and I ran all the way back to Catterick without stopping. The kitchens were closed by then but cook had put out some lunch for me. That was the kindest thing anybody ever did for me here. They laughed at me with their big open mouths but gave me a pass mark even though I didn't finish the run. I think that's what got me in to the Basic Training Course.

Another thing I was good at was assembling my SLR weapon. Fifty-six seconds was my record. I could do it twice over by the time anybody else had even finished doing it once. The Armoury Sergeant would look at me with a big open mouth but it wasn't laughing. He was sort of proud of me. I could tell. He was a yellow and I wanted to ask him how he ever made Sergeant, being Chinky and that, but I never got to speak to him, and even if I had I probably would have lost my nerve.

I was still pretending to roar but my voice was getting swallowed up by the wind and I could hardly even hear myself. Now the Corporal had emptied Smithy's webbing on the ground where he had just been pissing. He was adjusting the straps and still shouting.

I'd been sitting outside for ages when suddenly a great big barn door opened to let the smoke out and inside there was music and laughter, and pretty women in nice dresses were being danced by Officers in nice suits with red stripes down the middle and clinking boots with shiny brass spurs. I was watching that and lost in how beautiful it was, when I heard a familiar voice behind me.

HEY, PRIVATE AKRAM, RANK AND NUMBER AND QUICK TO IT.

It was the Corporal and it was the only time I had seen him on his own. His voice was a bit drunk and his body swayed from side to side.

I bolted upright.

"PRIVATE AKRAM. 24778345."

"Sit down, you daft bastard, and don't fucking salute me. I'm not one of those cunts in there." He pointed to the barn where the doors were now closing. "I work for a living." His finger did half a circle and stopped at me.

I looked down at my trainers which squelched as I wriggled my toes. For a moment I felt like I was about to cry, but then I realised it was only because I wasn't used to him being kind and I didn't want to give him another story to tell the others.

"About the piss." Noisily he summoned up a gob ball and spat it to the ground.

"I'll dry out."

"You're in the Army now, boy."

"I've seen worse." And I had, as a kid at school and on the estates. At least the Army had rules. That's one thing I liked about it.

"You egging me on?"

I knew he'd say that. It was typical. The minute you stood up to them they got all tough again.

"Just saying." I shivered.

"Recruit, you're doing OK. You don't give no bullshit backchat. Don't start now."

He pointed to a building from where I could hear laughing. "There's a pint in there for you. Come and wet your whistle."

"I'm wet enough already thanks."

He did an about turn and whistled as he walked away. Just before he was out of earshot I saw him look back at me.

KEEP IT UP, YOU PAKI CUNT.

He made sure the last two words were really loud so his chums in the NAAFI could hear.

Later, they were all marching back to bed and the Corporal and his mates were all shooting at me with finger pistols and laughing with their big open mouths so I just turned my back on them. I should have followed them back to my bunk and they couldn't have stopped me, but by then I had been out for such a long time that I wanted to brave it out and show them that I could do it and that I wouldn't come back in unless ordered to bed by the Corporal, but he was too pissed to care. I imagine the minute his head hit the pillow he slept like a bear.

I had learnt as a kid that people can be mean. He would hit her until she had no more noise inside of her and on top of that, the kids on our street would never leave us alone, breaking our windows and putting fire through our letterbox. One night she was crying; she said she had accidentally cut herself on a broken bottle. That was a lie. I was nearly a man and wanted to confront him and maybe try out my spring action Kung Fu-style but instead I went to the shop to fetch bandages. They told me she lit a milk bottle full of petrol, threw it inside and locked the door on my dad, and that she was about to light another for the next-door house when the kids on the street knocked her to the ground. He was rescued and went back to live in Pakistan. She was sent to a hospital for the rest of her life.

I was nearly seventeen so they showed me to a room at a hostel and there was a pool table downstairs and one day soon after, a man came and asked me what I was good at and I said running. He laughed but it was no laughing matter. I could outrun everybody I knew and still go further and if I paced myself I never needed to stop. At the hostel I would just take off and run all day, having adventures and pretending I was a soldier on an undercover mission, and I would find places to hide, in case the Ruskies came in their tanks. From a ditch next to the motorway I would fire grenades at them. Boom. Boom. Boom. One by one, the tanks would split open and burn, and by the time they had worked out where the fire was coming from I had escaped and was ten miles up the road. I told him I wanted to fly helicopters in the Army Air Corps but he said the best runners were in the Infantry, and anyway, if I applied myself I could work my way up. He promised to make a few calls and the next thing I knew a letter arrived for me with a rail voucher and I was free and for the first time in my life I took the train and the bus, all the way from Old Hill to Catterick and it was all paid for by the government.

The MO didn't like my chest. He listened to it and said it was too hollow and that my heart didn't beat fast enough, but I knew things about me he didn't, like how I had trained my body to the rigorous routine of an endurance athlete. I measured my heart rate every day and had got it down to an average of forty-five beats per minute and that was dedication, and I knew if I carried on like that then one day someone would notice and maybe put me into the SAS, but I didn't like buckets of sand because to get in you had to run with them for ten miles and they cut your thighs to ribbons. I knew I would have to practise for that. Maybe there was a special way of holding them or you just let yourself get cut and they fixed you up afterwards, once you had earned the *Who Dares Wins* badge on your beret.

I'LL TAKE THE PAKI.

The starter pistol went and we all started running and the Corporal was running alongside me and shouting nasty words in my face. I stopped at the first station, got into the prone position, trained the sights of my rifle and discharged one round at the pop-up target. It fell down. I got back to my feet, slung the rifle over my shoulder, climbed an obstacle, stopped at station number two, and fired from the standing position. One round and the target went down. I got up again and started running, and then with my rifle six inches off the ground and held in front, I crawled through a tunnel full of rat piss and shit, hit the ground again and made it to station number three. From the kneeling position, I banged the target in one. I was enjoying it and started running again but as I was running the Corporal kept punching me. I ignored the first two that landed but then I made a mistake and looked over at him and the sun caught my eyes, and just then my foot didn't see a ditch in the rutted ground and I toppled over. My rifle went sideways and accidentally discharged one round into the air.

I heard a whistle and the Corporal was screaming at the top of his voice.

STOP. STOP. STOP.

Everybody stopped wherever they were and unloaded their rifles, holding their magazine in one hand and presenting a clear chamber in the other. They all looked at me and their big open mouths didn't even need to say anything. I knew they were going to kill me.

And then the Corporal was kicking into me and my hollow chest was bruising and I didn't like that because I knew it would hurt for weeks after and stop me running my fastest.

YOU FUCKING PAKI. YOU COULD HAVE FUCKING KILLED SOMEBODY. I'M PUTTING YOU ON A FUCKING CHARGE, YOU CUNT. THE CO WILL HEAR ABOUT THIS.

Finally I was allowed to get up and my nose was bleeding and my chest hurt so much it felt like it was cracked.

He retrieved my rifle, removed the magazine and after checking the chamber he thrust it back at me.

I DON'T WANT TO SEE YOU AGAIN, YOU CUNT. GET UP THERE AND DISASSEMBLE YOUR WEAPON.

He pointed to a small wooden hut on a mound overlooking the range about a hundred yards away. As I was limping away I heard him instruct the others to reload and for a moment I thought they were going to shoot me, but instead they carried on with the Live Fire Exercise.

The hut was full of metal ammo boxes. I had never seen so

much ammo in my life. Miles and miles of belts full of hundreds of sparkling 7.62s, all neatly folded up like the biggest pack of felt-tip pens you have ever seen. Lying on the grass outside and pointing towards the range was a big gun on a tripod and the minute I clapped eyes on it I went, *Whoa fucking hell the GPMG!* And I was really loud but thankfully no one heard. We hadn't learnt machine guns yet and I had never been this close to one before, but I knew the GPMG. Who didn't know about the GPMG. It was German-engineered and in uninterrupted issue since World War Two. It spat out seven hundred and fifty 7.62 rounds per minute and could kill an enemy at more than a mile away.

I touched it and no one saw. The recruits were too busy aiming the muzzles of their rifles into the sun and every few minutes, upon reaching a station, they would all fire. Bum. Bum. Bum. I placed several heavy ammo boxes next to the GPMG, fell into the prone position and swung off the cover-tray. I pulled an ammo belt out of its metal case and laid one end inside a depression in the tray. It fitted nicely. I clicked the cover-tray neatly shut and switched the safety to off.

Jamming the butt tight in my shoulder and adjusting my eyes to the sights I trained it on the Corporal. Bum-bum-bum. He clutched at his chest and his face was all surprise, then one last round and he toppled over. Then Sergeant Skitt, who had been laughing with the Corporal. Bum-bum-bum and his head split open. For a moment he swayed on his feet and then he fell down. Mr Moyles, our Lieutenant, was talking into a radio receiver. Bum-bum-bum. He fell over when a shard of shrapnel flung off the radio and split open his eye. Then I picked off Smithy the dunce and one by one the others: Elliot who had two babies, Norris who I had never talked to, Gordon who had a motorbike, Clappison who was posh, Griffin who knew all the names of the plants and flowers, Sharp whose dad was once in the Regiment, Cryer who had been to college and could have been an Officer, Binnington who had thick arms, and Nonce who was a loud-mouth. They ran in straight lines and never took their eyes off the wooden targets and as they stopped to shoot they made easy prey.

Bum-bum-bum, bum-bum-bum, three rounds each, two in the chest and a final one in the head, and when they were all down the rain started and washed the blood and brains and guts and eyes into the green of the grass. It was then that I remembered art class at school and the teacher saying, *Red and green should never be seen except with yellow in between.*

I was still thinking about that when I felt a red-hot electric shock in my temple.

Before I could even blink I realised I couldn't move because the Corporal had the blunt tip of his rifle jammed into the side of my head. I felt a smear of warm blood trickle from my ear and tasted it as it seeped through a crack between my lips and into my mouth.

HEY RECRUIT, WHAT THE FUCK DO YOU THINK YOU'RE PLAYING AT?

There was a pause and it gave me time to take in the ease of my capture. I thought about rolling to one side and attempting a spring-action Kung Fu-style flying kick. I thought about the jailhouse by the gates and Siberia.

HANG ON – IS THAT THING LOADED?

Dead Leg
MAGGIE WOMERSLEY

Eileen began each visit to her gym like a mouse in a lab maze, scurrying across the spongy blue mats of the warm-up area, dodging between the shoulder press and the thigh cruncher, and weaving in and out of the phalanx of StairMasters until she reached the cycle machines against the far wall. Here she would hoick herself into position, ideally on the third bike from the end if it was free, before settling her water bottle, phone and towel around her like talismans. She didn't enjoy going to the gym, but it was important at her age to stay active; everybody said so.

Flickering images from the bank of TV screens caught her attention as she cycled. Two of them were showing the same pop video: a half-naked singer with skin the colour of Bourbon biscuits, undulating like a boa constrictor down a wet pole. Looking at that was no good. It only reminded her of Joan showing off – Joan dancing round the maypole when they were children, Joan giving it some sex in a Footlights review.

One of the other screens was tuned to rolling news. Eileen watched and pedalled and clenched her teeth as three flag-wrapped coffins were unloaded from the hold of a plane. The precise movements of the pallbearers, stepping forwards then sideways then backwards, was like a slow-motion quickstep. The camera zoomed in to show the men's faces, pale and serious under the stiff, starched peaks of their stuffed-down hats, backs rigid with the sacred task of carrying their fallen comrades. Eileen puffed out noisily and stared at the brave, sad scene, angry at Joan all over again, not just for making a tasteless joke out of death, but for roping her into it as well. Meanwhile a ticker-tape beneath the images reeled off some midweek football fixtures.

Normally on a Wednesday Eileen was at work, standing in her navy-blue courts behind the reception desk at the BBC's White City building. For eight hours a day, three days a week, she helped visitors with their enquiries, doled out name badges and gave directions. Sometimes she was so busy she barely had time to take the weight off her feet. She didn't like to talk to visitors sitting down, it felt rude and unprofessional, although her younger colleagues had no qualms. "You'll give yourself varicose veins, if you don't watch out," they said. But Eileen didn't think she would. After all, she had joined a gym, hadn't she?

Now it was time to hobble over to the slalom machine, a deeply unpleasant apparatus that always reminded Eileen of a science fiction film she'd once seen by mistake (Joan had made her go) in which the heroine put on a set of robotic arms and legs to fight an alien, in the same way Eileen might pull on her old overcoat and Wellington boots to take the compost out.

She slotted her feet into the giant ski paddles and clambered aboard. A dapper little man with a face like a squashed toby jug appeared on one of the TV screens. The camera cut away to an auctioneer holding up his gavel, and then to a close-up of a grotesque figurine. Eileen liked the *Antiques Roadshow* (who didn't?) but disapproved of this programme which was just a silly game. Joan had been on it once; a celebrity special. She told Eileen afterwards that she'd had the time of her life running around the car-boot sales, chatting up the auctioneer, giving out autographs. The Victorian commode she'd paid a couple of quid for had made sixty-five pounds at the auction, causing Joan to shed melodramatic tears.

Eileen tutted under her breath and looked back at the news. The coffins had gone, and a procession of long black cars was gliding out of shot. Going, going, gone, thought Eileen as she bore down on the exercise machine with renewed vigour. Then a horrible thought occurred to her – what if Joan expected *her* to act as some kind of coffinbearer? Well, Eileen would simply refuse.

She had reached her limit over the whole horrible business.

Three days before her sister's operation, Eileen had visited her in the hospital. The leg had been caged under the blankets like a malevolent pet.

"It's me or it," Joan had said. "How do you make a choice like that?"

"Well you don't want to die, do you?"

"I suppose not." Joan had lunged across the bed and clasped one of Eileen's hands. Her grip had been slimy with hand cream, or was it sweat? "I know you think I'm crazy, but I just couldn't bear it if they incinerated it like a hunk of old steak."

"Joan!"

Ever since her sister had divulged her Great Idea about the leg, Eileen had felt queasy just thinking about it. To distract them both from the topic, she pretended to hear her mobile ringing in her handbag.

"It might be work," she explained, freeing herself from Joan's clutches and fumbling about in her bag for the silent phone.

Joan raised her eyes to heaven. "Why do you always have to get so embarrassed? I'm the one this is happening to."

"I'm not," Eileen had said defensively. "I just don't know why you want to draw attention to the whole thing as if it was some kind of performance. And if you must go ahead with it, why do I have to be involved?"

"We're sisters for Christ's sake. Why can't you support me for once?"

The way Joan looked at her then had reminded Eileen of when they were children and Joan was forever trying to make her do things she didn't want to – like climbing very tall trees or running into the sea when the waves were too big.

But who'd ever heard of holding a funeral for a leg?

Typical Joan; she wasn't happy unless she was having her cake and eating it, and now she was getting her own way over this leg business too, even though the doctors thought she was crazy, and the priest – poor man – clearly disapproved.

"You'd think I'd asked him to conduct a black mass, the way he went on," Joan had complained. "But then the papers got hold of it and the people at the radio station sent a reporter, and now it's all going ahead. I've had to pay for a full-size plot but it's close to Mum and Dad. I know I always said I wanted to be scattered on the Heath but I've changed my mind – burial's best. Look, here's the brochure. I've gone for the white casket with the gold handles." She held out a pamphlet with a Post-it note sticking out. "It's a bit more expensive than the others, but I'm only going to do this once, so what the hell."

She could have been talking about buying a new dress or ordering a birthday cake. Eileen looked at the picture, appalled.

"Joan, do you realise this is for a *child*?"

Joan shrugged. "Don't make it sound so morbid, Eileen. Can't you just look on the positive side for once? Everyone else thinks it's a wonderful idea."

Her voice trailed off and she looked down at the boxy object under the hospital blankets.

"But *why*, Joan?"

"Why *not*? And anyway, when the Day of Judgement comes I don't want to have to hop into heaven, do I?"

Eileen threw the brochure onto the bedside table. "You're not even religious. You haven't been to church for years."

"I'm deeply spiritual." Joan fiddled with the buttons on her bedjacket and pursed her lips.

Eileen had known there was no point pursuing the subject, so she pretended to be interested in some of the Get Well cards on the windowsill. One of them was from an actor Joan had once had an affair with.

"I just think the whole thing is undignified," she said quietly, as she arranged the cards so that they were all facing front.

Joan slumped back on her pillows looking sulky. "I'm sorry you feel that way, but that's just how I am."

And there was no arguing with that.

Eileen was in the shower now, standing under the pummelling water. She'd kept her boyish figure, unlike Joan whose curves had spilled over considerably since the menopause. Not that Joan seemed to notice – she still wore the same floaty, Bohemian styles that had suited her thirty years ago; too much crushed velvet, not enough structured underwear.

At the lockers Eileen towelled herself off and ran a comb through her short, wet hair, the same colour now as the wirewool pads their mother had cleaned the pots with when they were children. Eileen didn't think there was much point dying your hair past a certain age, though Joan of course still dyed hers an optimistic shade of auburn.

Outside in the car park Eileen placed her gym bag in the boot of her car and inspected the front passenger seat. Joan had said her wheelchair folded down neatly, but in Eileen's experience Joan never got that kind of detail right. She couldn't help wondering a little bitterly why not one of the many male escorts that her sister had flaunted over the years was now available to drive Joan and her leg to their final adieu. Why did it have to be Eileen? Eileen who hated fuss and emotion, who got on with things, however unpleasant or tedious, who had never lost a leg, or her heart or her inhibitions.

As she drove towards the main road, Eileen thought again of the dead soldiers and their mothers waiting in the wings to bury them. An uncharacteristic welling-up of grief threatened to stick in her throat like a dry cake crumb. She had no children of her own and neither did Joan, which all things considered was probably for the best, but just sometimes she wished there was somebody younger with a future to care about and plan for.

She edged out into the afternoon traffic and hoped that an accident might happen. Nothing too serious, just debilitating enough to put a stop to all this nonsense. On the invitation Joan had scribbled something about a finger buffet before the service. She'd hired the same caterers that Eileen had booked for their parents' wake, and actually sent invitations – black-edged and written in Gothic script. *Joan Elizabeth Rose requests the pleasure of your company at a memorial service and burial ceremony for her leg. Wednesday 23rd March at 3pm, St Christopher's Chapel, and afterwards at The Good Companion for light refreshments.*

She pulled into the bottom of Joan's road, and glanced anxiously about for a parking space. There were some people she vaguely recognised lolling about on the steps up to Joan's block; smoking cigarettes in that dogged way people adopt when they are about to do something unpleasant. They watched her as she drove past, making her blush and hunker down in her seat.

The party announced itself as soon as she stepped out of the lift. Joan's front door was open and people with drinks and loud, look-at-me voices had overflowed into the communal hall. Most of Joan's friends were theatre types or "telly folk", a lot of them much younger than her and, as the years went by, the men invariably gay. Sometimes Eileen saw them at the BBC, coming in for a meeting or to record a show, but they never remembered her as Joan's sister, and that was fine by her.

The tinkling of Joan's piano could be heard coming from the sitting room, so putting her head down as she might in a hailstorm, Eileen set her course in that direction. There was a fug in the air that made her sneezy; a medley of perfumes, patchouli oil and sausage rolls. But around the bathroom door a faintly medical smell like disinfectant or Elastoplast cut through the pong like a knife through butter-icing. She pushed on through the crowd into the sitting room and there was Joan, in a wheelchair next to the piano, her coppery hair backlit by the spring sunshine and her complexion distinctly rosy. She spotted Eileen straightaway.

"Here she is, my long-lost sister Eileen. Let her through please, ladies and gentlemen."

People turned to stare, broke off conversations and moved out of the way. Eileen felt mortified and sweaty.

"Hello Eileen," somebody from the back of the room shouted out, and then everyone was saying it. "Hello Eileen! Look, Eileen's here, now we can really start the party. Get her a drink somebody, it's Eileen!" Laughter rang out and somebody pressed a glass of wine into her hand. A young foreign-looking girl in waitress garb offered her a tray of blinis smeared in grey paste. Eileen's throat contracted.

"Come over here and meet my new best friend," Joan called out to her and obediently Eileen stumbled towards the piano. Joan tilted her face to one side to be kissed. "You won't mind if I don't get up," she said, and the young man sitting on the piano stool laughed out loud, spraying the air with tiny molecules of grey blini.

"Your sister is amazing," he said.

"Yes," Eileen replied, attempting to lick some life back into her lips. "She's very brave."

"Oh shut up!" Joan said, jiggling around in her seat. "I'm not brave at all. I've cried for days and I'll probably cry again later, once this wears off." She waggled her wine glass in their faces. "Eileen, this is Bruce. He's a lovely, lovely boy and he's going to push me up the aisle later so we must be nice to him. Bruce, this is my little sister Eileen. She works at the BBC."

A hawkish interest entered Bruce's eyes. "Really? What do you do?"

"Oh not like *that*." Joan laughed, then to Eileen she said in a mock whisper, "Actors, they're all the same – one-track minds."

Bruce wandered off to "see some people", and said he would meet them later at the cemetery. Eileen perched herself on half of the piano stool and out of habit opened her handbag and checked her phone. There were no messages.

"So you came then," Joan said, a twinkle of triumph in her eyes. "What do you think?"

"Of the party?"

"No, stupid, what do you think of my new leg?"

Eileen took a deep breath and looked down at her sister's lap. Joan was wearing a long, dark-red taffeta skirt that fell in deep folds around her ankles. *Ankles*, thought Eileen; she hadn't expected that.

"This one's just for show – the hospital lent it to me. I'll have to get a proper one fitted soon."

Eileen stared at the shape under her sister's skirt. "It looks very realistic."

"Yes but it feels a bit odd. I'm not sure it's on properly. We'll have to be careful when we go into the chapel." Joan was scanning the room now, sipping away at her glass, waving and smiling at people who were waving and smiling back. "Quite a good turnout," she said vaguely. "More than I expected." A camera flash went off and Eileen blinked like a mole.

Joan squealed with delight. "No pictures!" she said, pretending to be cross. "Oh go on then, take a proper one." She rattled the wheelchair. "Does my bum look big in this?"

A howl of laughter bowled around the room.

"Isn't she *marvellous*?" somebody said.

The lunch party droned on for another hour until finally someone shouted, "Oh my God, look at the time," and hurriedly, giggling and staggering, the guests began to reach for coats and bags and artistically knotted scarves. "See you there, Joan!" they called as they banged their way out of the flat. Eileen was glad to have some air at last; the windows had all fogged up and she had a distinct headache.

Joan sighed and looked suddenly tired. "Come on, you'll have to help me to the bathroom."

Eileen got up and went behind her sister's chair to push. The thought struck her like a sly kick: she had never pushed a wheelchair before. She applied a bit of experimental pressure, but the wheels merely rocked in the thick pile of the sitting-room carpet.

"Are the brakes on?" she asked, her mouth dry again, her head throbbing.

"No, silly, you just need to give it some welly."

Eileen tried again and this time the chair wobbled unenthusiastically forward. They made a slow journey into the hallway as the slim young women in black skirts and white blouses buzzed past them carrying dirty plates. At the doorway to the bathroom the chair knocked against the skirting.

"We're on foot from here," Joan said. "I need to get the doorway adapted for the chair, or the chair adapted for the doorway, I can't remember which."

"OK," Eileen said, uncertainly. "What should I do?"

Joan shot her an impatient look; she seemed deflated now that her guests had gone.

"You'll have to come round the front and help me out. I think I'm going to detach this leg now." She was already fiddling with something through her skirt. Eileen looked away.

"Shouldn't you have someone coming round to help you with all this?"

Joan was beginning to pant with the effort of loosening the false leg. "I will have from tonight. I told them I didn't need anyone today because my sister would be here to look after me. There, I've got it." Something pinkish slithered to the floor. "Prop it up against the wall in the bedroom, and hurry up for God's sake. We don't want to keep Bruce waiting."

"Heaven forbid," Eileen muttered, stooping to retrieve the leg.

It looked a bit pocked in places, as though it had seen rather a lot of wear and tear. There was a slipper and a pop sock over the foot, matching the one on Joan's real leg.

"It's not how I imagined," she said, stroking the shin and running her hand around the knee joint.

"Oh don't look at it, Eileen," Joan snapped. "It's just a prop really. I'm getting my own one soon."

Eileen placed the leg carefully against the wall in the bedroom. Then she moved round to the front of the wheelchair and took hold of Joan's arms. There was a frightening moment when the chair lurched about, but then Joan was upright, clutching at Eileen and looking directly into her eyes.

"Still taller than you," she said with a half smile that almost broke the tension. She was stiff and light in Eileen's grasp. "You go backwards and I'll hop towards you."

They made their way into the bathroom like two drunken sailors dancing a reel. Eileen got her as close to the lavatory as she could and then manoeuvred her around so that she could sit down.

"I can take it from here,' Joan barked, a little breathlessly. "You'd better wait while I pee, if you can bear it."

Eileen scurried to the bathroom door and drew it closed. She pulled the lock across and then stared at Joan's dressing gown and shower cap hanging on the peg. She could hear Joan's laboured breathing a few feet away, and the sounds of skirts being swished about. Her headache prowled inside her brain.

A sudden burst of laughter and footsteps in the hallway made her catch her breath. Some guests had returned to retrieve something. A female voice just outside the bathroom said, "Oh here it is, still on the hook. I thought that bloody critic from the *Telegraph* might have snatched it." There was the sound of coats and jackets being moved about, then: "Oh look, she's left her wheelchair behind. Don't tell me she's going to try and walk on that dodgy falsey." Another female voice replied, "Oh, you know Joan. She'll probably do a can-can down the aisle." More tipsy laughter.

Eileen turned slowly to look at Joan, who held a finger up to her lips and shook her head.

"I don't care what anyone says about Joan, though," the first voice continued. "I think she's bloody *marvellous* for doing all this.

I'm so glad we came. You get that feeling that she's not going to be around for much longer, don't you?"

Joan's eyes were wide and frozen into a stare. Eileen wondered if she should perhaps cough, or call out and let the harpies in the hall know they weren't alone.

The second woman was speaking again. "Still, at least she's got that sister to look after her – she won't have to go into a home just yet."

Joan winced.

The other voice laughed. "Talk about chalk and cheese. I don't envy Joan being stuck with that dead weight all her life. Do you think she's wearing that navy-blue suit for a laugh? She looks just like a traffic warden."

More shrill laughter. "You're such a bitch! Come on, hurry up, the taxi's probably here by now."

The front door crashed shut and only the distant sound of someone vacuuming disturbed the silence in the bathroom. Eileen opened the door and peeked out. Her coat was lying in a heap on the floor. When she looked back she saw that her sister had closed her eyes and slumped slightly against the wall.

"Are you all right?" she whispered.

"Yes, just give me a moment."

Eileen stepped into the hall, closing the door gently on the tentative sound of her sister's pee. She went through to the bedroom and saw that the leg had slipped onto the floor. She picked it up and cradled it in her arms.

Fifteen minutes later and they were in the car, pulling out into traffic on the Finchley Road.

"I need cigarettes," Joan snapped from the passenger seat. They were the first words she'd said since getting into the car.

"Well I can't stop here, it's a bus lane."

"There's a space over there in front of the bank. You can get fags in Waitrose."

Eileen slammed on the indicator and dived across two lanes of traffic.

"Just ignore him," Joan muttered as a black-cab driver tooted furiously.

Eileen felt her stomach lurch with embarrassment. It had been stressful enough getting Joan into the car. She'd had to ask the porter from Joan's building to stand in the road and watch for traffic as she double-parked and then quickly but slowly, carefully but clumsily helped Joan hop down the steps. There was a set of crutches but Joan wasn't used to them yet, and the wheelchair had to be abandoned at the top.

"We're getting the ramp in next week," the porter yelled up at them from his lookout in the middle of the road. "Ten bloody grand for a bit of cement and a handrail. It's a licence to print money if you ask me." He seemed personally affronted, as if the money was coming out of his own pocket. "Better hurry up, there's a bus coming."

Now she was leaping out of the car to get cigarettes for Joan who would no doubt want to smoke them straightaway, even though she knew the smell made Eileen feel sick.

"What kind do you want?"

"Don't care." Joan shrugged, not even looking up. "Marlboros or Bensons – no, get me Superkings. And some chewing gum – not menthol."

Eileen slammed the door and tried to avoid getting knocked down by passing traffic. She was getting a bit sick of Joan barking orders, missing leg or no missing leg. Perhaps Joan wanted to be late on purpose, like some kind of blushing bride. Eileen pictured the chapel of rest at the cemetery, and Joan's so-called friends sniggering in the pews while they waited. At least the leg in its obscene coffin would be there already; discreetly delivered by the funeral directors at no reduced cost whatsoever.

There was a queue in Waitrose and Eileen resigned herself to it. Glancing through the shop window towards her car she thought she saw two men getting into the back and another one leaning on the passenger window. But that couldn't be right. A woman behind her coughed meaningfully and Eileen stepped forward to close the gap. When she looked back at the car she was even more confused. Why was Joan pressing her face into the windscreen like that?

"Can I help you, madam?" the shop assistant was saying now, but Eileen's attention was split. There were definitely two strange men sitting in the back of her car and another one hammering his fist on the roof. Then she heard it – the shrieking of sirens and the wailing of bells. Something must have happened in one of the shops. The man was trying to open the passenger door, and waving something around in the air. It looked like a gun.

Eileen dashed out of Waitrose and raced towards her car. A fourth man in a ski mask was sitting in the driver's seat, banging the steering wheel as though he thought that was how to make the car go. She could hear screaming now, not just Joan's but from the men too, their high-pitched swearing and shouting almost as piercing as the alarm going off in the bank.

The bank.

Eileen had reached the car now, and Joan was gazing out at her with a drowning, desperate expression on her face. The three men in the car all seemed to have their hands on her at once, pulling and pushing her about. They hadn't realised that Joan wasn't going anywhere without Eileen to prop her up and push her wheelchair.

"Get your hands off her," Eileen screeched at the lot of them, before whacking the man who was still on the pavement with her bag. He crumpled under the attack, more out of surprise than from the force of the blows, but at least it stopped him hammering on the car roof with his gun, and screaming at her sister to "fucking open the fucking door and get the fuck out".

A swarm of blue lights swooped around a corner, and a new aural assault rang out across the Finchley Road. Traffic screeched to a halt in every lane and policemen were suddenly everywhere, diving in and out of the traffic, sprinting along the pavement, and yelling at each other like football players in a particularly spread-out game. The robbers reacted in an explosion of arms and legs, making a run for it in four different directions. All in all it was an exhilarating sight.

A whimpering sound drew Eileen's attention back to the car. Joan was winding down her window.

"Eileen," she wailed, her eye make-up all over her hot pink cheeks. "Have they gone? I've wet myself. We'll have to go back and change."

A couple of hours later, in a pleasant room at Hampstead police station, Eileen and Joan sat drinking tea and giving their statements. A very nice young policewoman had helped Joan sort herself out with a change of clothes, and had even recognised her from one of her old TV shows. In fact Joan didn't seem too worse for wear, considering. Eileen thought that if *she* had publicly wet her knickers she'd probably have to kill herself, but Joan was an earthier type and the excitement of being caught up in a real-live bank job had done much to diminish her earlier waspishness. They had of course missed the whole service at the chapel of rest, which according to Bruce, who had phoned shortly afterwards, had actually been quite moving. The priest had evidently risen to the task, despite his religious misgivings.

As she watched her sister flirting with a young detective, Eileen remembered how the drunk woman from the party had called her a dead weight, as if she was the part of Joan that really needed amputating. The comment hadn't upset Eileen in the least – the woman was clearly a lush with a poor sense of self-control – but Joan had been upset on her behalf, and remembering that now brought on a sudden rush of love for her sister the like of which Eileen hadn't experienced for close on fifty years. She found herself thinking back to a picnic when they were children. She'd been about ten or eleven and Joan, of course, a little bit older. They'd gone off on their own to explore and Joan had found a particularly challenging tree to climb. Eileen remembered the way her sister's legs had felt in her arms as she boosted her up towards the lower branches; the knuckle of Joan's bony knees in the hammock of her hands, the soles of her bare feet, dirty and dry. All so that Joan could pull herself six, perhaps eight feet above the ground. Frighteningly high up, Eileen had thought at the time. Until finally there was Joan, triumphant and laughing, sitting astride a silvery-green branch with her two perfectly matching legs, slightly chafed and red with Eileen's thumb prints, dangling down around Eileen's head.

"You can see for miles from here. Why don't I pull you up?"

"No thanks," the ten-year-old Eileen had replied. "I'm all right down here." And she still was.

Violet
ALEXANDER KNIGHTS

AMT_15,330,364.seq

"When I do count the clock that tells the time, comma. And see the brave day sunk in hideous night, semicolon. When I behold the violet –"

I hold my quill poised.

"What's the matter?" I ask. "Why have you stopped?"

"Violet," she says. "That's my name."

I lift the quill away from the page; the tip is worn and the ink might drip.

"Yes, it is."

"The sky is violet."

"Yes, that's true."

I place the quill carefully down onto the aluminium workspace and look out through the window. The sky could be said to be violet, though there are also hues of lavender and plum. Across the canyon, in the tower that obscures the setting sun, a handful of ember flares has already been lit; thin streams of smoke trail southwards. On the window before me, two drops of condensation draw together and roll down the pane.

"The sky is violet," she says again.

Down to ground level.

"Violets are blue . . ."

The ground to which I'll return.

"Sugar is sweet . . ."

Where will she return to, I wonder.

"And so are you."

When the lithium runs out.

I reach for my stick, and use it to pivot in my chair until I am facing her. In the gloom, her pale skin is luminescent. Shadows traverse the tendons in her neck. Her ears are suspended in her straight black hair like white half-moons.

Not long before the harvest moon.

"Look at me."

She looks up.

"Don't be sad."

A pout, a smile.

"I'm not sad, Alan."

I turn back to the workspace, the parchment, the inkwell, the quill. Through the tears my eyes follow the quill's curved shaft, from the top of the feather to the tip of the calamus where the black ink gathers. I flatten out the parchment – calf skin, flayed, soaked and stretched.

"Shall I continue?" she asks.

I take up the quill.

"Please."

"Past prime, comma. And –"

"Hold on, stop a moment. Thank you. Could you start again from 'When I behold', please, Violet?"

"When I behold the violet past prime, comma . . ."

Her voice carries to my ears, ink flows from my quill, words appear on the page.

"And sable curls ensilver'd o'er with white, semicolon. When lofty trees I see barren of leaves, comma . . ."

An image forms in my mind – dead leaves.

"Which erst from heat did canopy the herd, comma. And summer's green all girded up in sheaves, new line. Borne on –"

"Stop. Is that 'borne' with an 'e' or without an 'e'?"

"With an 'e'."

Dead leaves from dying trees.

"OK, start again from 'borne'."

"Borne on the bier with white and bristly beard, colon –"

"Stop there, Violet."

A memory of ground level. My hands, encompassed by larger hands. Dead leaves gathered in piles. The hands lift me; I swing between them and scatter the leaves. In the air, the smell of burning.

My last memory of the last trees.

"Oh, Violet."

From my quill a drop of ink has fallen, like a tear, and spattered across the parchment. I must let it dry as it is, and hope the Society will let it pass.

"Oh, Violet. Don't leave me."

I heave myself, stick push by stick push, across the room. Slowly, gracelessly, I lower myself onto the camp bed and lie across it, my head in her lap, looking up to the shadowed curve of her neck. Slowly, gracefully, her fingers pass through my thin white hair, as they have done since it was as black as hers.

"We'll get the lithium."

AMT_15,340,216.seq

The acrid tang of spent embers hangs in the air. Light from the harvest moon filters through the glass roof. Just enough to illuminate a circle of men. Heads bowed, they are silent, as they always are before a reading.

The circle breaks and a cowled man steps towards me, his eyes shadowed wells.

"Alan, good evening. How are you?"

I look down at the folds in his cowl.

"Mr Chairman."

"You look tired. Burning the candle at both ends?"

"I don't sleep."

"Ah, well, a man in your position has greater things to occupy himself with."

"I think too much."

"And how is the dark lady?"

Blood draws through my capillaries.

"I'd rather you didn't mention her."

"But we're so grateful to her and her voluminous memory."

"Could we get to the matter in hand?"

"We're so curious to meet her."

"Mr Chairman?"

"Yes?"

"The matter in hand."

"Ah, yes, the matter in hand. Very good. The matter in hand. I like it. Hand me the matter in hand."

A hand emerges from his cowl, I pass the roll of parchment, it disappears within.

"Have you made any progress, Mr Chairman?"

"Will you stay and join us for the reading, Alan?"

"On the lithium, Mr Chairman. Is there any progress?"

"We have world enough, and time, Alan."

"You said it was being shipped."

"An ancient method."

"I was to finish half of the re-inscription of the Sonnets for the harvest moon."

"But we like the ancients, don't we?"

"Mr Chairman, please."

"Settle down, Alan."

Saliva draws down my pharynx.

"Violet needs the lithium, very soon."

"We can't have her running out of steam, can we?"

"She won't be able to produce any more poetry."

"Maybe it's you that's using her up."

"No."

"Surely, you must –"

"No."

"Let us sport us while we may."

Gall draws into my stomach.

"How do I know the lithium is coming, Mr Chairman?"

"The grave's a fine and private place . . ."

"Mr Chairman."

"But none I think do there embrace."

"Why should we continue with the re-inscription?"

"It's coming, Alan. Be patient. As you know, we meet next by the hunter's moon. Bring us the completed Sonnets, and we will honour our little bargain."

"Thank you, Mr Chairman."

I turn to leave.

"Oh, and Alan?"

"Yes, Mr Chairman."

"Do bring Violet."

Tears draw through my lachrymal ducts.

"That wasn't part of the arrangement."

"But we're dying to meet her. She can speak poetry directly to us."

"I can't agree to that."

"How does she sound? In full throat?"

"Mr Chairman."

"I do hope she's not coy."

"She can't come."

The Chairman laughs.

"A coy sex robot."

My fingers draw into fists.

"She's not up to it."

"But we are, Alan. Bring the Sonnets, bring Violet, and we will bring the lithium."

AMT_15,361,579.seq

I pull off my gloves and pick up the Meal, Ready-to-Eat carton, keeping it tilted. I hold it for a moment while the exothermic heater warms my hands. Then I pull out the MRE itself and lift the lid. Steam rises from the grey contents, the smell gathers in my nostrils, my mouth salivates.

"Would you like some?" I ask. "It's maple sausage."

"You first, Alan."

"I'm not that hungry. Go on."

She holds my gaze as she forks a sausage, raises it to her lips, bites and chews, bites and chews.

"Mouth-watering."

The light from the candle refracts across her cheekbones and reflects from the lacquered surface of her eyes. A low wind drones through the breeze blocks.

"Do you remember the first time we met?"

"I remember, Alan."

"At the Cave of the Golden Calf."

"Yes."

"I asked you to come with me."

"Yes."

"And you came."

"Yes."

"After the performance, we talked. I knew it would be pointless, but I said: 'Shall I compare thee to a summer's day?' And you said –"

"Thou art more lovely and more temperate."

"I never asked you why. There were others. Why did you come?"

"I love you, Alan."

"Really, why did you come with me?"

She leans forward, her pupils retracting as she nears the candle. There is a tear in the neckline of her dress.

"I'm very obliging, Alan. Would you like to see?"

Another line from her book of responses. I feel again as if I'm talking directly to her author.

"No, thank you, Violet. Not tonight."

"Are we going to finish the Sonnets now, Alan?"

The wind hums with greater force. The candle flame crouches and spits.

"It's too late."

I turn to the window, look across the canyon and follow a trail of embers upwards, all the way to the hunter's moon.

"Who made you, Violet?"

"You made me who I am."

"But who actually made you, Violet?"

"Sublunary Sex Systems, Shilong IDA, Beijing, China."

"Who am I talking to, Violet?"

"Shakespeare."

"Who is your maker?"

"God made me, Alan."

Notes on Contributors

Nick Alexander grew up in the seaside town of Margate. He has travelled widely and lived in the UK, the USA and France, where he resides today. Nick's first five novels – the Fifty Reasons series – were self-published from 2004 onwards and went on to become some of the UK's best-selling gay literature. In March 2011 his crossover title, *The Case of the Missing Boyfriend*, reached #1 in Amazon's Kindle chart, and was ranked #27 in the overall UK ebook chart for that year after netting over 70,000 downloads. Subsequent to this, Nick was signed by publishers Corvus Atlantic, who have taken over his full backlist and committed to publishing future titles. For more information please visit the author's website on www.nick-alexander.com.

Jenn Ashworth's first novel, *A Kind of Intimacy*, was published by Arcadia in 2009 and won a Betty Trask Award. Her second, *Cold Light*, was published in 2011 by Sceptre. She was featured on the BBC's *Culture Show* as one of the UK's twelve best new writers. Her third novel, *The Friday Gospels*, is the story of a Mormon family living in Lancashire, and is due out in January 2013 (Sceptre). Jenn writes an award-winning blog at www.jennashworth.co.uk/blog.

Julia Bell is a novelist and Senior Lecturer on the Birkbeck Creative Writing MA. She is the author of two novels – *Massive* (Macmillan, 2002) and *Dirty Work* (Macmillan, 2007) – and a co-editor of *The*

Creative Writing Coursebook (Macmillan, 2001). She is currently working on a new novel and a collection of short stories.

Phoebe Blatton grew up in South-East London. She studied Fine Art at Goldsmiths College, and has worked for a number of years in the art book trade. In 2008 she co-founded *The Coelacanth Journal*, and publishes this alongside a number of related projects, publications and collaborations. She is currently a student at Birkbeck on the MA in Creative Writing.

Tanya Datta has travelled to some of the furthest reaches of the world in her former incarnation as a foreign-affairs journalist. These days, however, she's more likely to be pushing the boundaries of her imagination since returning to her first love – writing fiction. Currently studying on Birkbeck's MA in Creative Writing, Tanya is working on a collection of short stories set amongst the Indian diaspora.

Born in Croydon, South London, **Terence James Eeles** is an '80s child, Crystal Palace season-ticket holder, Amiga nostalgist, mp3 hussy, West Country graduate, library connoisseur, slow reader and Wikislut. He works in the West End in retail visual display. Writing subversive, lyrical and motif-driven fiction, in 2011 Terry was commended and shortlisted in the Manchester Fiction and Bridport Short Story prizes. His story "Lemming" (which he is expanding into a black-comedy novel) will be appearing in an upcoming anthology edited by Chuck Palahniuk. "The Trojan Horse Mixtape" is from a collection of linked stories. His parents are awesome.

Paul Flack grew up in Stevenage, Hertfordshire. He has an MA in Creative Writing from University College Chichester, and is currently looking for an agent to market a dramatic coming-of-age novel, set on a French Mediterranean island (very unlike Stevenage).

Phil Gilbert lives in South-East London and splits his time between working in a PLC, completing his MA in Creative Writing at Birkbeck, climbing, surfing and writing best-man speeches for his coupled-off friends. He has recently turned thirty and is contemplating the onset of adulthood.

Susan Greenhill studied bookbinding and book restoration at Camberwell School of Art, then spent thirty years as a photographer to the book trade, photographing authors and literary events for publishers and national newspapers. She writes stories and poems, and lives in North London – with a biographer.

Victoria Grigg writes short stories and poems about the search for momentum and voice in our modern lives. In 2011 she won second prize in the Cinnamon Press Travel and Land fiction competition, and two of her stories appear in the anthology *A Thousand Natural Shocks* (Troubador Publishing, 2011). She lives in Hackney and works as an English teacher.

Thaddeus Hickman lives and writes in London. His short fiction has appeared in Issue 8 of *The Mechanics' Institute Review*, in the anthology *A Thousand Natural Shocks* (Troubador Publishing, 2011) and on the short-story app by Ether Books. While completing his second year of the MA in Creative Writing at Birkbeck, he's finishing a collection of stories and starting his first novel.

Lucy Hume grew up in rural Kent, studied at Durham and now lives in North London. She works as an editor for a play publisher and tries to write in her spare time. Reading Lorrie Moore made her want to write short stories and she hopes eventually to complete a collection. "At Bistro Joe's" was inspired by an eventful summer working as a waitress at a pub restaurant in East Sussex after graduation.

Erinn Kindig lives in London and Brooklyn. She holds a BA in English from Mount Holyoke College and is currently completing her MA in Creative Writing at Birkbeck. "Broke" is her first published piece of fiction.

Alexander Knights is currently working on two projects: a screenplay about BASE jumpers in London, and a story about protest. He is also Digital Publishing Manager for Insight Guides, a travel publisher.

Chris Lilly was born in 1953 in Dartford, home of Mick Jagger and the Vox amp. He left Hull University in 1976, and moved to the Isle of Dogs. He taught in Tower Hamlets until February 2011. Chris currently studies Shakespeare and Contemporary Performance at Birkbeck, and received a Certificate in Creative Writing from Birkbeck in 2009.

Alison MacLeod is a novelist and short-story writer. Her story collection *Fifteen Modern Tales of Attraction* (Penguin, 2007) was "highly recommended" by *Time Out* and deemed by the *Guardian* to be "as inventive as it is original". Her stories have been widely published and broadcast, and in 2011 she was shortlisted for the BBC National Short-Story Award for her story "The Heart of Denis Noble", while in 2012 the same story was longlisted for the International *Sunday Times* EFG Short-Story Award. She is currently completing her next short-story collection, and her third novel, *Unexploded*, will be published by Penguin in April 2013. She is Professor of Contemporary Fiction at the University of Chichester.

Jamie M-Richards gained a first-class degree and won the Arthur Scott Prize for Creative Writing at Brunel University. He is currently studying for an MA in Creative Writing at Birkbeck, whilst working on his first novel. He has previously had a short story, "Dirt", published in *Polari Journal*. Much of his recent work explores the correlation between addiction, sexuality, mental health, love and shame. He lives in North London with his partner and two very particular cats.

Nadim Safdar has worked in factories and as a carer, medical volunteer, soldier, stand-up, businessman and dentist; as a director of Fathers 4 Justice he occasionally finds himself in handcuffs. He is writing a novel about a Paki in the British Army who returns to find his people as volatile as the Taliban he left behind.

Veena Sharma was born and lives in London. By day she saves the world one spreadsheet at a time; by night she writes. She is currently a student on Birkbeck's MA in Creative Writing. She is working on her first novel set in the masala jungle that is cosmopolitan Mumbai.

M. J. Whistler is a writer of British and Guyanese descent, living in London. She has a background in journalism and the arts, with degrees in History/Art History and Psychology, and is currently writing a novel while completing a Master's in Creative Writing at Birkbeck. Her work has appeared in *Poetry from Art* (Tate Modern, 2010 and 2011), *Decongested Tales* (Decongested Books, 2010) and on the Writers' Hub. In 2011, she was shortlisted for the *Wasafiri* New Writing Prize.

Jack Wilkes left school at fifteen to become an electrician. He's installed showers, sold and fitted water softeners. His first creative job was as an animator for computer games but still no writing involved. When his children came along he made up stories for them, but was unsure of his English so didn't write them down. Sixty-two was a bit late to learn to write fiction, but he started nonetheless. Now after nearly four years of various courses he's getting close.

Rachael Withers lived in Japan for six years and has written articles on travel and the expatriate experience for various magazines and books. In 2011 her story "The Klinefelter's Adventures: Chromosome of Havoc" was shortlisted for the Bristol Short Story Prize. She is currently working on her first novel.

Maggie Womersley grew up in West Sussex before moving to London in the 1990s to work as an archive film researcher and TV producer. In 2011 she was a runner-up in the *Guardian*'s summer short-story competition, and longlisted for the *Mslexia* Unpublished Novel Award. She is a regular contributor to the Writers' Hub website where she blogs about being a writing mum.